Praise 1
is a Ti.

MW01532430

"This collection is a powerhouse of language; its sentences sing with heat and precision. Elizabeth Kirschner expertly crafts the unexpected. These stories leave the reader feeling haunted and moved. They are a mediation on loneliness and the unspoken. Kirschner's voice is poetic, lyrical, and singular. A monumental exploration of beauty in unpredictable places. Kirschner exposes the vulnerable and damaged through the lens of hope and redemption. A stunning collection that will stay with me for a long time."

—*Erika Nichols-Frazer, Editor,*
An Anthology of Mental Health Recovery Stories

"Reading Elizabeth Kirschner's *Because the Sky is a Thousand Soft Hurts* is like being enveloped in layers of jeweled robes— each layer intricate with emotional depth and magnificent prose. Kirschner's characters brave their lives—family violence; childhood trauma—in scenes so immediate and chilling, the reader is dared to both look deeply, then look away—in awe."

—*Sari Rosenblatt,*
author of Father Guards the Sheep

"We need more voices like Elizabeth Kirschner's, whose words connote the reality of trauma, illness, neurodivergence, and beauty through the juxtaposition of her own associative metaphors, similes, and images. A published poet and memoirist, she also proves adept at fiction. These are not conventional stories but quantum fictions."

—*Kevin Richard Kaiser, editor-in-chief of Punt Volat and*
author of An Ethics Beyond: Posthumanist Animal Encounters and Variable Kindness in the Fiction of George Saunders

BECAUSE
THE SKY
IS A
THOUSAND
SOFT HURTS

STORIES BY
ELIZABETH KIRSCHNER

Elizabeth Kirschner
June 26, 2022
for Terri
With great cheer
Elizabeth

atmosphere press

for Ken, Anne, and Dean

TABLE OF CONTENTS

I.

this skeletal structure holds me in the dark
after the dark, the cold after the cold. . .

IN THY KINGDOM CUT

When Tup tells me, "It's time to go," he looks at me, squarely, like a beast in training.

"Why?" I cry in a voice that's deceptive as the beauty in the turn of the woods.

Thin as the eyelid of a tree slumbering in its own gold, I pull down the window shade, and just like that, I give into him.

Beyond our darkened doorway, the sea throngs, waves rising like cakes, a stench that's otherworldly, yet when Tup's face rises with a peculiar glow above the crumpled bed, the only thing I understand is how meager I am.

Because I'm afraid that this will end, fear rings me, like lions that weave their music at a run.

These moments are so brief. Only space, smooth as a woman's hand, belongs to us.

At midnight, everything's blue. The grand boulevards

are deserted. The sea goes off in search of the moon, a happiness so heavy and disappointing it hits me, like a rock that disintegrates without a cry.

The beaches are full of those bodiless eyes we meet near dunes and remote sandbars, red from the blood of a flowery flock of rocks. Corpses of beloved days, crater of emotions and red, red drunkenness, but still the heart beats, a thin bell.

Orange smoke seeps through our windows, like the mushrooms we used to hunt; the woods are quite close and the spectacle of alpine variations, the leitmotif of the chamois, the lace crevasses delighted us.

Because Tup says the monstrous is near, we board the train the very next day.

The embankment cracks under the swift railcars and the soot, fiery from all the steam, flows far above the trees. No one knows that the smell, which seizes us by the throat, is from the animals the train roars over.

Courage for the cries of hysterical locomotives and for the groans of tortured wheels. Courage for the trees which have the unambiguous vertigo of crowds on an eternal voyage.

At every signal, the beasts stay hidden and look through a single eye at this great noisy train gliding over streams of diamonds and the pebbles of aerial mines.

The lake we cross, the unsettling iridescence of the earth—all this makes us want to disappear while a man walks down the aisle cracking hazelnuts. At times, he folds in on himself, a fan.

His hands are sorrowful as a snail's horns; he clasps them in front of him.

Everything illumines his lukewarm reasoning. As if in

4

the body of a dying bird, he listens to the contractions of stones under the train. The glassmaker's spittle gives him a starry thrill.

Tup's fingertip on my temple isn't the barrel of a gun. *Are we listening to each other thinking?* Less high than the stars, there's nothing to stare at.

The sea, which to the human eye is never as beautiful as the sky, doesn't leave us, but in the depths of our eyes, lost calculations aim at the future like those of prison walls.

What are we waiting for? A woman? Two trees? Three flags? What are we waiting for? Nothing.

Hypnotized by the multiple splendors of Tup's anger— *brought on by what?*—I hear a door slam like a schoolboy's eraser.

This is when I tell him that I know about a horse who's been split in two; how he runs through fields and snorts flames through his powdery nostrils. His gallop is stronger than night, more powerful than the ethereal vapor of love.

When will we mount that mammalian monster, that Tibetan goat which climbs the Guari-shankar to the sound of metal flutes sweeter than any human cry?

We look around, see pastel-blue faces. Their eyes are the pale gray that makes men tremble and women miscarry.

Among the severely dressed passengers is a young woman who has around her neck the little flame of a scarf. *Desire, desire,* it says, *make your mess into a message.*

All around us, omnivorous, dazzling human voices— coarse cries, airy falsettos, heady blues and solemn low rumbles, which remind us that the obscure human soul is happy and sad at once.

Everything is swarming, venal, frivolous, vexing, crude, hypocritical, but one must never cease to look, listen, feel.

Beyond each ash, avocado, and pepper tree, there's an uplift of transformation, radiance, unlike any sterile meditation on life.

I keep my hand on Tup's, whose lips and groin are pink as a criminologist's. The entire history of me is in him—viper of memory, stab of regret, and a showy joy.

When the blizzard hits like a cobweb's mesh, the train's muzzled, slows, derails.

Either I flee or suffocate. Like a soldier, I writhe, moan, wiggle out of a window the size of a porthole.

I hit the ground where the measure of my body is like hot sand, or a hand leaving its mark. Water, a scary vortex, swirls beneath gondolas hung from a cable.

Stunned, the few of us who got out look like shocked clocks. Tup isn't one of them.

Of all things, it's the bland span of black and white spats that catches my eye. In it, I see a murmuration of birds, a swarm of swallows swooping in unison, caught mid-swirl over the swollen river.

The image does what murmurs do. It changes shape as my eyes bring into focus the outline of human heads, two of them, floating, like bodiless gods over the earth's crust.

One belonged to the man who cracked hazelnuts, the other to the woman who knew how to make a mess out of desire.

Now that she's made up of floating fragments, she echoes the lockstep laws of the universe—everything's created to fall apart.

When I turn the black and white image upside-down, I recognize it as a sign.

I'm standing under it—a tiny rainbow only twenty-feet tall. It arches across the narrow causeway, touching down in the lake on either side of the two-lane road.

Above the rainbow, the sky bisects into before and after: on one side of the lake, the expected white clouds. Gathering on this side—a royal tower of black jet—the train, exploding.

Yet what I see in my head is an explosion-in-reverse, a universe of fragments all fleeing backwards in time to a beginning where everything's waiting to be whole again.

Bereft, we cling to each other, our voices, an asphyxiation.

When I see one of Tup's shoes, like a scratched brain, tumble into the lake, I scream. The sound of it, like slamming a book closed, or a forgettable character invented out of spite or misunderstanding.

When I go in after the shoe, the lake's lipless. My body thrills to the silence, gilling.

When I'm dragged back out, I'm clutching it, like the moldy heel in a very quiet loaf of bread.

Days later, when I see a set of egrets—the score of them, nested as they are in the treed twilight, I want to discover a pattern, or a dogmatic order to instill upon their random arrangement. The birds' necks are curved, slender, the elegant sway of a tangent function.

There's nothing more orderly than the number one. Unity, identity. When we mix every beautiful number, it comes down to only one, hence my incantation is serial, primary, a set of numbers I chant recursively.

To be a celebrant in a wake of buzzards, isn't this enviable?

Which leaves me like a baby drained of all suffering. Only I no longer know how to speak. The speaking has scattered into the woods where my eyes flee, like grains of yellow pollen, and the wind has gone out like a candle.

I look down at my wrist to find time has become a single white bone. And my bones have floated away, like Tup's, into a massive landscape.

"Cut it," Tup said, as if to say, *If this is thy kingdom, it is more precious lessened.*

"Love," he said.

"Trouble," I replied.

"Once," he said, "there was another world. It came to us like lions through the common things, lashing their tails, their blonde chins on each other's wintered withers."

"But," I said.

To which he replied, "Winter, it's always almost winter."

And because it is: I live on, like a feral thing in the fir trees, intricate, bewildered.

Until something shifts, opens like the once-stuck front door. Slides, finally, and keens like the sharpening of a blade.

I shake off the tender ache—eyewitness as I was to bodies stretched out like pairs of pants. The sound a plate doesn't make, flying. The sky, a pink funeral in which the brightness broke, an egg on the lime walls.

It's true, I took to Tup like a floating staircase, smoke framing a mouth and now my quandary is to live without him under the dark recess of clouds, elliptical and nervous.

Still, I want Tup in the multiple, in the glacial carriage,

in the snake cloister, in a closet full of guitars and stomped hay.

I want him in the exhalation of others, all swaying, but changing midway in the words I address to him, my hand pressed to his, much paler than before, an orchid offered beneath a warring sky, an orchid that yawns, cracks, and falls apart.

I want him in a bed of soft clothes where his shoulders were two steps, dawns, fruits, rivers, full glottal and his hands two countries and my legs murmured like grass, a dumb enduring, while the moon floated, a white beast stretched out between slow-burning lanterns.

When night runs off with itself like another crucial planet, death is something that storms in from the outside. The universe inside is bigger, it's deep and I float inside it, an unspoken terror.

So soft are the silks of eternity, which like the gilled mushrooms Tup and I once hunted, are rife with the scent of wood rot.

Nothing can ever happen here again, especially not during the season between pleads when I find a note on the counter that says, *Try to put winter away.*

Which I cannot do. Because it's heavy, like a tonnage of kings, a bondage, or a sword wanting out.

All wrecked, all alto, it's in the lake which held Tup's shoes, or thy kingdom cut, where I was with the lions, like a gold scar that sexed my bones.

Now everything pours out—gold fruit roiling in a sky sunk hard as a hallelujah, and the lions, haven't they left my heart like a chain and throne, beating?

Because I love Tup, there'll be no hotter canyon of hunted feeling. I can vouch for that, nor will my flesh ever bride anyone else.

Darling, look at this cavalier scene, the lions in the tree-line, their blonde chins on each other's wintered withers, their trembling tails and tell me, isn't this us—golden, delirious, like smacked sunflowers?

A THOUSAND WAYS TO DISSEMBLE

When I find my father's dress shirt in the back of my closet, suspended from a hanger like a mocking little noose, I tear it to pieces while feeling him crawl up through a vein in my neck.

I take the shreds, burn them. The ashes lead me to the edge of a powder-blue coffin that held the corpse of a boy who loved the Dave Clark Five. The coffin wasn't actually powder-blue, but it should have been, the color of his high school prom tux.

Someone made my dress, but not my mother. My mother doesn't sew. In fact, people refer to her as "Mister." "What can I get you, Mister?" the kid at the hot-dog stand says. "You want ketchup on that, Mister?" And my father, right before he died, looked nine months pregnant.

My prom dress was turquoise covered in white lace. Or was it white dotted Swiss with orange accent flowers, the color of churned butter? My sister used it two years later for a wedding gown.

She married a short, charming x-ray tech with a huge mustache, a man who snuck into the back bedroom of the house trailer where we were living and tried to kiss me. I was seventeen.

"Don't do that to my sister," I said, which was another way of saying, don't do that to me, which was another way of saying, don't do that to Marie.

Some in this town believe my mother is of a mixed race and treat her as such, my father a hidden Jew, his father a Hitler look-alike, his mother a Jehovah's Witness, his grandmother a kleptomaniac who steals carrot peelers and crucifixes and sews them into her mattress.

In short, we're below average in just about everything and subsist on cans of pork and beans. Marie sells Avon door to door. I wait tables.

A man named Jack, a regular, always comes in. He smells like fruit flies, mercury, and the water glittering beige in the street. His nose is a black prow, his shoes busted with spider legs.

His face, plundered, forgotten the way the earth cracks, tries to make itself into a dim fable. A minor bible that face, dog-eared, and somehow chewy.

I pour him a coffee, which he cups as though someone might kill it.

He doesn't say much, Jack, but when Frank, the boss, pinches my ass like a tootsie roll, he lowers his head, licks the grease in the bottom of the cup, brown odor of camphor lining walls brittle as old paper, as the paper Jack reads. The obits I think.

I can't start over or take on a new body as brilliant or

as pitiful as the one I inhabit, nor do I remember the moment of impact when my prom date's head slammed into the steering wheel, but his blood spilled like coffee from a percolator.

We'd been hit by a car with one headlight. A *pi-diddle*. Which got me one kiss.

The other driver, a drunk, had furry ears and eyes blacker than omission, how could I not want to kill him? But my own brain was wounded: gray, seeping.

Like Jack, who comes into the restaurant every day as if making the Stations of the Cross. How he sidles in like the saddest excuse for an apology I've ever seen. Even sadder. Like a scarecrow or an abandoned space station falling to earth.

When probing a monster's brain, you're probably probing your own—Jack is no monster, this much I know. He squats at the counter, a warped shrimp. The napkin. This he folds into the smallest anchor.

I don't dare ask, "What can I get you?" Don't dare cock my hip as if a baby might land there. It might.

He brushes everything away, off the sleeve, off the overcoat, huge ensembles of thought, like jars of spilled buttons, or a recurring nightmare of straw on fire, but who is the scarecrow, the scare, the crow, hovering then gone, gone the glances, gone the moths, the dust, the wheat?

Some of it explodes, is a vein in the brain, but not Jack. Like a vow, he just sits there, until he leaves me a nickel for a tip, then sets the gift on the counter wordlessly.

Like the last thoughts before sleep, maybe my best, Jack walks out of the restaurant in snow that is flash, breach, blow.

When he walks off, abject, he grows smaller, like a grotesque, wanton somehow, a spindle, or reluctant wolf. This leaves me with the gift.

Wrapped in brown paper, I take it into the kitchen where I tear it apart, make slow work of it—just one eye weeping, a single chip on my shoulder and the usual screeching in my brain.

Exposed. Idiotic is how I feel when the paper falls away, a crepe hood.

The gift is a statue of Jesus. About the height of a groundhog and no better looking. Homely, with homemade holes.

Picking up the statue as though it's a trophy, I know I'm a part of Jack—not of this world, but in the world of dying on rocky spurs of land in a blueness that refuses to lift the center out of the word *pain*.

I understand that Jack loves me, not as a god or a devil, but as one who must attend to the difficult harvest of a life, to its losses and simple gains. He believes that if I listen beyond the howling in my own heart, I'll hear him singing about what he carries down the road.

A crucifix made out of phantom limbs? The hum ringing in our bullet-borne language, ringing like static, a late-night ringing and the carpet's hiss and steam, as I vacuum, my body ringing, humming about my prom date, his gravestone.

Gone missing, but still this ringing in my eardrums, rifled, symphonic, this ringing of midnight and of brake pads gone useless, and Jack's muzzled singing, this threading in and out of muscle and bone, this ringing, this hum, this ringing and in the midst of it, Jesus.

Whom, when I get home, I hide in the closet. Of course

it's a disaster. An unbearable secret always is. Dangerous when we try to leave it, but for a short time, Jesus seems to be alive. Misled, misused, lied to, and cheated, but alive.

For a while, he doesn't weep. For a while, I don't tear him down. Because love never helps in the way we need it to and because we all die and are put into the earth forever, I need to eat the wildness in his sweet body, so I can reach the body within the body, like molten glass.

And so, I eat him like corn on the cob. The waxy kernels glut my teeth while I spit the way Jack spits, more or less a spew.

I've been told to love Jesus. Down to the bone, to the marrow. Which I do. What's left, of course, are the thorns. A crippling clutch of thorns. To nest in, like a mental patient.

Not knowing what else to do, I bury Jesus in the backyard. Under the cobra-faced lilies while my memory fins around and around like the shiny obsessive lassos of a goldfish banding the narrow perimeters of its too-small bowl.

I never see Jack again, but my dreams, like my dead prom date, these remain powder blue. Formal. Like a tux.

Coming home from school one day, Mom waits for me just inside the front door, holding the bare-assed statue of Jesus, sweet Jesus, like a bone the dog dragged home.

When she hits me in the face, screaming about sacrilege, I'm almost glad. Because I still pine for my prom date—no, for Jack—it's okay when Mom presses her knuckles into my throat.

There's a quiet violence bleeding through the sky—a wash of China blue lifts into the purpling dusk among the cobra-faced lilies and while yelling at her to stop, I'm afraid of what the world will do next.

I don't think I've done much, I who hold nothing but air, which I give back. All for the belief that I'm a home-made catastrophe.

Like Jesus, like Jack, there are a thousand ways to dissemble. Like this. Under the cobra-faced lilies.

THE GENIUS OF FLOWERS

In the bathroom, I lifted the gray folds of my brain to get at the pink parts—stuffed toilet paper into all the tiny holes I cut so it looked like a field of red flags waving—*paper tulips, love notes!*

I ate the toilet paper while my face, bright as a pill, fell like dominoes.

In order to stop my own screams, abstract as an overture, I balled up my arms, tight as a pin curl and hot as an electric fence.

I was five years old. While hanging onto the toilet, madness, mean as a bull, pulled me out of this world.

In the back room of my skull, a golden prowl commenced, like the skin on my mother's fists. Which had landed on me for soiling my underpants, the color of a beat-up door.

I covered my head, let nothing invade it, not even the genius of flowers, dressed in wire jackets, heckling leaves on their demented stems.

As I crawled out of the bathroom, I remembered the gopher, a baby, whose footpads had scrabbled as I dragged it from where it was clamped to the shiny green trap.

Spun from the same cells as me, I noted its ears, tiny colorless petals, and at the tips of its articulated fingers, ten frantic claws.

When I struck it, as my mother had me, its mouth opened stunningly wide, a scream so silent, it was sucked down my throat.

I hated that I couldn't salvage a thing. Couldn't skin and eat it, stuff or display its fur on the mantel—it was just a bit of breath I buried under a stone.

Of course, I memorized its breath, let it become my text for decrepitude, my usher unto death, companion for ten thousand years.

I've always been too weak for human touch, especially after my legs, faster than a rabbit's were splayed by my father, followed by the slap of his thrusts, urgent as a thug's.

The smell of apricots thickening in the air and my mother's voice, an ice pick.

There's a Buddhist story about a woman chased by a tiger. When she comes to a cliff, she sees a sturdy vine and climbs halfway down. But there's also a tiger in the pit below.

And two mice—one white, one black—gnaw at the vine. No, they're rats.

When my father hooked into me, like blood from a wrist—he smelled like the inside of an ear, like hospital curtains, or a flagpole in the dead of winter.

And, sorrow upon sorrows, in went the vinegar of the

damned.

Because I pooped in my pants, my mother bought me a new set of underwear so jumbo I called them thunder pants.

Wherever I went, I wore them. I loved the way they left deep red runnels around my midriff and made my bottom look like a Greek column of clouds, or billowy rainbow parachutes.

I was six when I showed off my thunder pants to grocery store strangers, believing my bottom was factory-perfect. Inside my eyes, a red tapeworm wiggled, slipped into my brain.

My mother's hair was wavy as a seaport, her teeth tombstones, as she dragged me like a potted plant out of the store.

She shoved me into the car which had a grille like a shark bite. As it roared up the road, I shivered the way petals do when wind grasps a stem too thin, too breakable to hold.

Inside my mother and me, something gathered like a scar. We were an ache—a gash sealed for someone other than ourselves. Remote and lonely as a star.

She cut her brakes. How they screamed, like banshees. My thunder pants, I wet them as she beat me.

After she kicked me out of the car, I got lost; my head dummied, as I wandered among that which rises and vanishes, oblivious. Like children.

Here is the question—my question: is humiliation the Buddha's first noble truth? Would I find it among the forest's deep ponds, glittering like butterfly eyes, the cosmic flight of bats, the apple moon, a drowsy owl, the tang of the blackbird's song?

When I got home, my bedroom door was ajar. My mother against its inner wall, cracked, the way a map shows little can be useful.

She straddled me, "shall my life twine break?" My leg slid off the mattress.

While the moon dropped into the swamp holly, I walked into the back of my eyes. Through their gun slits I could see the faux faun tethered in the front yard.

It too had been punched. Alongside it lay a dead sparrow, intent as a scholar.

When did I deserve this? When did I not?

In the living room, there was a painting of a nude woman. While her back was being flayed, she pissed jewels onto the floor. From her turquoise beaded crotch.

Weren't her cuts called *attese*, meaning wait or expectation? Didn't she also wear thunder pants?

That night, I fingered my welts: an inch above the elbow. Left toe. Ankle. Ear to ear. Like a swinging bridge.

I thought of it as cinema. The stuff in between the bones. To move and be elastic. To leap. To land when you fall.

The next day, my mother came in, yelled, "You've ruined me." The vein running up her neck stood out, a blue cable.

Was she teaching me what was good to know: that life would be low pitched and solo. That dream was just another word for tunnel. That being born means the same as to barrel—the way a train does from its station, the way I had from my mother.

My father, when he splayed me said, "every thrill in us creates unease," which gave him permission to risk the journey; to go a little farther.

Hadn't he tied up my hands so I couldn't bite him? Above us, a mud-dauber wasp nest hung, like a pan flute; and above it, a cloud.

But then he asked, "what of the childhood made larger in us? Is it like a cello left in the woods?"

I wanted to say: *don't,* but I was only a child, my head a silent chaperone.

When the wasp nest fell, we were pinned to each other, an armless sleeve.

While the wasps stung me, my screams peeled back like wallpaper. Or was it my hymen they punctured, a communion wafer?

As I tore into the house, there was a jar of mums on a table near the window.

Their yellows were yelling at each other. It was as if someone was calling from the end of a long pier where the docks were vertical, warlike.

While running I became texture. I was clawing at the palm of one hand and the bee stings with the other. Ahead of me, my mother with her magnified eyes.

"My soul," I yelled, "it's just the length of a baby's."

I ran up the stairs. On my mother's hand, an amethyst: a cube of lilac in hospital light. Maddish, reddish, her fists were clenched, but her body was an album of liquid astonishment. Or decrepitude. Which I loved.

While birds swept across the sky like pot-bellied angels, I fell into the abyss. I went straight into it, was even pleased to be falling, and found it beautiful. And so, in that very instant, I became an incomprehensible bloom and the voice that howls out of it.

Of course, they locked me up. No one came to see me.

My madness, was it contagious?

When did it begin? Was it when shadows darkened the yellow walls around my crib: a ripening pear? Was it when my mother frowned, touched her fingers to her nipple, placing the word *milk* there, then took her hand away?

The syllable drifted to the floor of my body, a shiny lure swiveling through the dark—my first intimation of need.

When she leaned down to kiss me, she pressed her face onto the pad of my silence; then withdrew, jostling the planets wheeling over my head.

The mornings in the psych ward are no less strange: I shiver in my blanket, still puzzling out what's in this thing—if you can call it a thing—this brain that cracks like a criminal.

It's been winter for a long time—and no pulse in my pillow, which is hard as a shark's fin.

Here, where I dream I'm turned by the corpses of three girls, girls who starve after devouring a bowl full of a thousand flowers. I wake up screaming while swatting at the wasps seeping into my hair.

The nurses come in smelling of spoiled milk. As the needle, long as a proboscis goes in, bits of my body migrate: bone dust, breakage.

Here, we pass through each other like weary sweepers, haunting through glass doors, arcing across gray floors faint trails of dust—from these cold floors, a film rises, like smoke from altars.

How easily the myth of one life wills itself into another—how strange to witness my own nameless shape. All night I wail. As I had in a crib heavy as a submarine.

There's something like a museum about me, a feeling

of great space and how can I cut away the razored insistence thrumming inside my head, the birdlike torturers in the elevators, the labial ear fallen to the ground, the decapitated hat of the black rose, the blind muscles, the blood and urine in a cup?

Can I draw the cuts. *Attese?* While pigeons alight across the street on a cathedral slim as a heron?

I can't because when the madness tells me that my eyes are dismembered silk, my saliva, a bubbling apocalypse. I know I belong to those of us who sleepwalk beneath glittering shelves of ice, dressed in cold light, confounded by doorknobs, by the part that hallucinates eel and angel, and the strange blue fin that sweeps a camouflage of dust into us.

When the lightbulb pops, hard as candy corn, I use a shard to cut a smile behind my knees. This while the stars prick the dark like a rash.

From the TV in the community room, a babble like a nursery rhyme. While the world is talking to itself in its endless repetitions, I begin to recognize that the plot of my life is the subplot of madness.

Cut and cutting, I dance in the TV's blue, fatal light. My madness, which is full of bounty, takes it all in. Moon with a faint dent. Clouds squishing like grubs.

This is the beginning of seeing past sight—in which what's interior becomes the visible architecture for the living self, like a photographic plate.

When I say, "let's go," no one turns the lights on. No one holds me, or tells me that the flatness in my brain is a metaphor for every kind of death, a pulse which rings louder than a mouth full of ulcers and steel.

Eyes wider than graves, I remember my mother setting fire to the wasp nest while my father practiced a duet with me near a window that opened onto the lawn.

Fragments of music collected like a water stain above our heads.

"Again," he said quietly. His fingers slim as a miser's.

I counted time like bolts in a bowl. We stared straight ahead, as if driving through a country we'd seen so many times we forgot to look.

The wasps writhed in the dusk's pink torso—my mother stood with a can of gasoline in her hand, piano notes tangling with the oily smoke before thinning out over treetops, and she let them go like that, without listening too hard, without trying to piece anything together, especially not me.

But my soul, this remains the length of a baby's, is still an album of liquid astonishment, soft as dismembered silk, in the slightly-windy, mostly-calm gray rain.

O' how it humbles me to confess that want is want, and mine is for those hours when I walked by the riverbank, giving and receiving stories, hours I might be myself or soon or not.

BECAUSE IT'S NOTHING TO KNOW ONE MOMENT ALIVE

My hands, like two terrible letters, are on the steering wheel as I drive my friend Mick and her baby Sammie in mountains which cubbyhole the sky.

Our day is uneventful. We have lunch in town, take turns with Sammie. We walk around, my legs in tights like a funeral of knees. Church bells clang, are hollow bamboo.

On the way home, fog descends, elegant as an evening full of dead things. Mick talks about the husband she fled. Brilliant, funny, abusive. He doesn't care about the baby. Of course.

I talk too, but not about my family. I talk to no one about them. No one. When I say something about Mick's husband Iver, she snaps, "We're not to mention him. Ever."

"Okay," I reply as driving is difficult. Fog embalms the car, is theatrical. I slow down, mindful of the baby. My concentration grows. I let the car find the road, painfully aware of the seven-month-old baby whose safety depends on me. Depends.

"By the way," Mick says, "your goddam perfume smells like air freshener. What is it—Pinesol? Listerine?"

"Thanks," I say while the windshield wipers, which I repaired with a hair tie, flip flop. I keep my hands on the steering wheel. The baby whimpers. I want to whimper with her. But I must drive. The world, I want to tell her, affords little consolation.

When I see the house lights, I exhale. We have made it. What exactly have we made? As I pull up, the baby begins to cry. I don't blame her.

Once inside, Mick goes into her room with Sammie, locks the door. With eyes the color of hairspray, I stand in darkness. The darkness Mick secretes. As if she was born to do so.

Because I might as well let every moment ache, I pour myself a drink while watching the sky rinse off its pulp.

My cocktail glass, pale green, dutiful—I gnaw on its crisp lip, for haven't I been three or four years old for decades, I who long to press against my father's knees with my shoulder snugged into him as he wound down the clock of the girl I was, I who skipped, blinked and curtseyed before ticking down?

Over Sunday brunch, I stared at him, then my brothers and sister. Didn't the four of us exist like a split lip? Weren't we meant for something better, we who grunted while eating our toast?

After breakfast, my siblings headed out into the summer morning where the light was lusterless and somehow luckless, leaving me with Dad whose groan became my truth which, like extreme lightning, hit my eardrum.

"Get the kitchen scissors," he insisted, "it's time to cut my hair." Everything jumbled together as I fetched the scissors Mom stuck in a pot of ivy. The blades were sharp as my favorite Sharpie.

With them, I cut his hair. Pepper-blanched and wind-scuffed, I imagined the noise of small brown mammals each time a lock landed on the floor.

When I trimmed Dad's sideburns, bristles stuck to my fingers like icky scraps of his brain. The floor, with tiles black and white as an Oreo cookie, was littered with what looked to be wooly bear caterpillar fuzz.

Grabbing a hunk, I went into the backyard, which was about as big as the area we kids chalked out for a game of four-square.

I stuck the hair in dirt next to the orange seeds I planted not long ago, orange seeds bright as the lantern that should glow inside every child, the one Mother tried to blow out, like the candles we put on our birthday cakes.

Marking each spot with a popsicle stick, I patty-caked the soil down until each mound looked like the black tulle on a ballerina's tutu.

My father, who believed in gardens, came up behind me and said, "if you're not happy in your own backyard, you won't be happy anywhere," meaning, of course: if you want a happy ending, you have to know where to stop.

Where or how to stop, this was beyond him, whose hands, whose hands.

After he went off to work, I was left with Doug, who was mowing the lawn. The grass hissed as he marked lanes Olympic swimmers might go down.

When Doug stopped the mower, the puzzle that we are

came to life—all the assorted, confused and tumbling pieces, kaleidoscopic pieces, jagged as jigsaw, these pieces left me elated, puzzled, shocked, dismayed, confident, loving: every minute of the hour—each fragment was a whole made so by one's actions, thoughts and feelings.

My brother looked at me and said, "Why don't you take the Chevy for a spin?" His lips barely moved. Was he a ventriloquist?

I pinned back my butterfly wings, the ones with white veins in them and climbed into the car. My feet couldn't reach the pedals. Even so, I made car sounds while I gripped the steering wheel, hard. It was black, sticky.

Doug, laughing, reached into the car and released the clutch. The car rolled into Sherman Road, backfired into a blossoming bomb, just like Dad's hands.

When it hit the opposite curb, Doug laughed some more, a laugh loud as a fart.

"Bumper cars," I hooted as Mom came flying out of the house, heat-rash-fast. She had the flyswatter and was wearing an apron over her blue sheath. The line in her silk stockings was a fat worm. It squiggled, like the creepy crawlers I made with my Creepy Crawler set.

"You," she yelled, as she yanked me out of the car. Doug had gone back to giving the lawn a crewcut. He pretended he had horse blinders on and didn't dare look my way.

Mom kept on yelling while swatting me. Her breath was everything I couldn't bear, as she, who was but atoms combining and recombining, atoms which glowed a deep orange-gold against a blue so sheer a single bird ripped it like silk, said, "I may have to break your heart, young lady, but it isn't nothing to know one moment alive."

She was right, it wasn't nothing, as she beat me. While wind clamored in the trees, I understood that one moment alive was to never have enough of enough.

Standing by the kitchen sink, holding my cocktail glass like my mother's, I know that things that are lost stay lost. When I weave and stumble into my room, my dog Useless is right behind me.

When I get up to pee, Mick's door is wide open. The baby Sammie is on the bed. All alone. She has just learned to roll. This means she can easily fall off the bed onto the floor.

I go in, sit on the edge of the bed. Mick is on the phone. In the kitchen. Her voice has resin in it, fury, hail. Is she talking to Iver?

"You" she yells, "are a flea bag. Your own daughter, never, don't even think about it."

Sammie's ears are damp with sleep. Her eyes, pale as starlight on the gray wall, are evanescent. Drunk as I am, the scent of her sugary milk-breath nearly knocks me off my feet. Her yarn-soft skull glistens as she yawns. I long to touch its luster, but Sammie, she lets out a squeal, clean as an orange peel.

The sounds Sammie makes are glitter-spritzed. I don't touch her. I just don't want her to roll off the bed. Useless agrees.

Mom, I want to ask, *aren't I your clever girl?*

"Clever," that's the word Mick uses to describe Sammie. "My clever girl," she says, when feeding her. With a creamy ovoid for a mouth, she's all eyes as Mick floats the plastic baby spoon toward her mouth.

"You, my wee little one," exclaims Mick, "are full of malarkey!" The baby spoon holds soupy oatmeal. It slides down Sammie's bib.

The baby, whose breath is of lime and peppers, smiles as her mom laughs, "Aren't you my funny kick-about?" That smile, it's a mothy flicker.

The air in Mick's room smells like a hammered mouse. Worried and fed up, I wander to the window with its strict bang of Venetian blinds. My hands fidget. And then I see myself: I want out. So does Useless.

As she comes out of the kitchen, Mick's voice is no longer the high-pitched one she uses with Sammie. "You," she yells as though there's grit in her teeth.

Her voice holds my wrists down, is the sound of two knees hitting a sandbag and when she walks toward her room, I know she will come at me.

"You goddam drunk," she starts, "get the hell away from my baby." Her face, like rock candy, glistens while her words bury themselves inside my mouth.

"The baby," I sputter. Because I'm slurring, *baby* probably sounds like *wading* or *baiting*.

From where I am, I can see Sammie's eyes and the up-turned corners of her mouth. Her lollipop bright hands are neither spectacular nor sad. Surely they are not the hands that pet and shape and slap.

Mick, whose skin is tough as boot wax, says, "your breath, it stinks."

I try to speak but can't.

"You friggin' drunk," she says, again. "Get the hell away from my baby."

Staggering, I fall onto Mick's bed. Dust goes up my nose.

I land next to Sammie. Minx-like, she prattles. Useless jumps up on the bed next to us. His ears, alert as hers, are souvenirs.

The three of us sit like bread in a stay-fresh wrapper. Sammie, does she bite the inside of her cheeks? Useless, does he bite his?

Mick comes closer. "You," she yells, "never, ever are you to come near my baby again. You're wasted," she continues, "it's obscene. Get out! Get out of the goddam house!"

"Sorry, but you can't throw me out of my own home."

"Like hell, I can't."

When her hands go not on me, but my dog, when she strikes him, hard, not once, not twice, but three times, when her hands paddlewheel him the way my mother once struck me, this is when I yell, "Stop!"

"You asked for it," I scream, as my hands grab Mick's throat. My breath chuffs, "is this what you want?"

Because I aim to bloody her, I do. Hands hit, whirr, slap, dance.

Backing off, I stomp my way out of Mick's room with Useless swaddled in my arms, crawl back into bed. While my fingers drift in the shallows of his hair, it's clear that almost all of us have lost the way and none of us are entirely good.

When I get up, my bedsheets smell like the day after the dark has died. The room where Mick and Sammie stayed is deserted. Only wary insects remain. Insects and a gloom. I walk by their room, let out the dog.

Once in the kitchen, I gaze out the window. As the stark light sifts through the plum tree, I see the buck, his head a grape hyacinth, his antlers fissured by snow and rain as piercing as a slap burning my cheek, a fifty year sting.

Seeing the dog, whose teeth are white as sticky rice, I rap on the window, hard.

Useless looks up, scampers on in while the buck, whose head is a rack of crowned sounds, flicks an ear to hear a rustle in the underbrush.

Like a voice the odor has changed, the buck's antlers are one shaft of light among many shafts of darkness, the forest toward the end—worried moss, sodden firmament.

When I pound on the window a second time, he lows musk, snorts black fire, then bolts.

He vanishes among trees downed ages ago. Ages. And in his absence, there hangs the fact, hard as a raw bullet, that he has gone unharmed. As did my father.

When I go to make tea, which smells of cardamon, licorice, a shaft of light hits me, piercing. As it steeps, the dregs become worthless, like me. Purple shadows bruise while loss, stiff as a male, breaks in.

The dog sleeps. Starry snow mats his brain. While I sip my tea, steam, bright as a gut full of shiners, leavens the air, let's the earth grieve.

What unpleasantness—an earth let loose and loss the only record of its evolutions, a sky rinsing itself from the pointless trash of winter.

And then I hear it—the word, *beautiful*, tumbling out my mother's mouth. More and more I hear it, while imagining my body slumped beside hers. It's peaceful. Years and years of never rest and it's peaceful.

A SIN WORTH HURTING FOR

The mustard sofa, this was an island in our factory-big family room. Here I sat next to my mother on foam cushions, ear-plug-thick and covered with a striped beach towel. And my smile was bright as a salted crust.

The picture window, the size of an elevator. It framed our winter scene.

The family room was so cold it assassinated my future, but still I smelled the lotion Mom put on her hands. Columns of ash tumbled from her wasp-hot cigarette while her mind guillotined, slammed shut, became the plant matter that transformed pain into prayer and ash and misery.

I was trying to be a child next to her. The child. This, after I had shoved books down my pants to soften her blows.

My mother. In the dusk of her cold, unfocused mind— the moody, livid pining I bit through, but for what?

I rubbed my hands together, right on top of left, as if to make a small fire. Nary a spark, nary a spit of flame. My cold hands attempted to hold onto the homey miracle a child of God should be.

Lily Day. I loved that my middle name was the same as my mother's maiden name. When she called me, I pictured the thicket of day lilies that cropped up alongside the house. Each bloom was an orange trumpet and reminded me of Easter, which I loved because rebirth was more exciting than birth.

Birth, she told me, just sort of happened, but rebirth had a mystical quality and took an extra special effort. You had to die first.

Even my dog Daisy, who had tumors, bumpy as the popcorn stitches on my sweater, knew this. All winter, I'd been wrapping her paws in gauze, which left bloody footprints in the snow, like Valentines.

Sitting next to Mom, I stitched a pillow for my brother Ed. The orange and yellow yarn were bright sun rays. As I worked the needle, I longed to tie one to my finger.

It was snowing. Flakes fell like spiders from their hidden wells.

My brothers and sister were outside, loose hair flying. They'd taken juice glasses and were out catching snowflakes, yelling, "Car, car, c-a-r, stick your head in a jelly jar!" They filled the sky with hilarity and laughter while I tried to stitch myself into their winter scene.

"Oh!" they exclaimed each time they caught a flake. Of course, it melted as soon as it touched glass. They continued to pursue what they couldn't capture, like the physics of a breeze. How could I not love them for this?

My world was steeped in veils of snow, oblique as the

December sky. The snow helped bury my small helpings of feeling, which were clean and empty as a scrubbed cup.

While my brothers and sister ran about, full of delight and pathos, Daisy wandered off as if drawn into the vortex the snow was sucked into.

The night she disappeared happened to be Christmas Eve. When my father came home from work, bits of snow blew in the doorway with him. My mother, where had she gone? Was she powdering her nose?

My father sneered, "You know, you look like her. It's in your features."

"What features," I wanted to ask, "TV features?"

Before I could say anything, Dad began taking my hair apart, one follicle at a time. He worked his way to the neural tissue, then threw me down with his cannonball looks—up against the coffee table, he pressed the rough country of his lips against mine. They tasted like Indian rubber erasers.

"Listen," he said, but I didn't. His words, these tied me to him, a flower to a wolf.

I could smell the Shake and Bake that was in the oven. Mom had shaken the meat in baggies to get the coating on.

Dad pushed me away. "Get ready for church," he said, so I went to my room to fetch my chapel veil and Communion missal, the one with the cathedral on the inside cover, a cathedral that was raised like Braille and was the color of my panties.

I was three shades paler when I walked back into the kitchen. My brothers and sister came in, fresh as snow globes. I expected the dog to come in with them.

"Where's Daisy?" I asked.

"Dunno," they responded in unison. "Who cares,"

Doug went on. "She's older than dirt."

I stuck my tongue out at him, like neat meat.

In church, the creche on the altar was surrounded by lit candles. It hurt me to look at this Nativity Scene, for my family wasn't that family. Mine was unmanageable, frightening, lacking both warmth and light. Unlike the Holy Family, we were real. Our realness, this was what frightened me.

Once or twice, when the Christmas candles threatened to go out, I shivered.

Didn't that mean ghosts were passing through God's house? Wasn't I one such ghost? Couldn't one harsh wind blow down my own house, as though it has been built from the manger's straw?

After Mass, I begged Mom for a quarter, then went up to the votives where I slid the coin into the metal box. Down on my knees, I lit a match, touched it to a candle, but it went out before I could pray for Daisy's return.

This was when I knew that every single light under heaven would and could be extinguished, even mine, which was the littlest of them all.

In the morning, Mom got up early to prepare Christmas dinner. Dad and my brothers and sister slept in.

When they stumbled out of bed, we opened the presents. I gave Doug my Indian head penny collection. Marie got the belt I hand tied myself and Ed the pillow I made with bright yellow and orange yarn.

The attention shifted from us kids, who sat among piles of wrapping paper and new toys, to Dad in his Christmas green chamois shirt, his legs in a victory "V."

He stared at me, then Mom, whose forehead was stillness chained to wrinkled darkness. She was wearing a lavender cardigan, pale as a chilled egg, as she handed me my gift.

I tore it open, "A dictionary?" I asked, "really?"

Mom's face turned into a hot iron. "You don't deserve it," she said.

I didn't know what to do. That look of hers, it scarred.

"Can I help paste up the bird?" I asked.

"Yes," she said, "but it's baste, not paste."

I helped her get the turkey out of the oven. I stood on a stool to squirt the bird with the bloody juice. Something smelled funny. I was about to say something but stopped.

Mom, she staggered. Next to the sink was a bottle of bourbon and Murphy's Oil Soap. I realized the rag on the turkey had been soaked in the Oil Soap. No wonder it smelled.

I didn't say a word and let her serve the turkey anyway. No one caught on.

Over dinner, while passing the salt, I blurted, "Daisy." I knew I sounded like a baby with a pacifier stuffed in its mouth.

Doug rolled his eyes. "C'mon, he said, "this isn't *Lassie*. You know she's probably a goner."

I lowered my head, pushed the peas around with my fork. No way was I going to eat the turkey, but Mom wouldn't let me leave the table until my plate was clean.

I was used to sneaking food to Daisy, but because my dog wasn't there, I balled up what was left on my plate into my napkin until it looked like a mumbling nun.

"Garbage duty," commanded Dad. His nose looked like chewed up hamburger. He was still working on his martini.

"You," he said. His finger was pointed at me. Everyone else had left the table. His glare, didn't it make the air a bullet made of silk?

I went out, dragging the trash bag behind me, a ball and chain.

I paused in the garden, in gossamer snow, fingering the pearl necklace Dad had stuck in the bottom of my Christmas stocking, thinking, *moon chip, milk tooth, tiny pellet of angel shit.* Why me?

Aching in deep cavities of snow: *spit ball, egg case, the Glory-be-bead on a child's white rosary,* I ripped the necklace off, buried it in snow the way Daisy buried her very best bones.

I trudged over to the trash cans. A bird flew up with a leaf-shred-howl, after which I heard the sound of an animal in pain. I hoped it would go away. It didn't. I knew it was Daisy.

When I realized she'd burrowed under the barn, I ran into the house to get everyone else.

Because I was the smallest, I crawled under the barn to help the dog. I pushed from behind while Dad yanked on her front paws, as though she were a seam of comprehension in the ordered world.

Daisy snarled, tried to bite me, but once I got her out, she stood up, trembly as a newborn. Little flakes of snow stuck to her flanks like sequins.

When she lowered herself back down to the ground, Dad said, "You know we're going to have to put her back down."

My brothers and sister were on either side of Dad, as in a stand off. They huffed, went back into the house.

I fell to my knees, hugged the dog like a church for the

disinherited. I wanted to get her paws moving toward the language of trees, bring a steady rhythm back to her pulse, the breathing she knew before she was born.

I wanted to mend her, to reverse the dark that grew behind her eyes like an old rubber tire does after much wear.

The cold walked around my upper lip and with my tongue, I licked the ice off her paws. It was like licking the watery tracks that someone left behind or walking backwards in the snow.

When her eyes fluttered open, I felt like I was at the edge of the mouth of a cave with every intention of jumping in.

Snow fell in a scatterplot, or was bird shot pinging her collarbone, its cracked glaze. Like burnt sugar, a ring of luminaries collared her, a golden torque while her jaw unhinged as if to eat its way out of its grave.

Under the shaking aspens, butter weather, but cold like herringbone, and in the brain's eternal lodgings—the dog's, mine—radiance, which is never quite as warm as light, but who hasn't tasted the silver in sea mist?

Someone should have told me the child is what delivers us from death, but all I could see was Daisy's face, swollen as a bored ocean—it was black, but with plums inside it, as if they were floating in blood.

Because I needed a lot of death, I felt as though I was entering an order that no one could see and the feeling of becoming music was something nobody else could know. It was a lonely thing. Painted with ink, the white heavy snow.

With my arms wrapped around Daisy, I heard a sound, like washing calves in cold water. It smelled of whales and vapor.

It was written. A flower fell from her eye and bloomed in my mouth. It was written. A swallow rhymes with hunger and cannot hatch an egg. Like a hundred white stones turning into chrysanthemums and nightshade.

As I held my dog, a bird lifted from her and passed through my body. I imagined a dark surprise growing on its wings. This, as clouds floated down, smelling of skin.

I half-carried her back to my room where I felt the world rising to evil and falling asleep to sin. In the mingling between us, the world.

Clutching her head, I rolled toward her. Outside the wind howled, a rope burn.

My faith was in her face. And her ears. Weren't they soft as ferns where water seldom goes?

Sometime after midnight slipped off the horizon, when the air was soaked in blackness; sometime after the clouds hovered, like boulders, and the stars crawled up and studded the sky; I left the dog, a sleeping puddle, and unlatched the window.

I walked into the forest, my dark hair a flag. I walked for hours, my feet light-stepping through puddles, over hard-packed dirt on snowy hills, over sticks and pebbles, over lakes and frigid streams.

I went from nothing to nothing. I just wanted to get beyond pain, beyond graveyards and clearings. All around me, the eyes of startled creatures gleamed, a herd of candles.

No echo of a bell lulled me, no spirit, nor scent of a word whose storm fell to drown me—which blood star, which thread of water, which trickle, which sorrow was being clotted, which pain dammed, which wall spread its ivy like a veil to blind me?

When daybreak came, a clarinet sounded, like a wounded mare, and the violins were lifted and the flutes blew their hot dry breezes while the cellos chewed on the sounds of thunder.

This music milled about, an orphan. Then a lute began groaning and dawn lost its meaning.

When a bird started singing, when the branches like lollipops tilted sunlight into my eyes, I let go—listened to the bullfrogs' opaque, plumbeous, tympanic slurps, how they were harped with pings and plops, making the unseemly froth go berserk with a foofaraw under the blue-green film, spongiform but formless, boiling with botched air-bubbles, the surface, glopping up slicks of glossy, palatine pops and liquid circles.

The chickadee. Her song, this possessed the lassitude of an angel.

In the fable, the animals smell fear and so does the child. I thought to myself—I am both. I am both. I am both and I can hold it together.

That's when I heard it, the whole world filled with swallowing—me, my dog—only by leaving nature, could I still keep it—Daisy was dead.

And my mother, who's anonymous as a bedsheet, even she knew that birth is easy, but death that's special, rebirth, even more so.

"Listen," she said, "I'm dead and in hell. I've known that for years."

Dead and in hell, I still wanted to ask her, *Am I sweet? Am I yours?*—she who was a story about everything, like a sin worth hurting for: fever, vapor, atlas of bone, fields of muscle, her body opalescent with what once lived and will live and live again.

Like a forgery in coral, this beauty I'm eager to hoard becomes slippery on ordinary days, comes not at all, comes never, or is a pearl made by the tears of my smallest self.

IN EXIT TIME ONLY

The moon leaked yellow onto the road the night Tom shattered the bottle he was drinking from, then fed me the glass gingerly, as if it were seed. All of it.

After kissing my forehead, which tasted of gum and rose petals, he came into me as if to puncture a flap of heaven. As he emptied himself, I smelled ashes, buried music.

It was all in the synapsing—the way the fluids in his inner ear swished with vodka, how his breath, a caught, fathered object thrashed in space and the crowns glued in his mouth were like hitting a switch. Or me.

When the condom broke, letting the hot wax of him grime my thighs, it dripped onto, what, what was it, filmy, but stiff, like a flag?

A mushroom-sized corpse, it smelled of leaf mold, damp moths, and a spider's dank interior. I seized it, wrapped it in moss, then tucked it under my school blouse.

The long walk home was chaperoned by stray dogs. While Tom's cum rotted in my hair, I knew we'd made the world smaller by garaging a body, quiet as an abstraction—even the trees were disappointed, for they too had been tampered with.

When we got back, I didn't say a thing. What was there to say? My brothers and sister had moved out long ago. My face, had it been felled?

Up in my room, I just waited, breathed. My body was speaking. Expressing the thingness of a thing while my mother down in the kitchen washed what the garden had produced. Nubbins shaped like turrets.

Outside, the gate to the garden was ajar. In it, what I had left there, like pocket lint. In the ache of oblivion, in rain cold as cabbages. As though a fork had been driven into it.

We could have drawn a chalk line there. But, this is not conceptual. This is. Tom is. I am. The hesitancy. The history. The undoing.

And the secret: humiliation is release.

Because of the way I walked, with that littleness under my blouse—sometimes mariposa blue, but mouse-like— the town was talking, talking like dentures, *clack, clack,* but nothing was really said.

As I walked, I thought about how everybody longs for a catastrophe. I thought about cracked statues, blonde fireflies, voyagers, gold, yes, I thought about gold—listen, whoever does the telling stops time, like days with little in them. And I'm the teller.

Who considered how everyone is astonished by what has shot through them, like those sounds I sometimes heard from that cocooned otherness, its muffled ocean. Or was it from the sad turbine of my womb?

Without hesitation or mercy or any form of compassion, I got into a taxi. A purple fragrance came in, like battered wine.

The driver drove and drove. The hills, like tyrants or dark owls. The sea swept by—an apology for genius, the waves white, bright as excellent children. The roar, like the way we love, translucent as the claws of turn-tossed surf.

Under my shirt, this barely perceptible thing, ghosted at the threshold of being: *here, not here.* Like the single breath we hold onto at the thinnest verge of sight: *here, not here.*

A curve nearly naked of arc, of almost, a wisp of becoming, a wand—we drove into the city, where the blue buildings were parked, as if weighted by ashes.

When the cab pulled over, I got out. The air smelled like wintering frogs, filmy, insubstantial. Dismal, it seemed, the sky, a mythic image shrinking, pulling in on itself, all incinerated fragments of breath and bone resting heavily.

Not knowing what to do, I walked down blocks long as nooses—isn't the smallness of being our only greatness?

I somehow became a room, listening to my one heart beat. Like a pebble thrown down a well. Fickle was the word that came to mind, or speechless.

As the day ground its way into my back, I made my way into a park. Sat down on a bench, hard as a bas relief.

In a river thick as quicksand, two swans worked wings that were a bleak, dirty canvas, their beaks pricking the water like greasy hair combs.

I thought about Tom. How I'd swallowed glass, brittle

as a beggar. Of what I had come to do.

The statue. Here in the park, like a sick child. The gray of it, whispery, flinty, like grated shale. And those swans, vicious now, fighting.

Tossing out hunks of scummy bread, I remembered how I had walked across rugged terrain over to the hen house where my mother's prize guinea hens were brainshocked by sunlight's quick jig.

My face, it was neutral, as I palmed eggs before placing them in my pocket, as if each had hatched out of the turbulent mess that comes attached to a womb.

I clucked, hissed at the hens who teetered across islands gravid with pointillist snow, an early snow which fell the way light denies the day's clear profit.

Casting out grain, which the hens devoured, I looked up, saw my mother raise the rifle.

She aimed at asses, harassed and plucked—raw, red pomegranates, and fired. The sound the gun made was furious with precision.

A hen reeled up, then another, another, while carmine blood flecked specks of armpit snow.

I threw an egg straight from my pocket at Mom's razor-boned back. It splattered, a red and yellow pinwheel.

She turned her face toward mine. Between us, a massacre of birds whose bridal groins were bullet-bled. The vomit of their blood slopped onto a vacant apron of bonemeal snow. The pits of their eyes look key-holed.

Between me and my mother, a carnal tension, wordless, alien. Her frame duped mine. She held the rifle, swinging it, a teeter-totter.

"Are you going to do the favor of killing me too?" I yelled.

"Maybe," she replied, her voice light as a hanky, but I knew she had better things to do.

My eyes, were they on rerun? Could I gun the gap between us? Better yet, could I pace off my heart?

The horses, dark as nacre-torts, were alarmed. Did they see from under the far side of their eyelids, which were gelid, quivering?

Their keening sounds arose from the zenith of their genes, they who knew that the wind, on this desultory vista, could reduce everything to a tatted mystery.

Solid as solar pegs they stood in a Ruebenesque landscape. The mares, were they masquerading as recluses?

Guillotine-red, the blood of the slaughtered hens airbrushed stones. The bullets that tore through their brains were nails pounded into figs, each hole left a velvet depression. That's how my insides felt, riddled.

I took an egg from my pocket. It was still warm, like a monk's tonsured head. I took the safety pin I used to hold my coat closed, punctured the shell, opaque it was, and smooth as an infant's cheek.

The trick was to puncture the egg without shattering the shell. Little pinpricks, like the ones made to see an eclipse.

As if drinking air from a whistle, I took sips of yellow syrup, saw the one drop of blood, Venus-bright. Might this make my own eggs fertile, little moons in the offing?

The pinpricks, all the pinpricks, and what Tom drank after he upholstered my body with wounds no one could see. The dirty trickle, its famous gravy.

In that red hour, when all those moons fell out me like sick tulips.

Because I couldn't bear what I'd never bear, I took that

smeared thing from under my blouse and packed it into that cracked statue, which was a room as good as any coffin.

Wet black gold. Wouldn't this statue be canted with wet black gold and might a slurry of eggs, slick as excrement, be bedded, like secret eyes in secret places, until they incubated into angels the size of dragons, the size of ants, or frogs, or butterflies so meek and lightly scaled, so beautiful and rare that nothing else mattered, but that slight flurry, ghostly, winged?

Of course, there was more. With my mother. When my favorite mare was due to give birth, I slept in the barn. Noodled into her, as though her body were a hatbox from which might spring a cacophony of feathers eerie as diamonds or a bevy of emeralds.

I was there when her cervix dilated, like a pupil going blind. And her moans, these were curses said under the breath. Light steamed near her body, cast by the barred window.

She took me below my body where I recalled spring evenings, christened by the chorus of peepers and the weight of chartreuse air. With a gush, the foal slipped out of the mare, like a plum glossed silver by the birth sac's gooey tented fabric. It tore, a purple snood.

The foal, like pick-up sticks, rose onto her jellied hooves. Nodding blankly toward all that would nourish her, she latched onto a nipple hard as a hoe.

Her nose was warm and soft, her lips spoke to my fingers, sweet as the burst of grape upon a velvet tongue.

No one knows how the smallest life is akin to an agent of the mind, or the first radiance of planets: like the filly, who arrived, as if on a mission to save souls.

When I threw back the barn doors, curried light mustarded the fields. The glow was a russet flare, almost hellish, but in me was a vision of a place I could have left many times and still not be gone.

The neighing all around me was a dark romance, but when my mother came out to inspect the new foal, I wanted to hide her.

"Worthless," she pronounced, as she swatted me, "just like you."

I didn't argue, but that foal was all I aspired to be, a sleek presence, fern-soft, unfurling.

Not long after, when I came out to do chores, I heard a cry that pierced me. I ran to the filly's stall and found her, one hoof belled between the bars. She hung by that one hoof, as though it were the Ace of Clubs.

Her cries cored me. I knew, in an instant, that she had been riled during the night, either by an owl's cowled hoot or the horrid half-howl the coyotes make.

Spooked, she reared, snorted red fire, jammed her hoof.

I ran for my mother, who grabbed a crowbar and pried the bars apart. When the filly fell, I ran into the stall, cocooned her.

The vet, of course, came. X-rayed her. Bandaged the hoof, looked at me, said, "Lily, it's time you leave the world of horses and enter the world of men."

Which meant the filly would be crippled for life. A slow crippling creeping inward, which is what my father felt like before he left. Like rancid jelly where blood should be.

Which is what I was when I met Tom.

As I led the injured filly, round and round the ring, ribbons on her tail, like those on a kite string, or the ones in my own long hair, he called out to me.

Thusly, I was drawn, as though enchantment and disenchantment were the cause and effect of every moment on earth. How often did we ride across hills blue as suitors?

In the felted air, the days themselves were a burnished stratum, waves of color twisted into the white pines, a friction or frisson of time, which is nature's genius, as is every whistle, squeak, or eerie bark.

Ephemeral. Of course. Everything is.

We went on. And then that night. When I became those scraped cells in a Petri dish, the ones from under the nails of the newly raped. After which we found what we found and I betrayed it.

Memory has its own wet black gold, is the residue I left on that statue before going back home. Empty as a curse.

The day my mother left the hens in the fields, their bodies smelling like bouillon cubes, I watched as the filly, her hoof still bandaged, moved with a flattering exactitude from behind the massive semblance of her mother's rump.

When her face, full of greatness and doneness and an exaggerated sense of aquiline significance, lifted itself to sniff air headlined by blood, when this little horse posed with an expressionless perfection, I applauded.

Even if she couldn't be studded, she was my prize—black cherry-bright, a prodigal in a spotlight of light.

The high faculty of her forehead, her paperweight heavy head, this made her mine as I went and folded into her flanks which were a squandered ornament.

The gun. Up it came. With a displeasing ease. I couldn't help but imagine my mother's aimed joy as she pulled back the trigger. The noise-bearing bullet blasted my ears.

When the little horse heaved herself, a steel door, upon earth's chilly twilled tweeds, her blood, tenacious as napalm, stained me, she whose consequential, belled silence turned life into the aching maw of a reluctant miracle.

Unlike my mother, who stood in the hell of here. When she fired again, I screamed, "take me too."

The sound the mares made was full of a devastating sentience as I held the little horse. After her last breath bubbled up, her body became heavy as marble and placid as lard. It was opulent as the rarest poverty. As was my mother.

Who stood with her legs apart as though she were the champion of champions.

Her groans told me: *we are in it still.*

Then and only then was she done, as was Tom when he kicked me while I held that corpse as though it were my trousseau.

Before I dragged the filly's carcass away, I draped myself over her. Her blood, its wet black gold, storied me into an empty future, one where a scant, unadorned gorgeousness might be found, like a pond of melted gold. Under which a stirring quickened, piloting to stay in place.

Losing that little horse was like losing a baby so small it wasn't even human. To suffer, to bear from below, this alone is deathless and everlasting.

Like the filly, or my eggs, which Tom ripped out of me as though they were a confession.

The beautiful thing about this story is that it happened. It was summer and time circled like a swarm of gnats, but I destroy myself, destroy myself and have such a long way to go.

Which gives me a sad pleasure. Like those orange roses

I heaped onto the filly's grave. And the night is precipice. No, the night is a hollow sound, beyond all depths and silences.

CRY THE DYING VIOLET HOUR

Furious, my sister pulls our entire plastic kitchen down, crashes it to the floor, as if toppling a bookshelf. Dishes scatter, are flying saucers.

Marie. Isn't she a war novel entirely lacking in female characters? And me, I'm like the table that eats its own legs off because it's fallen in love with the floor.

Weight presses down on me, pushes the air out of my lungs as I yell, "What'd you do that for?"

Marie doesn't answer. Intact in immaculate blackness from head to toe, more marvelous than the Cheshire cat with her portion of life, like a red pearl shining between her teeth, I can see how she wears our mother like a scarf around her neck.

"Clean it up," I yell, but Marie, she grabs a plastic bag, slips it over my head, cinches it.

When I start to choke, she laughs, pulls the bag off, retorts, "Clean it up yourself!"

Feeling infested, like cocoons are clinging to the back of my throat, I run into the bathroom, gag, spit them out.

Out the door I go, beyond the foggy shrubs and into woods the color of tea. The boulders are there, a warren of barren rooms.

As I walk, a thought sticks to my skull, as real as a bruised eye and what I have, there's no name for: mystery, suspense, insects, blood, curiosity, death, like layers of sky—crushed ice on branches sloshed with gold, some sun under it, making it all gleam.

Bloodless and bright, snow petals the ground, which is pleated like an accordion. Calm as a morgue, I find Mom, sprawled face down in the snow.

Bracing her, I see a puff of ice on her chin, as she coughs, drops again.

What good is she in her shower cap, pink bathrobe, as I push her shoulders back against the trunk of a tree. Her chest's so cold it cracks—in her shadow-etched face, sticky sap, the color of pee, oozes from her mouth.

I don't know what to think as she produces cigarettes from the pocket of her robe. Cigarettes and a lighter. Her bones don't make a sound as she lights up.

I huddle next to her. Shaped like an inverted triangle: her gaped mouth, a great white fish on the verge of striking, poised to devour and feed on skin, on all.

"Go home," I say. As I do, she staggers onto her feet, her face, sketchy as antenna, presses into memory.

Left to rot, my childhood, like the tree's speckled skin—and staticky, that sound my mother makes as she gets up, leaves, her eyes two small coffins.

Her smell—parasitic ash, swamp woods—runts me until even the hollow my body makes in the scant snow is a slight violence.

I too go home where softness makes a trap for me, like the scarf I love, the one my sister wears as she snores—her mouth, this makes tadpoles.

Her shoulders swell their small tides. I want to trap her sighs, divide the stillness in a mason jar: breath like smoke against the window—but I cuddle next to her, listen while the wind chatters down the gutters, noisy as gum balls.

I lose my edge mouthing Marie's name. To love what we can no longer distinguish, to cry the dying violet hour; I think about this as I peel a scab the size of a freckle off of her shoulder.

Through the curtains, I hear a voice, through folds and folds of fabric, a voice, like a slash of lightning—"Am I the most beautiful?" It's Mom, of course.

"Am I the most beautiful?" comes her voice again. Scratchy, like a broken toy.

How can I tell her that my father craves me, how when he comes for me, I'm silent as a gargoyle.

While I eat my screams, my sister pulls the covers over her head.

When he leaves, Marie stuffs her scarf between my legs, then slaps me. That slap, it burns as it hurdles through time and space like an over-bright comet made out of stones and plastic and boxtops and eggs.

After Marie storms out of the room, I pull the scarf out from between my legs. It smells hairy, is dotted with blood, is moldy Swiss cheese.

I turn it into a sock doll, use a magic marker to make a mouth, loud as a scowl.

All over the bedroom floor, pieces, a waterfall of pieces

from when Marie tore down our entire plastic kitchen. Plastic cookies. Plastic forks that look like claws that have crept out right of hell. Plastic cupcakes, tiny as Tater Tots. Holding my sock doll, I try to feed her a cookie, "Don't despair," I whisper, "you're almost there."

Why must I tell this? I'm just a girl who knows nothing. Bright as the sun, I gaze through folds upon folds of curtains, which trap the light, cry the dying violet hour.

It's the trapping, and the darkness so huge—but the light—*grilled, dished, dazzling, the wish of it, enough.*

MIRROR, MIRROR

Half-drunk, I get into my car, drive in coffin light, the sky drab as a nun. The lines on the highway wobble, my vehicle swerves. I don't care.

I'm wearing spiky black high heels. Like my mother, I choose my obsessions, which are train cars the size of boulders. I drink until my bone marrow pickles and my eyes, their lids, turn into thin tourniquets. I drink, my lips lush as a gun full of mist and dumb want.

When I arrive at the theatre where I'm to model, I leave my water in the car along with my slippers and spa socks. This way, I'll be able to drive home in comfort.

Up into a room bright as guilt I go. There's a bevy of women. Older, like me, with a worn, worried glamour. We dress, drink champagne from plastic cups. Red, red lips are painted. Diamond studs go in. Chatter chitter-chats.

Our clothes have paintings on them. Industrial windows. Ladders the color of yellow rain boots. Yellow like the sleeper pajamas I wore when all of thirteen. PJs with feet in them, suede bottoms so worn little balls formed on the padding.

In a tent the size of a merry-go-round, we played spin-the-bottle. Two girls smoked. The cigarettes glowed, were red batons. Our faces, lean and hound-like, were gaunt in charcoal gray light. Beyond the tent walls, the lawn hissed and stars barked, like barkers hawking cheap goods.

Which is what I was. My sister had shaved the back of my head so far up my neck, the kids in school taunted, "Girl or boy?" My breasts, these were as tender as a baby's teething gums. The liquor bottle, brown, grimy, was spun. *Round and round it went, and in coming round, did not come out right.*

It kept landing on me. Again and again. Girls sat on their thin haunches, bared their teeth. Off came my mood ring, smoky with a thin band of light. Off came my monkey knot bracelet. Off came my tongue, my mind, my heart.

Each time the bottle pointed at me, like a teacher's stern ruler, I was ordered to guzzle. "Ten, nine, eight," went thrashed teenage voices. Faces were in florid horror; anthrax and manna, festschrift, floating on air. I drank. The liquor sizzled down my throat.

"C'mon, girl, show us some more!" I unzipped my sleeper pajamas a half inch, then another. The girls kept at me. "More, more!" Tobacco smoke came at me. I shrank inside, was deflation at depth.

The air swaggered. My breath had obscene billboards in it. I swigged more alcohol, fell down, got up, a pop-up punching bag.

The girls, they laughed at me, shipwrecked hyena laughs. Susie Zompa, whose blonde hair was soft as dental floss, heckled, "She still calls her Mom, Mommy."

Drunk, my eyes stitched closed. I wanted my doll, the one whose hair was like the stuffing inside a cattail.

I robot-walked toward Susie. In school, we communicated by tapping our mood rings on our desk tops. Because they were too big, we had wrapped them in yarn.

I pawed the air as I walked toward Susie. I believed if I walked toward her, I could walk into her and leave my body behind, for it was the stuff snow disowns. My mind, it was zombie-like and full of the mechanics of disintegration.

"We want you naked, girl," came a chorus of voices, loud as a squawk box. When someone yanked on the collar of my pajamas, I shrank some more. I didn't want them to come off. My father might get me. This scared me so much, I passed out.

When I came to, I had peed in my pajamas. The pee was still warm. I was not. The other girls slept, were heavy tubes of paint. Susie snored, a chime held underwater.

I didn't know what to do. My head had garbage inside it. I stank. The girls around me, young and cruel, cute as toy guns, these girls were somehow normal. I was not.

Because I didn't know what else to do, I stripped, stuffed my sleeper pajamas in my sleeping bag, the one with fat cats in the lining. I then rolled it up, tight.

I put on the outfit I had arrived in for the slumber party. A plaid skirt with my bright-as-rented-light school blouse.

Ducking out of the tent, the sky was a scab with purple scallop edges. I took my sleeping bag with my yellow sleeper pajamas tucked inside it down to the river that smelled like a river. I tossed it in, a log. It bobbed, played

Dead Man's Float.

Birds flew in elegant mobs, tragic, sinister, their heads, migrating jewels. These senatorial survivors were feathered delicacies as they flung themselves, like musical geniuses, into wind that hefted their voices into glass ships.

Into the cornfields I walked. Into my country of phenomenal women, even though I was anything but phenomenal. I was just a girl who stank, a girl who already walked in the valley of death.

At the fashion show, I strut onto the runway, as though it too were the valley of death. I flash a smile like grass in a summer essay. My heels click, a nightmare of staccatos. I dance a little, turn, wave my scarf at old men whose smiles are weak lifelines.

Three times, I sashay out onto the runway. The other women do too. They are polite, demure, and smell good. I take up too much light, bare too much leg, smile way too hard. Aren't I what the lipstick lights?

I forget to eat. Little trays of appetizers go by after the fashion show. I ogle the wine, guzzle a glass or two. *Good night, beautiful peoples, good night,* I think as I head toward the door.

I'm stopped by the bartender. "Sorry, lady, you aren't going anywhere." His eyes are almonds, hard on the edge, but sweeter in the middle. Mine, I suppose, are glazed.

"You," he goes on, "are in no condition to drive."

"Excuse me," I say, "but I need to go home." I wink at him and in that instant, I remember: brother Doug, once he was so drunk he slammed through a neighbor's sliding doors. The waterfall of glass was tinsel on a Christmas tree.

I am that tree and my words are an authentic corpse

as I smooth-talk the bartender. "My little dog," I start. Surely a woman who has a dog to care for will be allowed to drive home. Surely.

The bartender body-blocks me. "Go sit down," he orders. I'm put into a side room. People gather. I keep talking. "My feet are killing me. Can't you see that from these stupid heels?"

Faces contract. Am I slurring my words? "I've got slippers and water in my car," I argue. "I'll be fine."

"We're not letting you drive," come more voices than I can count. Are their voices slurring? Blurring?

A big fat hamburger is shoved at me. It's bloody and the bun looks like a monkey's bum. I shove it away and do what drunk grownup women do. I cry.

Mascara streaks down my cheeks. This is a scene and I'm making it. A cop comes in. I notice his gun, snug as a penis in its holster. *Please put it in my mouth. Pretty please?*

"Just blow," he orders. I blow into the breathalyzer. Will I make bubbles?

"Good God," says the cop.

"Uh-oh," I answered, "uh-oh, spaghettios."

I'm driven home. All the way I talk, but the driver, he just yawns, a fly flinging itself against the pane.

At home, I get undressed, put on my nightie, pour myself a drink while listening to myself howl, like having fangs is something to regret. So what if ninety percent of my blood is pure alcohol? Aren't I the one who chooses my obsessions, like boulders the size of train cars? I choose and in choosing, I walk in the valley of death.

When I walk into the bedroom, what I see in the mirror on the wall is more ghost than anything else. My face, it isn't mine, for in it, like an exit wound, is the tarnished face of my mother. *Mirror, mirror.*

From my own face, *mirror, mirror,* rises the holding pattern of my mother's. *Isn't she the fairest of them all?* Clutching the dog like a feather duster, I crawl into bed. The foam mattress sinks into a "U" as I fall into drunken sleep. My drool trickles down my cheeks as though it's a lifeline. The faithful work of my drowning has begun.

Still, I remember: when my brother Ed married his college sweetheart, there was a party. Back at the hotel, Mom and Dad drinking. Ed's friends. Me in my shirtwaist dress, prim as a school teacher. Cigarette smoke. Beer bottles. Chaos. Calamity.

A sordid joy. Dad stood up, "Toga party," he exclaimed. Bedsheets came off the beds. Ed's young friends donned them, masquerading as strobe lights with Smiley face grins. Wreaths were fashioned out of lamp cords.

My father was among them in a toga splotched with tarantula-brown cigarette burns. He staggered, moved, as though he were a bone fracture. His sickly hands flew up.

He went down. His groan, it filled me, for he was a muscled quarrel with the muscled sea. Bearish and unbearable, Dad stood up. His toga twisted around him, a loin cloth.

Ed's friends, they took the party elsewhere. Mom, she moved, a flip-book, tiny, drunk, stuttering, slobbering. She sharpened my sight, blocked the fact that something too violent is always attached to something too alive.

Each punctured moment punctured her mouth: deplorable and utterly useless, it opened, closed, a dare.

Dad went down again, as if bearing a crucifix. I felt its

enormous weight, felt the ruin in his hip bones. I watched him, my hair up in a knot, he who once came at me like a knife thrown into a tree.

Let him fall, I thought, *like a blowdown ocean.* Even then, I knew his erasure would make me a frequently asked question that entirely misses the point.

No one helped him up. I stood there, let his flesh and mine sink accurately. His breath, it was misplaced weather. And his face, a hurt woman's who makes the doorknobs go silent.

When my father went down a third time, when he lay there on the floor, like a strange image of the body stroked dark, did I wish him dead? Maybe. Because isn't this the world my family has arranged and isn't it horrible, how we carry on?

Next morning, when we checked out, Dad was dressed in pink golf pants, a lime-colored shirt. Mom was in golf clothes, too. I noticed her sleeves, the clean buttons, how each seam gleamed. Her eyebrows, these wore a suit of summer dusk, a quietus.

When the manager came out, the bristles on Dad's un-shaven face moved like the legs of vanquished insects. He took a long pull off his cigarette while I considered how little flesh is needed to make a song.

"Sir," the manager started. His smile had gone missing. "Sir," he started again, but Dad interrupted. His face was a wet cut.

"Nice operation you've got going on here," Dad stated flatly. Ashy laughter came from his spineless throat.

"Sir," the manager eked out again. "Complaints," he murmured. His lips were cheap receipts. Mom, she put on her movie star sunglasses.

"The bill," he went on. "Damages. Here at the bottom."
When he waved the bill, my father grabbed it. "What's the problem? You should be congratulating me. My youngest son just got married."

Like the briefest of doors, the manager moved. When he put his hand on my Dad's back, I almost slapped him.

"Sir," he said, as though he were the priest at High Mass, "you're not allowed to come back to this hotel."

Who was he, this manager? Was he the hole in my heart, or the hole in my grave? I felt my tongue sharpen with each sharp breath I took.

"Go to hell," I yelled.

Dad smiled. It was a cutting-edge grin. So cutting, I smiled right back at him and when I did, God opened his blankest eye upon us. Mom, Dad, me.

Like the congenitally spoiled, the three of us walked out the door. The sun was shining. Birds chirped while memory slipped into a hand grenade.

This was the world we arranged. Horrible, how we carried on, like well-groomed, old fashioned guns.

Horrible, yes, but glorious too for this was my family, that is, my genius, helpless, wretched, like a short-thrifted goodnight kiss or a paltry sorrow which saw our partial horns, saw the cut sky see us, rueful, singing.

WHAT IT IS LIKE TO LIVE

Alone in the school yard, a blizzard suddenly blows in, and within moments, puts me in its calculated coma. A small circus bear, I paw the air with my red mittens while my lungs cry like feathers. I spin and spin, a top.

My stocking cap, the one the boys like to yank off when they sneak onto the girl's playground, this the wind takes with ease. Snow begins to fall under my skin. I shiver while my brain stem hardens.

The blizzard halts me in the stasis between fight and flight. To be lost in a storm, any storm, is to know that the angels, like pregnant women, dispense with us freely.

The boys, they chased us while our skirts moved in a thievish rush of wind. Underneath: *the beginning of all mystery.*

We all got caught. Sister Claret, who had no niggling tenderness toward any of us, said, "You girls have no modesty. I can even see your Kotex."

Our punishment was to come to school that Saturday to scrub the school's corridor with a toothbrush. Down on our hands and knees, each tick-tack-toe tile was beige, boring as God.

I scrubbed and scrubbed while glancing into a nearby classroom where I saw myself ferrying down aisles, like a small Venetian, past desks long bolted to the floor, gondolas in deep canals, in order to brush the chalk dust from the good Sister's veils while the globe atop her desk, needled by its axis, spun and spun its little world.

Every morning, we girls kneel to show her our skirts are long enough. A yardstick is used to measure the length from floor to knee.

While kneeling, I long to step inside Sister Claret's confessional, to watch her undress, tissue falling from her sleeves, her breasts clear, tiny as raindrops.

Walking home, the road appears, disappears, caked by briskets of snow. Lonely as an orphan, the voice of the storm tries to erase me.

When I walk into the house, a bottle tears through the air, shatters when I grab it with my hand. It splits a vein, turns my fingers purple.

I can't even make a fist. I use the other hand to indicate, *I'm okay.*

Mom's giddy, the way people are when their lives go up in smoke. Her eyes, drawn into tiny brown sacks, gleam—the alcohol on her smells and her meanness, it's a loop of razor wire that closes around the circumference of a shaken snow globe.

"Your father," she says. In that instant, she has pinned the tail on the donkey. "He lost the job again."

When a boom comes from the wood stove, *red roar,*

blue applause, I stand, clutch my hand. With a ferris wheel smile on my face, I see him, fingering his pant zipper like a snake's tongue. Up, down, it goes. The sound, it rips stitches.

She harrows me, "Go to your room," she says, as if her voice could penetrate my private parts, which are many— my teeth, my hair, my tears, which are dirty as a sock, but I just stand there, staring at my father's head, which is bald as a bulb of garlic.

"Do as I say, Patty, or else."

I go halfway up the steep stairs, squat. My parents look like clay figures dipped in oil paint. I watch Mom's hands go up.

When her fists come down upon my father, I remember the Playhouse. Down in the woods. Where I held tea parties with my Patty Play Pal.

"Lift your little finger," I said as I held the cup, which was wreathed in Banded Peacock butterflies, "just like this."

When she didn't answer, I wanted to slap her, but she was too pretty. She was also bigger than me.

That's when I heard snapping sounds—quick, neat, like a turtle's mouth. "Patty," came a voice, "oh my little Patty-melt, guess who's here?"

I didn't answer. Instead, I ducked behind my doll, made her my human shield. Peeking out, I glimpsed a hunter's hat. Bright orange, a boiling sky. "Patty," came the voice again, "Come out, come out, from wherever you are."

Sickly sweet, that voice made my stomach turn like a cherry cough drop.

It was Dad. In his Hush Puppy slippers with the backs

broken down. Into the Playhouse he came, fast as a gash.

There was no one to make him reasonable as he ripped my doll out of my grip. No one to make him reasonable, as he got out the razor and cut the hair off her head.

No one, as he said, "You're next," while holding the razor to her throat.

I could hear Mom saying, "Everyday is like this," just as Patty's head hit the floor, dull as a door with a hole punched through it. It rolled, the way heads do.

Holy dum-dum, silly ottie ay. This is what happens, *Holy dum-dum, rum-dee-dum.* To people like me, *silly ottie ay ae.*

The sound of his Hush Puppies. *Silly ottie ay,* like squishy seaweed as he went away, *Holy dum-dum, rum-dee-dum.*

Big as a block, I cradled that head—it couldn't talk, couldn't walk, that head, which like a ball with no bounce, stayed dead, played dead.

When I walked back up to the house, I wanted my girlhood to circle me like a coat, but my mouth, rotted and anonymous, felt thicketed in sludge. It opened, shut.

Smelling brittle, I snuck into the house, right past Dad who was polishing the shoes. White and eyeless, the clock ticked. Had someone wound it with a knife?

"Soybeans," he said, "the future is in soybeans." His face, this was the color of my old sandbox.

I went into my room, closed the door, got into bed where the streetlight blazed, a neon fig.

While my brain split, I wondered: had my father stolen my screams? Would I wear what he did to me like gills or a new way to breathe? Weren't my siblings, all but shadow selves and aren't minds like family, which makes dying one of the exits it can take?

In the middle of the night, I crept down the hallway into my parents' room where they lay on the bed, smelling like the fungi on ingrown toenails. As I walked over to their bureau, house flies brained them.

Inside its drawers: the smell of pine; of lavender. Inside the lavender: nests of stuffing. Inside that: my mother's nylons, a dot of semen, violent longing.

Inside that—a roach nibbling through silk, the sound of it, dust on a bat's wing.

Because death is utterly banal, like an arm pulled through a sleeve, I wanted to be against it, but I wasn't, not entirely, nor were my parents who curled, a question mark, under a ceiling that leaked yellow light.

Because I wanted to do what my father did to Patty, I padded down the hallway out the front door and ran away.

After years pass like a mute correspondence, I end up in an apartment, dark as porn.

In a house with no before or after, no faith in, no walls, no shelves—I live alongside a cripple named Lloyd and an imbecile named Elmer.

On Catlyn Avenue, the dark evergreen days turn and turn. The two men, they live upstairs. Elmer is next door to Lloyd. In a room that's soiled newspaper.

He has pictures of naked ladies. Wears sunglasses on Saturdays. Works as a dishwasher. Each plate a slice of moon. Each glass hot and ready for his cock. He likes my legs. Leaves me notes in the mailbox alongside penny candy, as I once did for my mother.

Lloyd sits in his green chair all night long. Tells of his broken body to a TV that blasts the news about a headless body in a topless bar. His face is as soft as my inner thighs, but the rest of him is a tarnished medal.

One night, I sit at my desk, grab one of my father's stubby red pencils, write Elmer and Lloyd a letter in the pitch dark, imitating a blind child whom I had watched write her name on the chalkboard. Each shaky line led to another until the words were more like pictures, which resembled the attitudes of the sainted sacred.

Because the cold comes in, this work doesn't last long. Shivering, I crawl into bed, pull the black bedspread up to my chin. I fluff my lozenge-hard pillow and lay my hair on it, as though it were a dancer's fan.

While the street lamp blooms in my bedroom, I listen to the *tap, tap, tap* of Lloyd's wooden leg thumping down the stairs where wallpaper, dimmed by old florals, peels off. His leg is a twisted cask, a complicated bramble. It holds him hostage.

There's a knock on my door. I get up. Wearing my mother's flesh-colored nightgown, I open it.

It's Triplett, not Lloyd.

"Hi," I say. My head is down. I'm afraid to kiss him.

"Can I come in?" he asks. His hair falls in long auburn waves. His face, white as a scare tactic, has blue, blue eyes. Forget-me-nots. Cornflowers. Like my Patty Play, he's pretty, way too pretty.

"Of course," I whisper, then take his hand, lead him to my bed.

I'm nineteen. My body is a dream, is the myth surrounding Catlyn Avenue. I pull my nightgown over my head. It leaves my hair a desirable mess.

"Oh," he says, as he kisses me. I unzip his white Chinos. The sound of it is skin pulled off a snake.

Because Triplett wants me, I let him. When the condom, soft as a mouse, breaks, the cartography of longing pulses onto my thigh. I wipe it away, as Sister Claret did her breasts.

And then, like a paler version of my father, he's gone. His vanishing is an abyss, one in which an infant screams.

In the yard, the landlord's dog is perpetually leashed. The dog turns manic circles, is a goldfish in a dime store bowl.

I go outside where the landlord's shape fills his window like a shadow self, then drops from sight.

I walk barefoot in the melting snow as though it were my genius to do so. I'm wearing my only dress. Blue birds weep in its torn sleeves.

I walk, hold each breast in my trembling hands while the snow starts to fall, huge flakes like voluptuous birds— and clouds the color of a romantic rose, these throb quicker than the human heart, throb, flutter, like a red ear on a wet pillow.

Flushed, cold, I return to the house on Catlyn Avenue, knock on Elmer's door. When he answers, my hand goes to his face. Cool as a clamshell. With no meat inside, but chubby as a club.

Nights, he clicks a spoon against the silver radiators. The rhythm of heartbreak, of distress, of broken bottles flying through the air, of glass shattering, a rainbow of glass, like skinned fish, the scales glistening, a stripper's pasties.

He steps aside, let's me in. "How about a Coke?" he asks.

"A beer would be better, thanks."

Elmer grabs two from a fridge that looks like a well-fed tomb. When he hands me mine, I remember how my father once courted my mother. Instead of flowers, he brought her a basket full of beer. A bouquet of bottles, sudsy, frothy, like scum on a summer pond. Frightened, Elmer backs into an overstuffed chair. Doilies are on it, like a latticework of shadows thrown onto a prison wall. The sound of him humphing into the chair, deflates. His jaw, it hangs, jowly, like a clown's.

I walk over, straddle him, hike up my dress. The birds, blue as a nightmare, arc their injured wings.

Sounds fill the room. Cries like kites slap against my head. When I kiss Elmer's thrash of a face, his sigh is as lonely as a red cello's string.

The beer bottle. This I smack against the coffee table until its neck snaps, the way a bird's does when a cat nabs it, the way my Patty Play Pal's did when Dad knifed it, the stalk of it, celeriac.

The bottle, brown as a scowl, this I press against Elmer's flabby neck, a low tech crown of thorns. With it, I sketch a zigzag of lines.

I'm about to cut: to score a single, sharp-edged pattern; but Elmer's fixed hysteria is rendered obsolete when little Lloyd rushes in.

Instead of batting the bottle out of my hand, Lloyd bats at the tinsel streamers on the electric fan, then drops his crutch. Looking obscenely green, obscenely jewel-toned, obscenely neck-like, he somehow possesses both grandeur and decadency as he begins to dance.

Like a space invader in an arcane video game, Lloyd, hapless and demented, flaps around the room with spittle on his lips. His fingers wilt like vegetables in a drawer and the look in his eyes—his thousand, groping green eyes—

as he step-drags, step-drags, this is the worst of all, lacerating and unforgivable, as if to say, *this is what it's like to live.*

Poor eyes. Poor eyes that see me weeping, the beer bottle now rolling on the floor, like the grossest of tumors and Elmer's lap, soggy as the Kotex Sister Claret insisted she saw when we girls forgot to cross our legs.

The smell has temperature and space while a rat reveals itself in the corner the way a woman tenses in and out of the light—like Lloyd, like Elmer, like me.

A LATTICE OF FILAMENTS

My cold cheek, hard as candy, is where this story writes itself nightly; where ghosts weave their oily hair into Dad's, then lay him fetal on the icy concrete—the afterbirth of stars glistened over him while snow blew through the high fever of belief and ended where our mother's lips went white.

We drained our flashlights on his scraped forehead, watched the moon two-step across his waxen eyes—from his mouth's shallow pond, his sobs were a monstrous fetus hung up in its own uselessness.

"Once more, just once more," he whispered, as he got up, bruised me into the car.

Through sleet and ash, Dad drove me under bare cherry trees, which were grand hotels closed for the season. Behind us, death, like a trickle of terror was layered, liquid as thirst. More than touch, less than labor, it was a lesson in tilt and lather.

At home, Mother, hovering, waited. My little brother Joey held his head, tight as a football. Neon Budweiser signs blinked, an ellipsis, in the fogged windshield as Dad drove, a tensed verb.

I don't know why we move around the world as though there were a single way for each of us, a kind of life stamped into us, like a childhood injection, a cure released into the blood with every passing year, as if to protect against any possible disobedience that might awaken in the body.

But the body isn't mere submissive matter. It's a lattice of filaments as I imagine threads of starlight must be.

What can never be touched: the body. Or so it should be, but whenever someone lives outside the law and that law is muscled and violent, a boulder plunging off a precipice and crushing everything in its path, how then do we manage to wander around, how do we feel confident in being what we are: blood, organs, sex, this species?

When Dad cleaned his mouth on my neck, sitting in the dark—pain didn't distance me, not with my skin on his sweater, both hands stripped.

The body is never an accident—Dad lingered, his thumb like a cat's tongue, his lips, the signature at the bottom of a painting. I tried to scream, but my voice only went as far as my lungs.

In that moment, I understood that no one knows the way to heaven, even so, we keep trying to get there.

When we do, it will be different, but we'll use the same words. One little word as small and large as anyone and if there aren't any words, then the soul of every living thing will be measured by the intensity it manifests once it's set free.

Strange, what Dad did to my face—he spit in my mouth when I refused to cry after Joey shot himself in the barn, a shard of light growing in the hole in his skull beneath clouds the color of wolves.

My brother's hands, these were five-legged spiders, knuckled starfish, grabbers of forks, the softest suggestions. They flew up like two birds when we spoke, two brown thrashers brandishing twigs in their beaks, lifting song the way pepper springs from the tongue.

Always, I held his hands, which smelled like caramel, cocoa, black beans, vanilla.

Like Joey, I had been looking for a way out—when I lifted my head as Dad stood above me, my jaw dropped, a ransacked drawer.

I said nothing because I was shivering and the rain, which felt like a translation of crushed hours, was falling.

I swallowed it, like the latex gloves Dad wore as he tied me up with the leash Mom dragged Joey on, down the road, a bitter store clerk.

Sitting beside this ancient gray fountain, I'm imagining him alive somewhere in the world, and I don't know how I feel about that. He's eating a peanut butter sandwich, peeling away the crust, like tearing the dress off a mannequin. He's sinking his nails into the skin of a peach, licking his fingers.

I need to stop thinking that this fountain is made of the same material as tombstones. I need to stop thinking that if Joey had ever met the moon, he would have grabbed it by the throat.

Does it matter? Even extinction is temporary. Rain as it touches ground.

Because dark clouds don't fade but drift with ever

deeper colors, I've given up on happiness and meanwhile, meanwhile's far from nothing: the humming moment, shaking like eyelashes in a hurricane.

Now I watch a squirrel clean its face until its hands are Joey's, until the chemical energy of sunlight is gentle as a kiss on its cheek, or laundry taken by the wind.

It's true—what Father did, the yellow pills, how I went away. Anything can hold itself hostage. The question isn't *Why* but *so what?*

Still, there are ways of touching without bulldozing, ways of washing a body without making the person inside it feel like a plate. I did that for my brother and now I carry him in my pocket like a mint.

Even as children, we wore our skin like an anesthetic. Dad's licking, the sound of it, a velvet itch. And the hole in my brother's head, this was a thrashed halo, an emerald shrine, a gold ring.

If we could see into anyone's life, wouldn't it be through this hole, which is slag enough to crust the world with rotting and birthing and being born in the smallest possible once before once.

II.

Years and years of never rest and it's peaceful.

IN A SCENE DEAD FOREVER

The dog barked at the wind-loomed trees while I grew up stubborn, like jello molded in tiny doll dishes, each trembling bit different in shape but otherwise all the same.

One day, when foraging in the sunshine, I found a paper hat afloat on a cone of water. The orange and gray bugs on it were linked from mating, but they faced each other with antennae like horny peace signs.

Their scrambling, this amounted to nothing, which simply means that the imagination is more restless than the body.

In the afternoon, when the shades were pulled for my nap, the light coming through was dark yellow, nearly orange, melancholy, heavy as honey, and it made me thirsty.

That doesn't say it all, not even a small part. Yet it seems even more incomplete than when I was there. Half the day in half the room. The wool made me itch and the scratching made me warm.

The crib next to my bed held the baby like an apple. Scrubbed, polished. The paper hat was propped up next to him like a tent, and the sound of his breathing, this seemed sad.

I wanted the doll I had half-buried in sand. She was lying on her stomach with one eye closed, driving a toy truck along the road she had cleared with her fingers. Protected by the dog, protected by foghorns, I had played with her while a frog honked and crickets circled the brown hill.

When my mother called me inside, as if to receive a birthday present given early because it was too large to hide, or alive—a pony perhaps, his mane trimmed with colored ribbons—I obeyed.

Later that day, I raked the leaves beneath the trees— their shaggy branches scattered twigs in the deep cleavage between dirt and roots. The treetops hesitated, then swept the horizon, until there was just the singing of birds and the sounds of a natural scream.

The baby. My mother had left him on the front walk. In the stroller. The hot sun pickled him. And so he screamed.

That scream lives on in a scene forever dead. A scream, livid as meat. It has cankered my brain.

The baby. His bald eyes stiffened when I ripped the sun bonnet off his head. On that miserable eternity of a day, the pinched peaches of his ears twitched, ugly as scabs.

I carried the bonnet, big as a lung. Strutting around the yard, I needed high heels. A cigarette holder thin as an ibis. Lipstick the color of embers.

When I went back to the baby, his skin looked like a lizard's—gray-lit, gray, glistening.

His howling, I hated it. I also hated how his head looked like a kidney bean.

Pure as a brand new pair of underwear, I yelled, "Stop it, stop it, you dumb old baby!"

"Lie down," I went on, but that's all he knew how to do. Lie down. Howl. Like a crash of smashed crockery.

My arms, these were hard as paint sticks. When his mouth opened into a scream that whelped, all sound was sucked down like weights on a diver—all that could sink, sunk.

Afterwards, someone was crying, but it certainly wasn't the baby. He was quiet while I washed him with a little gray leaf that was a handkerchief for waving good-bye.

I washed him, feeling like a house rolling toward the abyss with two empty shells embracing each other for an endless journey.

Brighter than a globe of an enflamed thistle he was. Brilliant. Silent. Wrapped in his blue blanket, I condensed into his dazzling transparency like a ghost turned inside out.

When I picked him up, he felt electric. Smelling like a mild blight of violets falling uselessly on forgotten days and hours; his name, his persistent name, this my hand left behind on the familiar tree, its sound always green against the windowpanes.

In the very garden where the grass still grows, where his head so often rested beside mine in the thickets of darkness, everything's still the same.

Oh, how I miss his obstinate silence, his skin, desolate as a country—visited only by ash-gray petals that have watched, for so long now, the inexhaustible patience of ants going back and forth through the ruins.

This isn't the cold face of the terrifying snow nor the face of last night's dream, no, it's my mother's cry—its absolute loneliness, its absolute truth, as I carried what was wrapped in the blue blanket back to her, and this long future: staring at my hands like harnessed scorpions as they grow old.

THE SHIPWRECKED WORLD

As we sailed a small sloop in Chesapeake Bay, Dorothy Schaffer, whose homeliness—modest, unmentionable— was punctuated by pimples that populated her face like a sad brown town. Our sad brown town, the one we were earnestly sailing away from, was a story with rope burns.

All of fifteen, her greasy brown hair was parted straight down the middle and tied back too tightly. Had a razor been scored into her skull, the way a butcher scores a raw slab of meat?

When there was a sound like a bassoon with a mute on it, one girl started screaming, "Overboard, Dorothy has gone overboard!"

In water placid as a cucumber, Dorothy flailed, bobbed, went under. It was a sickening, baffling sight, this girl whose face was a homily no one listened to, whose coarse skin was malted by the light's bookends and whose will to live was an elastic that wouldn't snap back, well, even her flailing was pathetic.

I can't say she was someone anyone would want to rescue. Why, I wondered, was she trying to kill herself? Why, *why* was Dorothy Schaffer trying to die? Was she beyond clear meaning and any indication of the human? Would her beefy body simply sink, heavy as a tub of margarine?

Her hands were fliers, the kind you pin under windshield wipers, fliers folded into cootie catchers. Kelp wrapped itself around her arms like cheap bangles. Her mouth twisted into an inverted kiss as she made pufferfish sounds, little blows, weird little nonsense rhymes that set my teeth on edge.

Her reason, where had it gone? With whom was she wrestling in the water's well-argued allegory? Her father? Hadn't he hung himself from a ceiling even she could have punched a fist through? Her voice was the lisp inside a drafty flue, raspy, nasty.

Pathetic, I thought, cunning, too, but still I dove into the sea, yes, I dove into where I grabbed hold of her greasy hair and strapped my arm across her chest, her rough bookish chest, then dragged her while she gasped and coughed and peed, icky pee that made my stomach turn.

I lugged her, a booby prize, back to the boat where my shipmates Susie and Joy helped haul Dorothy back onto the deck, then me after her, and when I fell on top of her in a sick heap, I started to pummel her, yelling, "What the hell were you thinking?"

I beat Dorothy with a will I adored—glorious, victorious. I beat her while snorting a Chieftain snort which aborted my wretchedness.

While I pounded this half-drowned girl, who burbled like a Barbie doll, I could hear Dad yell, "The belt. You're going to get the belt."

I was screaming, "No, no," when Susie's arms grabbed me. She pulled me off Dorothy, yelling, "Stop it! Stop it!"

Panting, with my hands on my knees, I belched and glared at Dorothy as her eyes rolled back into her head. When I saw the bruises start to welt up on her face like leeches or jewels followed by tears which rolled down her cheeks—these wrung the world right out of me.

"Sorry," I whispered, "sorry."

Exhausted, I fell down on the deck next to her. What a mess we had made, yet when Dorothy started twining her hair around her index finger as though she could pin curl it, I started twining mine.

"Your dad," I said under my breath.

Her head went down. Drops of seawater beaded on her forehead, then fell into her lap, a lap full of worry and uncertainty.

Weren't Dorothy and I one of a kind and weren't we both hiding the part of us that stank like milk thick as leftover grease?

"We'll be going home soon," I continued. Our attachment to our fathers, wasn't this what made our future look like a mortician's face?

My hand touched hers. Our fingers laced together. In an evening loose with dreamy attention, we held hands gently, ever so gently.

"Dorothy," I said, "aren't we a pair?"

Her smile, slight, boring and small, was far from being swoon-worthy, but it was a smile nonetheless. It filled me with a thin joy as I added, quietly, "Will you visit me sometime?"

She nodded her head. That nod was the kind the birds

make when aiming to mate.

When I looked up, the evening wheel was flying, far off, dreaming. Soon, we would be, too. "C'mon," I whispered, "it's time for bed."

I wanted to add, *Safe, it is safe now,* but didn't, because for girls like us, it was never safe. For girls like us, there was only a lock with no key. The best we could do was hold hands and so we did, as I sea-horsed my lukewarm back into the washbowl of Dorothy's soupy belly.

We spooned each other, snuggling tight like chipped, unloved Hummels.

While the waves tumbled, were backup dancers, a flawless cheerleading squad from a more transcendent universe, I touched the velour of Dorothy's neck, but because she smelled like cat food, my heart deadened in its sack, patient, mute, a slave.

In the republic of pain, clouds piled up on one another, swallowed the sky like an eyeball—silent, powerful, better than me in every way, they hustled over the shipwrecked world until forever came out—*or not, or not, or not, or not.*

JONES BEACH

It should not follow but it does; my brother Ed is here; in the brief strenuousness, in a house like a cowl on the head.

"Well?" I ask, my voice, a song with hinges. Even though I'm wearing my heaviest sweater, I'm cold. Rain falls, like evening wear, while the season stretches out of shape.

"Spoons," he replies.

We take one another's hands, lift spoons over the gas flame on the stove, the blue of it, noble.

When our spoons glow like eels and soften into wax, we pour hash into them, throw a blanket over our heads, breathe. The coals are blisters, rippling.

At first I think it's a dream—in my brain, which is like cheesecake, the dead bark once.

If it's true what they say about memory being the weakest character in the story: then my first ones occur in a series of rooms—behind a locked door, my fingers trapped.

I was five years old. If cut open, if dissected, this is what would be pulled from me: a pair of handprints, a body, fossilized. Nothing much.

Afraid my brother will turn my smile into a knife, I plead, "Look at me! Goddammit, look at me!"

I want to tell him that I know it's hard to gaze at the speckled night sky and not wish upon dead light, but Ed just stares at the wall.

An egg, frilly as an apron, has been spattered against it, the blood a worn echo. The moral: *Live life like an egg: fried.*

I look out the window, see a man's pink tongue razing the horizon. Or is it raging? A tree, thin as a pin in the skull, tangos and spars, makes me paranoid about how much grief it can witness, withstand.

When I was buried in the sand, what was left of me sent up a demand like a corkscrewed hand. "Jones Beach," I say, "remember how Dad buried me?"

"You thought you were in a body bag. Your screams were so loud, we took turns kicking you." My face, wasn't it a pyramid—ear holes, eye holes, nose holes, mouth hole, plugged, spongy?

But I'm thinking about the waves. High as a church. Gothic. The color of swampy molasses. They screeched even louder than me.

"Uncle Richard." Dad's sister's husband. He dove into the ocean's black maw. To save, to rescue a man holding his daughter in a love knot. They bobbed, went under, her swim cap white as skimmed milk.

Didn't, as they say, come back. Death is funny like that: precise, dissolute.

The sound of almost drowning. A slap on the backside? A hiss, a kiss, sloppy as a jellyfish, the one that lights up before it lights down, like slashed lightning?

Buried in sand, I was a heaved under a mountain, heaved into a cave, my blue swimsuit heavy as the water flooding Richard's mouth like tears from the windowsill of a house, a window opened onto a bed, a small boat, a shipwreck, a current come to carry us away.

Bodies. Mine. Uncle Richard's. The swimmers he couldn't rescue because water, like a drain, lurked in them. Bodies like a shoal of fish kept in the depths of a ten gallon darkness. Bodies. Clearly, they're a system for cleaving until death opens for darkness to pass into.

And if darkness is the solution, I won't be like it, won't be a shell scooped of its life, won't be the sea glass punished for inciting violence.

Under sand heavy as cookie dough, I heard shouts: Richard's body was pulled up beside mine. Pigs-in-a-blanket, the dead girl and her father was lined up too. *Who's who?* I wondered, *Who's who?*

I kicked the sand away, sat up, swung so hard my hand landed in the mush that was Richard's face. Applesauce. Under cling wrap.

Taller than the wingspan of a heron, I stood up. Pointed. People began to gather around the bodies like seagulls. Their footprints burned holes in the sand. It was a strange parade: the dead strapped to boogie boards, followed by a flock of rowdy boys.

Some squawked and flapped their bony limbs while the waves waltzed, as if in an acre of bad wigs.

Stories. Like a top whirling so fast you can't see it stop. Fifty years later and all I know is that Ed and I love the sea even if it swallowed Richard like a collapsed waterfall.

Was any of it real? My brother's kitchen where I watched our hands turn into window blinds, cool as patients in difficult bodies.

"Be polite to the windows," I say. "They know we're beyond repair."

Were we? Neither of us knew the meaning of what was lost. Childhood like a spare tire. An Uncle.

We knew we wouldn't go back. What for? To see bodies shaped like a banana palace? Bodies hard as a rubber crotch?

The price of any lesson: to describe what happened such that it doesn't happen again. An SOS in the sand, that was me. Crushed like a grape inside a fist. And Uncle Richard. Water, a vise, held him.

We have gotten older, my brother and me. My breasts have migrated into tectonic flats, but I can always find hints of what used to be, and if I move with a wrongness any animal can see coming, this, I think, is what turns the wheel: the moon ghosting a hole in a rainbow, the rainbow's effort to efface the moon, the moon sailing, slow as a ship.

Loss. It lives in us like a question we can't answer, but keep trying: the secret is that it can't last but does, like a pile of trash or the chain of starfish I left plastered on Jones Beach, a bridge of starfish—arced, empty, dead as party hats, tossed up, unlucky coins turning in darkness.

MAKE LASTING FRIENDS

My friend Lenny and I are on our bikes. Mine's a blue ten speed, Lenny's is silver. She has dark brown hair, a good face, strong bones.

Our tires kick up brown dust, low sulfurous clouds. Hunter orange flags fan the stale Midwestern sky. They're propped on the back of our bikes on antenna-like poles. Warning, *warning*.

On an adventure, we pedal along a bike trail in Southern Wisconsin. We plan to ride for two weeks. To make a loop, a circle, a wild quest. Our backpacks hold water, hot dogs, buns we stole from the local A & P.

Pumping hard, the trail is banked by leaves, by cornfields stacked with hazy hay-heaps, by fields mobbed with hoof prints. Are the trees tall green goddesses? Do they move a little in milkweed-heavy air?

We continue to bike, leaving behind towns we refuse to try on. At dusk, when it's pitchfork and gray, we pedal into a campsite. The green goddesses have gone into the low lights of our imagination where they spark, quietly.

Lenny and I make a campfire. We drink strawberry wine, smoke pot. The scent of it hovers, like a needle on vinyl.

An RV is at the campsite. The man I've always needed to walk away from is in it. We hear him, smell the whorish scent of his liquor traveling, like blood, from his body into ours.

When he moves his RV closer, we caterpillar down into our sleeping beds. My breasts rest in the bellies of cats. We fall asleep.

When I awaken, that man's hands package my left leg. His odor parachutes out of him, the dust in stink bugs. The hollow in the hulk of him is a herring left face-up in its briny tin.

I touch Lenny. We bolt upright. She has a fishing knife in her hand. I have an eighteen inch flashlight in mine, shiny as a baton.

When the flashlight comes down on his head, I hear a pop. He doubles over. His puckered face turns ugly, like a child's when it cries. Lenny's knife, the sound of it going in, a heavy doubt, is sweet as swilled light.

The two of us flip him onto pavement, hard as my head. When I kick him, the sound of it is raw steel, a confusing clamor.

We flee the campground. We pump and pump on our ten speeds. Terror is a magnet fastening us to the same pane of glass. As we ride, I remember the tag on my mother's dish towel, *Make Lasting Friends*.

The cornfields slide by. And still we go on, our brakes

screeching, an avalanche of wind and fog. Moon is earth-quake thudding and tearing, hard as the shrapnel fists of our fathers who come at us, their voices, polite, loutish, assured, suave. They come at us, yes, they do come, breathing through mouths which are holes.

And still we go on. We jink over potholes and crooked nails. Even our hair is tired, famished.

We pedal by flat-chested corn cribs, barns collapsing into lapse-backed mules and randomly spaced trees, knowing that our fear of being broken is dexterous, dangerous. We would kill to save ourselves from having the delicate thing in us destroyed, and did we?

That man, has he met defeat? Will he stay away from us while dust rises among the roar inside us?

We go on, pedaling. As we descend, grunting like lost dogs, we bike past swollen creeks which suck down the better part of ourselves because the better part of ourselves knows that love is dumb luck that doesn't belong to us, nor our fathers, whose sick kisses we remember, like mausoleums pressed against our lips.

Lenny and I unreel as we ride. We feel how that man attempted to break into us with his brute hands and his torn, foil-backed eyes. He might have succeeded, but for the flashlight, the knife.

Who will welcome us in this nowhere place, its banal, tumbling, sour wind, yet when we see the town, we let out an almost-breath and in slow motion, we pedal, winded, toward the jail where we confess to the jailer, who seems made of glue and straw, and the cot in the jail cell is where we ought to be, young and frightened as we are, but we are turned away.

We camp on a park bench. The top of my head touches

Lenny's, like a precious lotus.

When we awaken, we see a baby bird, whose closed eyes are a grave over which a barely glinting fire pours.

I take the fetal bird, tiny, fragile. I take this corpse, like an itty, bitty opera into my hands.

"Lenny," I whisper, "it's still warm."

"We need to bury it," she replies.

Lenny kneels down, takes out her fishing knife, then carefully carves out a small hole in the dirt by the park bench. I wrap the bird in my turquoise bandanna, the one with the white butterflies on it, and tuck it into the earth.

"It may be dumb," I say, "but I want to sing a lullaby."

Lenny nods her head. We start, our voices small as roses, "hush little baby, don't you cry, Papa's gonna sing you a lullaby."

Our voices, young, ordinary, become the sweet abyss into which we fall because from it there issues a small whispering sound, the one we've been traveling to find, for it is what God slides into our bodies and even though we've been harmed, we do not care, for we are in the small whispering sound and because we are in it, this sound is the breezeway through which we go *on*.

DR. FLESH

People are harder than birds. They squawk more and it is
an unlovely sound. The light in the ward is institutional.
In here, the mad lament better than paid mourners.

I know their cries. One poor soul's sounds like a snake
covered in scabs. Others are Kyries coming from ordinary
men and women whose brains, like mine, are broken. That
Kyrie is also mine.

In the lock-up, I stand, empty as a shoe box before the
window. The white curtains are stiff cardboard, the sill
glued shut with frost. I press my fingers to the glass. So
cold it shocks me.

I watch the night grow black as a pirate's eye patch,
see stars gloat in three-quarter eclipse. I look at them, am
made madder by my hankering to hold a great blue heron
in my arms. The greater, the bluer, the better. Neck long
as a flute made out of glass.

The head bob that pushes yes to an edge. The ebony

vase of the slender beak. That stately strut. One golden claw working mud. The eel grass, like serrated bangs.

To hold a heron in my arms and not break its neck, now this is the challenge because if something is alive and throbbing and flighted, well, to not destroy it when every straining, unpleasant cell in my unpleasant body is passionately and dangerously driven to do so, oh dear God, how can I be stopped?

Suicide-proof windows do the trick. Glass thicker than bifocals helps. The screamers, pacers, cutters, among them, I become them, knowing that the body can sustain its own sick burning, its own hell for hours. It's the mind, the mind that cannot.

In the distance, nun-like hills, ghostly rain, Giacometti-thin trees. Even my hands cry.

The air is oil paint as I jump up on the bed, feel my silence break in jars. The floor, isn't it boiling with rats and won't their bites chew my breasts until they are thumbtack hard?

The rats gain altitude as I jump up and down on the bed. The mattress, is it my flying carpet? Will I lift off, a space woman untethered to the mother ship while horror leans in, telling me that the future is dark which is the best thing a future can be?

I eat my screams. It's akin to swallowing scarves pulled raw from a worn box. No music inside. No music. None.

As I jump up and down and eat my screams, the rats play me, are acrobatic. My eyes blink, rooted in a language all their own. The rats are yo-yos zinging off the walls like ping pong balls.

The male nurse Fred comes in. His sneakers squeak. I stop jumping, smooth my flannel nightgown, try to think of small talk. Will he baby proof my brains by nailing them to my lungs? One congested with smoke, the other, shut like a gun?

"Hi," I say. I fold my hands: *here is the church, here is the steeple.*

"Take this," he says. His hair is poppy red, rough, burred, and in his outstretched hand is a tiny blue pill. My father, didn't he take me like aspirin?

"No, thank you," I say. I'm still worried about the rats. Are they under the bed? I drink a glass of water, then some more.

"You know," says Fred, "you can die from drinking too much water."

I lift my glass, "Cheers!" My smile is wired, thin.

Fred shakes his head, leaves. The door stays open. A pie slice of uterine light comes in.

I'm in the psych ward in a room clammy as wet bread. The air I breathe is shrapnel and I am a mess of flesh. God wants this, my brain besieged, my heart broken.

"Let it break," he says, dropping my world like a raindrop in a storm of thousands. "With pleasure," he adds.

While the rats recede, my roommate, blind and confused, starts to scream. I pad over to her bed, place the foam slippers with smiley faces on her feet.

Her thin ankles are mottled with veins. I adjust paper-thin blankets, calm her by placing my cold hand upon the elusive foam of her forehead. Her smile is faint as the one on her foam slippers. Her eyes shut.

I go back to bed. Outside my window, the night erases God's words like an old lesson on a chalkboard and in my brain, green glorious dreams arise, impregnated by storms.

All night long, my dreams are punctuated by my roommate's screams.

In the morning, I enter a room where Dr. Flesh puts me on display for a game of Show and Tell. Aren't I supposed to tell my story to a group of students who want to be just like Dr. Flesh, who is special, very, very special, unlike me?

I'm still in my nightgown, the one I refuse to take off. The room is cool, ballroom big. Gray floor tiles match the grey sky hung above a low-slung red horizon. Ceiling lights are pillbox hats.

Medical students sit at café tables. One twirls a cocktail umbrella in his black coffee. Another folds his hands: *here is the church, here is the steeple.* Another picks beard bristles from his unshaven face.

Dr. Flesh takes my elbow in his, escorts me across the room. "Is this a date?" His mustache is mouse-gray. It looks like ash has been painted on his upper lip. "Did a preschooler do it?"

Perched on a stool, one eye weeps as I start to use words which fall out of my mouth in a knot of muddy milk. "My heart," I say.

Mother, I couldn't escape her. Drunk, eternal as a weed, she chased me down the hallway. My screams, brittle, paper-thin.

No one hears me, nor alas do you, Dr. Flesh. I see you yawn while my screams, acute, angled, leave a trail from pink to darkest red, like a smell which takes on human weight.

A SORRY SCHEME OF THINGS

Who I am when at seventeen I'm tunnel-vision drunk and only the stars and only the sea and only the light gush from its unknown source, this can be charted as precisely as a fever, even though it's absolutely colorless and missing a thingness.

Swerving in my father's station wagon at 3:00 a.m. Two-lane road, all curves and dips—dark woods, a stream, a patchy acre of burrs and grass.

I don't see the deer until it turns its head—road full of eyeballs, small moons glowing. I crank the wheel, stamp both feet on the brake, skid, jolt into the ditch.

Glitter and crunch of broken glass in my lap, deer hair drifting like dust. My chin and shirt are soaked—one eye half-obscured by the cocked bridge of broken glasses on my nose.

With the car still running, its lights angle up at the trees as I get out. The doe lies on its side.

I want to fix the beautiful body, color of wet straw, of oak leaves in winter, but here's what I do: pick the deer up like a bride, wrestle it into the back of the car—the seat folded down.

Somehow, I steer the station wagon out of the ditch and head home, night rushing in through the broken window, headlight dangling, side-mirror gone.

My head throbs, something stabs my side. The deer breathes behind me, shallow and fast.

A stoplight and I'm almost home when the doe scrambles, its long head like a ghost in the rearview mirror. It bites me, teeth clamping down on my shoulder. I scream, struggle and flail until the deer, exhausted, lets go and lies down.

A wonder how my own body, empty, clean of secrets, knows how to drag the deer out of the car, onto the driveway. Shaking, I pat it down, frisk it, like a fish slipped out of its net.

The deer shudders, bleats. By now the doe's eyes are hot tar and my shirt's smelly as dirt. Clutching the doe, I slap it, scream, "Say it doesn't matter. Say this is enough. Say you want this."

Around the driveway the trees wave like mute women trying to alert me to an emergency. Roots like jump ropes. Grass cut like a cancer.

My father comes out, yelling, "What the hell?" The odor has changed, enormous as a storm, as he walks to the toolshed, comes back lugging a concrete block.

When he drops it on the deer's head, I'm a river diverted from its path. And when God doesn't strike and the sea doesn't overflow and my voice is a kettle of hawks, circling, I see how death accepts a special kind of silence, and exhales.

While I unpin from my skin, we dump the doe in the woods, as though we were gangsters—her mouth grows more exposed, her spine, a column of clouds. The remains a brutal cave.

After rucking dirt onto her, I go into the house. All night I had danced in a bar full of misfits, squash flowers rotting in my hair.

Drunk, weaving, I broke open, a pecan full of beige meat. Smelling of dried sassafras, nutmeg, burnt flour, and clam shells, it was as though I held something monstrous, a two-faced daughter in my arms.

Shuffling in place, I danced with a man with bits of blue pigment on his teeth, the color of Mary's cloak. The floorboards wilted while he twirled, dipped me, as if into a vat of hot wax. The twirling, it lacked etiquette and felt like being bullied into a dead end.

Heavy as a worn saddle, I wanted to drink from this man's sorry scheme of things, touch the spot that bites back. And so, I did.

Like him, I had a wide, friendly face, yet when I smelled his dishpan breath, I swung my ponytail, a filthy tassel.

As we walked out the door, his voice, like pestilence, burrowed into my ears, "We're mired in this until we're not."

Next thing I knew, blood on the sullen ground, blood on the stones, blood on the slope and blood on the fist going into me without pain.

Blood in thick amber strokes, blood from my right ear, from his ochre nose. Whose blood was this? On the fender, in my shoe, in his breath?

"There's blood," he said.

"Blood here too, down here," I said.

Only blood, blood on his watch, would it dry? On his whitish wedding band. Would it dry?

Blood on his knee, blood on the faithful knee, the one readied for erotic negation. Blood at the age of seventeen. Blood that was mute and autistic and cauterized and smelled of tar.

Was this mine? Blood on the wheel—bronzed, dead, gold and diamond deep. Blood as fast as the car when I hit the deer. The thud was log-thick.

When I got out, her hide was frayed mohair, her petite feet, small as the ace of clubs.

Dragging her into the woods with my father, then standing in front of her body listening to her bones hiss like pumice stones, I wanted to drown my hands, for this is the work of daughters: to hold the dead inside them, then turn each sliver about on the tongue: a shape in a tangram.

My father's voice cracked, was candy in my brain. "You," he said while boring his knuckles into my eyes until they were ringed with purple, like reversed lily pads. Ash violet, my tears, alien as a teenager's.

Even now, a year or so later, my right eyebrow still bends wrong, a warped arrow. I glance at it in the rearview as I drive back home, thinking, it's a terrible time to be alive when all I can see is the deer's skull-mush like lemons squeezed into a pot of tea.

I go back into the woods where the deer was left like an underwater statue, the woodsy rooms, abstract. How can I stop dreaming about her, she whose hot package of breath rose up like a rocket and falls again, also like a rocket?

What I make of the earth is inferred and the undersides of the leaves on the forest floor are a rundown palace, the color eel-black. This is when I suspect I'll never get to see it: a bright future, never coming close.

My hands, these smell like smelt as I stand, a condemned building, while the hour half-steps its crippled way elsewhere.

KEEP SAFE, KEEPSAKE, MY KEEPER

Wearing all but the scantest flap of fabric, I once twirled, a rotisserie chicken, before a boy whose face was a warble of acne.

Pointing to giddy throngs of sugar-stoned yellow jackets pivoting above rednecked flowers, he smiled, rubbed his stomach. I mean he really rubbed his stomach, like there was a baby in there.

It was hot. His head shone like the song the whip-poor-will makes when it senses a soul dispersing.

A simple shame stitched us like a quilt whose threads barely held us—so human and frail, so beautiful and sad and small from this remove.

Remove, that's a word I love. It's all I have now, *remove.* The boy is gone. The yellow jackets. Me, dancing. There was a fire that night like a room with an open window.

Haunted by our hearts, continuously beating, but irregularly so, my body shook, a wine glass. I sang a little, let my hands go where they wanted like deranged pleas.

Just then, I closed my eyes, imagined that the boy smiled. I have not danced nor moved with such ease ever since.

In other words, I was both animal and windstorm, was hurdle and burn, burning through the night.

There was darkness, of course. There still is, always will be. Like a cordial sipped ever so slowly.

The boy, he entered me with a limb-letting thrust, found it marvelous. That is, until my teeth sank into his throat, a brick.

When his fist hit my belly, I felt it sink deep all the way to my spine and when he pulled it out, I thought I heard a sucking noise like a boot pulled from mud.

I knew he could no longer hurt me. No one could. Blood dripped, braiding us, hard as a cross bite. Why didn't he pop my jaw? Isn't such breaking simple as surgery?

While fingering bruises like bull's eyes, I couldn't help but think about the girl who was found frozen inside a hotel freezer. Did her killer wrap up her womb, gushy as a water balloon? Put it, like a turtle won at the Fun Fair, into a carton meant for Chinese takeout?

I once held one such turtle like a green rose to my chest. I awoke to sand in my mouth: gritty as nocturnal silt.

The turtle, hard as a super ball, was dead. Like a crumb, I had crushed it in my sleep.

While a bird's child-like voice insisted that my father and I knew one another by smell, I buried that turtle.

Therein began this breaking, in our skin, in the inches of our skin, like a fugue of lightning—which clapped, *clapped* against the inhuman acts.

After the boy left, I crawled out of the woods, feeling like a gut with an antler rammed through it. My body endured each crack, each crevice, numb, inarticulate—death came to me, like a scab in my mouth, and I was afraid. Wasn't my fear like ice sculpted by cuts so deep darkness grows teeth? Didn't it make the mind a gun which feeds itself closed, a nipped rose?

Skin like ruined salt. Pink skin. Brown eyes, like a window with a covering that refuses the passerby's gaze because horror was the company I kept that night when the shades were drawn—and the geese that carried a low sadness, curved, signatory, geese whose cries were radiant as a cleat, sharp as an ice skate, sprayed to a sudden stop.

I tried to read. Through the curtains, a voice, through folds and folds of fabric, a low voice, like a flash of gunpowder—*How have you been cut down to the ground?*

Thoroughly, I wanted to say, as I went into the bathroom, squatted to pee. Blood clots, like tiny parachutes, dripped into the toilet, smelling like tuna out of a can.

Oily as the eyes of dead sheep, these clots were pansydark. Before I flushed, one moved, light as a float toy, as though something was torn or tearing.

Down the drain it went. A squiggle of life, polka dot bright. As the water churned, it felt like hands, fat as tornadoes, were at my throat. They smelled, a corpse with no door. I ripped them off. Who wouldn't?

What I didn't see coming—the gun. When my father died, I went to the funeral. Staring at his fingernails, which looked like nervous fish, I remembered the sound of his teeth nibbling my ear.

I couldn't bury that sound as easily as I could bury him. Tight as a jackknife, his suit. With one frayed thread. I wanted to tug on that thread, unravel him like a skein. Instead, I hailed dirt on him with a shovel hard as a snout.

Back at the house, I went into his room. Floral wallpaper, dim as tobacco. His pillow, wallet-fat. Underneath, the gun. Bright as a penny whistle. I cradled it: *keep safe, keepsake, my keeper.*

The gun came with me everywhere. Fetal it was, curled at my breast like a sea cucumber. I went to the dump with the gun. To the gym. To concerts, plays where I patted it, a lucky rabbit's foot. It distracted me from harder pain.

One night, I got into my car, drove by the most beautiful hearse I have ever seen, cold as cod liver oil. Its elegance was akin to icy ripples on the river, which sounded like glass violins.

While snow jackhammered from a sky smooth as heartache, something like the Holy Spirit poured over me.

The street lamps were grilled lemons. Sucked out, they told me, the dead grow longer in the night.

Dark as a pitted olive, the gun came out. I opened the car window, fired.

The sound of it was whiplash. The exploding glass, electric. The *kaboom,* like a tick in my ear—this was miraculous.

It wasn't me who lifted the gun, not me, as its lightness was a gift from my father. Almost bodiless, wasn't it an ingrown ghost?

As I set the gun loose, my eyes flashed. Buildings, these I shot up, the bullets, bright polka dots.

I went into the corner store, bought cigarettes. The boy I once danced for was in there, behind the counter, his mouth, a key scraping a misfit hole.

"You," I said, flashing the gun like a pointer used to make mute objections. "Empty the cash drawer."

He did so quietly, perfectly. It made my teeth ache. He handed me the money, started rubbing his belly, I mean really rubbing his belly.

This was when I found the way to break the human who isn't human, like an escargot fork, until I heard the murmur, then the plea like a head in its mitt, *not me.*

My heart was trash in a puddle as I left this man balled up on the floor.

Once outside, I riddled the storefront windows with illiterate gunshots, then crossed the street and aimed at my own car, my finger, thickening, like a lock around the trigger.

Since my own life was the thing I wore around like nothing, I let loose one more explosion. It nearly set a fire in the sky sticking all over my skull.

The bullet blasted a hole in the window on the driver's side of my car. When it flew out of the passenger side, I considered it luck to be standing on the outside looking in.

The carnage my body would have been. Glorious. Dead. My blood, a map. No squiggles, polka dot bright.

Damaged was how I felt, as I saw how my car windows looked like white crocodile skin, or corrugated cardboard covered in plaster of Paris.

Astonished, I pressed my finger to the glass on the driver's side. When it shattered, a frozen waterfall, I screamed.

The scream was what made people come out. They

drew around me, spokes in a wheel.

"Look," I said, "someone shot up my car."

"If I were in the car," I went on, "I'd be dead." I then raised my trigger finger to my right temple, the one with the birthmark the color of a bruise.

Then they saw it—my death, like a popped blister.

I demanded a police escort home. The siren's wail, bright, expressionistic, the vast underbelly of wind sailing through the broken windows, bliss, this—barbarous, victorious.

The boy I danced for. The one I left on the store floor, fetal as a weak penis, was nothing. The gun was nothing, I swear, nothing; but the dance, that was *everything*.

IN A FOREST OF FILLETED BONES

Old now, and flawed, I want to be who I am, going where
I'm going all over again. Into a forest of filleted bones
where I couldn't have saved the boy. I couldn't have even
saved a dog.
From the window, I saw him. In the red snowsuit.
Heavy as a padded quilt. Scalpel cold, he shivered as if he
were a verb. Snow beneath him in a starched obedience,
but unkempt and somehow ruthless.
He was the shape of Wisconsin, a sad animal with its
head hanging low. Bulleted with pain, even I could see
that, and behind him hills rumored gold and the marsh-
wealth in a buzz of conversing—wing flap, ringed with
shouts faint as a cough.
The lost boy. An orange rind for a smile, was anyone
looking for him? His mother?
Outside, the voices faded, a stain. Leaving him alone.
Like the abominable snowman. Or a half-buried stone,

which has witnessed more tragedy than a filthy glass of water.

I watched him tuck his wings beneath boney plates, the kind you spin on the tip of a stick. To keep the story going.

Then dusk. A snore of it, cold as a collar. The ground, madras plaid. And the boy, crying now, sobbing really, his back shaking, a hammock.

I grabbed my parka, went out to get him. Under a sky red as menstrual blood, the wind boxed us, screamed like useless children.

Beneath clouds thick as mashed pulp, the mountains jutted, larger than ocean liners, mountains whose weight was a marathon sleep, heavy as violence.

The malt dark mountains crouched in serial silence. To get to the boy, I pushed out of myself into the nothingness that isn't silence because nothing sounds like silence.

As I grabbed him, the horrid bawling of the wind kicked up. While snow blew, thick as blind milk, I half-carried, half-dragged him into the house.

Into the kitchen we went, his snowsuit heavy, waterlogged. His boots, these sloshed, a gushy snow cone. When I pulled them off, one, then the other, sludgy water poured out.

I laughed, but the boy, he looked exactly like what he was, a small, lost boy. "Your name?" I asked, as I took his mittened hands in mine, like the paws of a circus bear.

The kitchen was no ballroom, but still I lifted him off the chair, and together we performed a sad *pas de deus* like mannequins whose arms were tight as rolling pins. Our bodies, cold pastry bags.

The politeness—his, mine—felt abominable. Yet there

it was.

The mittens, I took them off, each one soggy as custard, and his hands, looked skinned. The flesh on them, wax paper-thin. See-through. Like a negligee.

What can I say? That those hands lacked decorum? Or that I did? The rawness, the nakedness, it disturbed. Like peaches, bleeding.

"Your name?" I asked again, but the boy just took a pretend key out of his pocket, locked his lips, then threw the key away.

That gesture. Like clouds full of raw torment, it told me the world is at least half terrible, and for every kind of stranger, there's always one who's out to break you.

Was that stranger me? I hoped not. With his mittens off, and his arms hanging by his sides like pale cold fish, I could see the string hanging out of his snowsuit, the one meant to keep his mittens attached. Or his mother. Who was nowhere to be found.

Which was the best way to be. Or so I thought. As I tugged on the string, it stretched, like a rubber band, or silly string. Spools of it came out.

"Cat's cradle?" I asked, laughing again as I wrapped the string into tiny balls the cat might worry.

The boy's silence, stoic, unearthly, is what comes at the end of a loud suffering—or during it. This tunneled into me, boring holes, minute as dust mites.

Because that boy, in his abominable red snowsuit, continued to shiver, I grabbed a saucepan to heat some milk in. I waited until the skin formed, like the veils that veil us, one from the other, then grabbed a can of whipped cream.

As I squirted, only air came out, in puffs. Little puffs, like the sounds mushrooms make when they collapse, in a creepy, cretin-like decay.

While blasting the kitchen with air bombs, I tried to make the boy laugh, but all that emerged was a dry cough.

I sat him down. Gave him the mug of hot milk into which he dipped his fingers as if it were pudding. When he made the sign of the cross, x-ing his forehead, his mouth, his throat, and I too crossed myself.

While the pines groaned and the scent of metal became deep and close, like a silent-burial, I made phone calls. For the lost boy. Whom no one would claim.

Only after the storm abated, and light cracked the sky again, did I recall the cave. It was there all that time. And who would want to know what was in it?

Bats, like dreadful masks, a void sharp as a paper cut and in me, and in spite of it all, the whipsawing voice of obsession, my mother's.

The boy, like an old wound, carved a blood alphabet into me. For days, I could only crawl from one side of pain to another.

Had he come to meet what no one else can see—the cold, black absolute that life swifts into us, hungers which devour us until all we can do is find the hour where we do not matter anymore. To anyone.

The boy, mute as heartache, already knew that nothing stays, especially if you love it and nothing goes because you let it, yet the glory that is our portion here is dark and immense and gold and marvelous. And heroic.

When a truck gunned its way into my driveway, the boy's eyes were knots that refused to be chastised. Whaleboned to the world he was, a pin on a landscape—and if you pulled that pin, *if?*

The man who burst into my house, gruff, goat-like,

barked at the boy, ordered him into the truck. His arms waved, were tattered mops.

"Who are you?" I yelled, and that silly string, this I wanted to cat-cradle the boy into me.

"You," I yelled again, "can't have him." With every word I hurled, I went cold, then hot. Real hot. An aching fire devoured me. I turned to him, cooled.

When that man looked at me, I grabbed him by the face, the jowls, really, and yelled, "get out."

I bit my lip, let my shouts incinerate into hisses. The man, he shook me loose, placed his hands on either side of my face, as though it were an accordion and squeezed.

The groans, which sounded like birds trapped in a bag, these were mine, as he shoved me onto the floor, grabbed the boy.

Who said nothing. As he was yanked out of the house, a crow snapped its beak over and over again—everything became blurry, a splotch of red; the boy, his snowsuit, the man, the truck roaring out of the driveway, the gun rack, a wily swastika.

I ran out after them, but they were gone. The storm, too had passed, a mirror which showed me that the outer derives its magnitude from the inner.

Clearly, in the mysteries of what lives out here, the hunted and the hunter are linked, as if by a great white trope.

The man and the boy. Me and my mother, who knew the difference between the two darks and insisted that each day was like sitting in a roomful of dolls, who were quietly slitting their throats. They did not bleed, they did not die, they just kept quietly slitting their throats.

Who did I send that boy off with? I wondered this

while the bright, liable flesh of my mind told me to live as if already dead, under a sky which collared distress, hulled pain.

Life without that boy hasn't been wholly one thing or another, but his eyes, which were the color of butterscotch candies, how could I not be heartbroken by them?

Or the peaches. The ones my mother loved. Which, like pallid squid, carve themselves, year after year, between rosy petals of snow.

And when they fall, heavy as altos, as though slipping out of the skin into soul, like blood sliding its alloy through the veins—the gleam is like broiled marigolds.

The boy. The seer mistaken for the seen. With the scent of peaches on him, which is, of course, the scent of resurrection—quiet, muscly, furious.

Does he know that there's room for him to cry in my mouth like a finch that flinches a little from the cold?

Among the peaches, bosomy, plated, funereal. Or truth. Abominable or otherwise like a sweetness which makes the teeth ache.

THE HEFT OF MERCY

As the sun teases glitter from the river's face and mist clings to ringlets of moss, I lower my fishing line, sing about a man in love with a red horse.

This while grasshoppers tumble from the reeds, snap like electricity. Birdsong warbles from the spiked heads of trees, rippling, an anchor rope.

I watch the fish rise through a portcullis of branches—algae sheathes my line, beading it with emerald gobs. Shadows line-ate fins as the silver hook catches a bejeweled jaw.

There's a sloshing ache in my shoulder as I yank the fish aground—intestines fall out, like magic scarves, as the spine reaches up through the muscled back.

While a finesse of bones dam its throat, translucent, straining, the glum inkling of beauty loosens, and beside it, my irrational hunger for wonder, truth, and impermanence.

Because to name a thing is to say it will die, I let desire rise and risen, it's writ in a red so ardent the walled heart of that fish should've burst into flames.

But it doesn't. Instead, I squat on a shelf of sediment and release it, here where my father buried my face in the river's laces. Oh, so long ago.

Blanketed, one might say, the river became a figure for the weight of sin. Or, was the river was merely an old net? Waterlogged, was it heavier that night? Heavier than a body, waterlogged?

The pollywogs in their folds were hind-legged. They seemed quite incidental. One's tail was replaced with the absence of tail. Sutured as a doctor would a thigh.

How much later was it when a neighbor came to fix the fence, to mend the barbed-wire where the horse, the abode-brown yearling, had plunged through headlong, flecks of blood washed into the ditch by hours of rain?

The storm which bade her plunge, which fixed her eyes skyward in a rolling frenzy, hers alone, that terror, which had a texture like shorn velvet, sensuous, severe, alluring.

With a chainsaw, it took about an hour for the renderer to quarter her. I think the neighbor must've fixed the fence. Perhaps it fixed itself. No difference.

Not likely that one might call the panel-truck that removed the horse, a refrigerated hearse. Not impossible either.

I think often of the calm between waves, droplets lit by late sun, which might be incidental, the net as both artifact and artifice, its holes replaced with smaller holes, re-laced with something that isn't lace. How fake tadpoles seem when out of context, slick to the eye, dry to the touch.

He said the way I flinched resembled a gun-shy whelp. My tears, these tore tiny holes in the air. Air: the cloak the living wear? I said I love the uneven weight of grief, but I mean that uneasily. Loved. Something that bucks tense.

Come spring, the tractor lays down fertilizer. My father probably never saw a beast like this churn and spew in the pasture, absurd in its lack of context—pistons for tendons, driven by a man in what looks like a party hat.

It sleeps there all night. If I shine a light, I can see how close the coyotes live to the house. How their eyes in darkness enumerate themselves like stars, perhaps, or a droplet on a web. Of late it makes no difference.

The story goes like this: *who is the wrong question, as is why.* We skin, are skinned. By piece, or piecemeal.

Still, we light any way we can. Our bodies prism the world. As did that fish's which flayed—yoked mica, deafened glint—among leaves, sticks, twigs.

The yearling's skin, it too prismed like handblown glass. Floating, it never felt like floating—when I discovered the horse, spurting where the barbwire's infinite awls bored through her tan-brown hide: the stone of her flesh rolled back.

I ran, got a darning needle and a hank of yarn, stitched the horse right there in the pasture, letting my oversized needle zip in and out, a dragonfly.

I've since learned that there are dragonflies called Devil's Darning Needles. Maybe it's true—at least, it makes sense.

The one thing my father wouldn't leave me with was air, which is impossible to live without.

Air, that is—on the night my father dragged me into

the river, there was none. While my lungs boiled like frogs, waterborne spiders swaddled dragonflies, which weighed next to nothing.

All this is old and visceral and grotesque, but later, when my father took the old pickup down to the sandpit to feed the dog, which he kept chained to a rusted stave—this whelp, he was ribbed, like the fresh water mussels we dredged from the river bottom, a protrusion of need if not lack, and as we wended down the washboard road, I saw that it was serrated with sedge, that cleaned nothing and was itself unclean.

Peering through slats in the floorboards, the dust rose up and into the pickup's metal flanks—the dog too rose when it heard us rattle down the gravel road—creasing its bald forehead, oiling its joints with a few viscous licks.

As my father chucked rancid meat from the truck to land at the dog's feet, he snarled at that stake, which was polished by the gnashing of the dog's teeth.

Years later, when my father went into the river, I didn't scream my animal grief the way I did after I hauled myself out of the same river to lay in the dirt like a germ.

Instead, I was sheared by the shriek of that yearling who'd nailed herself on the fence, and beyond her, mud and bluegill carcasses, as she sharpened her voice on lionized air. Which sounded the way my mother's had before she left.

A shrill cry. No choice in the matter, I climbed down to lift that little horse up. I waded the muck and mire, knock-kneed and unbalanced, to save her.

Between the snap and buck of her gently coiled neck, I held her close to my chest, felt her blood coursing as I stitched her flesh, which hung, a shirt.

When she leapt free of me and cleared the pit, my stomach dropped. Who knows where life's logic comes from—that yearling, spotted like light below a stand of pines, she spoke only the wordless tongue of loss.

As she went down, impaled on the dog's stake, the knotted muscle in my chest undid itself and how my father got there while the fish flew and the birds drowned, I'll never know.

His monstrous eye, a *trompe l'oeil*, went over the horse's mane, its beribboned extravagance which, like consciousness, had been cut.

Her bleats, these she broadcasted, as her body jerked in an afternoon, thick as carrageen.

Because the nose bone's so close to the brain and the brain doesn't have a bone, only an oafish sea wall, I had to believe the yearling couldn't feel the bullet that bore into her.

But I could. Up above, buzzards rode the heat signature of dusk.

Even the trees went mute, patient as slaves, as the yearling's blood left sun spots all over the field beyond which the hills rose, were dark barbells.

Beneath the barbwire on that fence, there were poppies, or if not poppies, then the downy heads of dandelions, heavy with humid air, or if not air, was it the heft of mercy?

The sky was blown, my skirt white as a headache. My shoulders, these became thistle as my father carpeted my body, took delight in my pain, which was the color of dirt.

The trees, sandpaper-rough, leaned away from us—my father, he left a strange taste in my mouth, of bile, of iron— *where is she?*—tell me, where is that bitter girl we both trashed, rusty as a brown rose?

But the river, cunning cat, bristled its brittle fibers—as he pushed me under, no one saw the wound I had from my chest up to my throat, a garnet rainbow.

Above me, his face pale as a quail egg warped. I wanted to peel his skin off like a decal, but he was gone by the time I came up for breath.

As I crawled out of the river, I felt slimed by the under-water moon which had put its snake-nose all over me. On the craggy bank, I shed wet light, was slowly wakened from my dream of the ruined world by the sound of rain falling onto the earth.

Because I drifted for a minute, an hour even, in pure, or almost pure response to the rain and the insouciant life all around me—cloud, bird, fox, the flow of light, the danc-ing pilgrimage of water, the vast stillness of spellbound ephemera, animal voices, mineral hum, wind conversing like mist—I became a star among stars.

One of the smallest, perhaps, but still a star and be-cause our great earth is cold, not like a block of ice, or a dead cloud even, but like an empty walnut, it rolls along in pitch-black space.

A star among stars, I needed to grieve right then—I had to feel this sorrow—for the world must be loved this much if any of us want to say, "I lived."

While the slapdash landscape turned blue, I grieved—so sparsely blessed this life, wherein whole lifetimes are writ on the undersides of leaves, leaves clogged with the neat procession of lush and flutter.

Back at the house, my father's eyes, siphoned, dimmed, demanded that I accept desire as it was—a stilted, earth-scummed crippling that never stops.

I picked the dots of dinner from his beard because he was what I had to endure in order to survive. He who barreled into the dwindling novella of his days, as if already lowering his heralded bulk with little fanfare into the grave.

Time and disaster. A heavy landslide down the mountain. When my father stopped speaking to me what he really wanted was for me to stop speaking. To stifle the sound of my voice; he didn't want the nit of it in his ear.

Sitting on the porch, I asked for flight—and to learn how to make of nothing, the most, better: an ever-enlightening mark, like a piece of flint that, if rubbed the right way, would illumine that which collapses, gives up, lifts.

Like fire in the flue, we lived in the neck of an hourglass, its downpour, and pain, which remained so long in our home, it became me.

We succumbed to the dirt in the draperies, to the furrows on the wall's forehead. We succumbed to the ticking hands of the clock as it dismembered us. And life entered from a hidden door every night with a dull knife.

The moon was witness—as were the little cells moving through the capillaries in my fingers, as my father wrestled me into a life so narrow that we fell, finally, into the same pit the yearly leapt over. To her death.

Here, then, was where I shot him. The sound of the gun an affliction, or squalor—the bullet pummeled his brain like rawhide.

Here where a deer drank from the middle of the river, kissing her reflection like a saint. Her eyes, these were soap bubbles, as she looked up, bolted.

While geese honked overhead, I dragged the body into

the fevered currents, into water that was a sealed aquarium, water which turned predacious as it wept across the rheumy field, its moon-rings a dimly lit room.

Watching my shadow flow like ink from my white bobby socks, the river—it folded back, a virgin's skirt, no air there, none, only the livid carriers: wasp, mite, moth, and the gnat that instilled its eggs like rank seed pearls into his bald eyes as he sank, an anchor with no rope, nor fish nor birds nor song.

Yes, he sank, bulls-eyed, bedeviled. This, then, was the moment of suffering: when my father's face, like a fracture in the mythic, or an avalanche of axes, became negative space, or the sound of an ending, which is an odd sound, like sunlight striking leaves, or kisses in a dark old doorway, despite the mess of it, the hurt, the empty.

A SIEGE OF HERONS

The woods are austere as I glitter, dumb as a gecko, against a stranger's neck, my hair inside his mouth, revolving, a wet organism of sandy eels.

I look into his mud green eyes—brief cloud, brief other, brief the minute fiction of oneness as he cobwebs me with a glacial loneliness, never-ending and feral like childhood or the house we barely owned.

Insignificant as a footnote, I'm fingered like dirt—and perforate, trembling, while my womb, aesthetic and bald as a priest's, smells of wet dog and sandalwood. Perhaps a moth flutters inside, tasting of years without music.

The belt, it hurt like a dragged cross—any wound will do as long as I keep it open and remember where I come from.

Which is like living inside a dying bee, its wings, filaments and the sky a shell of thin, transparent glass enclosing the late summer day, a canopy of incandescent blue.

Upon which everything shimmers. Like prayer before it becomes a prayer: in the throat, the machine for lamenting, smelling of musk, char, as in: these hands are reaching, but all they can grasp is air.

How could this not make me a funeral before the funeral, the ghost it despises?

After this man leaves, I go home to my mother in her double-wide, captive to pumps, pipes, irrigation tubes.

The spotlessness of her gown, the immaculate hem of the nurses' smocks. Her body, a sling full of broken clocks.

While the hours wasp into evening, spreading like spilled salt, I touch her face, which is like holding emptiness, but her heart, hard as rebar, is dangerous.

Still, the way they pull the needles out like eager monsters—as if freeing her lungs from its escutcheon.

Hurricane calm. How the lawn is yellow as phlegm. And the blocks under the house have worried themselves loose.

The mark of death: the face of termination and the sound of earth closing its one good eye.

Her body, a defeated sunset. Carried out, over the abandoned sunflower field, and the moon in resignation. And no one, not my father, nor my brothers or sister, are there to watch her go.

After which, moths follow me to bed. I count them: twenty, fifty, block, choke. In the room where I sleep, the breath hangs low, coarsens the room.

No one knows where the air is charged and released into the world, but it thistles, which is how breathing fills a house with no one in it: as if to draw the buzzing to its source.

This is not a house, but a husk, a plugged maze. What

I won't tell you is how I was a flute when I brushed against that stranger's lips, but there was no music.

Only blows furious as juniper and the wind was free but kind.

I won't lie and say there are days when I don't curl into a ball and pretend it's only breezing outside under clouds like marbled ham while his smell, like salt sitting in milk, dwindles my skin.

Thinking maybe, just maybe, I can get out, I pack. As I drive in the middle of the night with the wild indifference of a boxer, the road smells like mesquite.

While driving, I remember how I used to bathe my mother with two quaking hands. It was like opening the hives to find them bare, not even a corpse. Mushroomed with tumors, I crossed her arms, like boiled starfish.

In a way, I was doing the work for her, and my own, eventual flight.

I used to think there was nothing crueler than the transposition of parent and child. But what of the child-less?

Or funerals where the only light sprays from grieving mouths? Even the river abandons its banks.

And so, my mother and I became strangers to each other, the way the angel of bare essentials turns into silver mist on the embalmer's table.

But her name remains as flowers do, a little while longer. It lingers like ice and stars in the morning.

When a river meets a river, the name of the smaller one dies. But the waters rise and when darkness falls, one light fades, as if the missing of some things could cure the loss of some others, like smoothing a rock to make a false eye.

Before me, a shuttered motel. Vacancy pulsing neon red into the night like the promise of a country I've traveled far to see.

Because my head's heavy from carrying its empty weight like a bell with no rope, I stop, go into the lobby, and get a room.

In that room, I sleep with one hundred tiny men, all of whom are identical. I stroke their little beards, which are raspy like red violins.

Under these men, I forget to listen to the light I've lost—my only child's breath, the one she never took. Her skin, on my fingertips, scent of heliotrope.

As she was: a soft vertex of gray on pink with the afterlife already curled around her wrist's slight stem. Immortality comes first. If ever it comes afterward.

When my mother saw me clutching my dead baby, she slapped me, the sound of it, the music of loss and defeat.

The baby, like my little brother Raphael, was noosed by its umbilical cord, which was the color of squid. It can be said both of them entered heaven the way a gila monster emerges, its black body dotted in pink, its ugly head flashing its tongue to see if the blood of our wanting has dried.

What binds us is the slow dying from top to bottom, the passageway where no one can tell the bones of the dead from the bones of the living, not the dove's, nor the winter hares, their fur stripped like the exhaust a thousand planes have strewn over fields of ice.

But the baby and Raphael, they entered the cadaver room quietly, lay down in the place of future absence.

I've never been more sorry. Even so, my sorrow is unremarkable, it comes like indigestion or shortness of breath—a cry, a deadbolt turning, the doorknob reversed so the lock is on the outside.

Sorrow, it's such a fat word, one that's filled with the bitter aftertaste of the tepid coffee I leave on the nightstand, the pink of my lipstick on its rim.

Outside, leaves are all around and there's a heavy chill over the ground's damp tapestry—sorrow is the death of beautiful things, it smells like a bevy of hatchets or strangled starlings.

Which puts me inside a delirium, pale as the horse harnessed to the field. That even a horse gets spooked and runs, the wind tearing through bone like a child running for its life. This matters.

Standing back from the windows, I stave away the flies, longing for the gift which erases every blow.

But my mother's face—that first looming of shape and shade was enough, like a tower of blocks diced down upon me, there in my yellow crib, which was melted butter or sunshine's ode to a culture of claws.

Her arms, these were massive as a wharf's pylons and her voice a litany of losses so epic that I cannot repeat them, her sorrow without tears, that was something.

Which is why when my mother caught me in the bushes where I was cradling a snake, rocking and rocking, she tore it from my arms, thrashed it dead.

Over the kitchen sink, where she scrubbed my mouth with soap, I gagged.

That night I snuck back into the garden, found the snake, a smooth corpse. Stuffed a crabapple in its mouth. The sour juice sparkled. Small fangs dimmed. The moon was balsamic.

This is when I saw myself. This is when I started falling, this is how I fall—gravity my heirloom, my bluntly conjured fate.

My sorrow, next to my mother's—merely insipid, persistent as the feeling that happiness is the prelude to tragedy—I can say that this has kept us together, like an organ of skin, and that I measured the baby before she was gone.

Twenty-one inches, like a resurrected fern. On ghostly days, I go into the wood's unlit spaces where she lay.

It only takes one touch, one trace of water across the lip of a leaf to reenter her world. This is how the skeleton regains its map of flesh and lucency.

If I must relive her death, and Raphael's, for one hundred years, I will do so, like a chapped eyelid closing on an era where nothing's affirmed, not even fire.

In that hotel room where the sun—inconclusive, elliptical—inches through the window, I'm completely ruined.

Outside, the crows on a moat of snow filch twigs and unpicked berries, flip snow, scolding, scolding, scolding, the grief I never forget to feed.

After the baby, my mother sent me the same letter the entire time I was in the psych ward, wearing an issued blue gown. She wrote, "I'm getting old." She wrote, "the house is falling down."

"The walls move," she went on, "in the middle of the night, and I swear when I put the lamp somewhere, it's gone like a halo on a gravestone."

I didn't write back, but after I made it out, I drove home.

Entering the kitchen, my mother's eyes were unformed skulls floating on the ceiling. When I kissed her cheek, my beautiful womb-faced lips tried to erase her slurred speech.

Like vapor stains, her words bleared: "When you were born, I wrapped you in butcher paper and all the stuffing from your squeaky toy."

"Enthralled, I dropped lit matches into your crib, watched you excrete white ooze like a toad."

"Listen," she continued, "you're no different than anyone else and, anyway, I'm dying."

She furrowed her brow, "Your baby brother, though, he was my glory and you, the hand of all my mistakes."

I wanted to tell her that I've never seen a siege of herons, nor beheld the manzanitas; that I know nothing of the gods; their tedium, their melancholy, their blood's leaden sludge, but I could narrate the rain as it blows through the pines, as it slips, stumbles, and sluices; the rain as a scattered body; the rain as shape-shifter; the rain on the face of the hunter and on the sorrowful face of the prey.

In that moment, I understood that the way out is *through*—the gate, the abrupt hills, ten thousand trees.

Which is never as hard as the journey *in*. My mother and I, what we shared was a heart, its spent quarry. By then, I was too tired to go any further and was re-begot of absence, darkness, death.

Late that night we talked: things which are not—the world's raw starlight. The river. The shape of the shifting sandbar.

The third glass of wine was a finer vintage than the first.

I told my mother that I was tired of grief's baroque rations.

Since the baby's death, and before that my brother's, she's waited to pit me against the putrefying force of her surroundings, to draw me into its extreme, deceptive, desolate eschar like a wound on the water; to bear witness to the wind screeching like babbling parrots; her aged life mendaciously smiling, its lips opened by vacated agonies; an aged poverty silently rotting inside her; an aged silence bursting with tepid pustules, the awful futility of our *raison d'être*. This while my heart flushed, pumped, went nowhere.

Sometimes the zebra wins. And the sound of the savanna goes on—birdsong, frog croak, beetle chitter, occasional grunt of a warthog, hard panting of the cheetah after the chase—as the lioness walks slowly away, bleeding from the mouth, staring ahead, looking for a place to rest and await a slow starvation.

Sometimes the savanna's ambient song is interrupted by a sharp crack that sounds like a gunshot, but it's the zebra's kick finding the lioness's jaw.

Sometimes the lioness dies. Always the sound goes on.

As did my voice. "Mom," I said, "don't drink the gnat that's planted itself in your cocktail glass. Don't leave the porch light on. It will call in all the things that want to eat even you."

"Mom," I went on, "Say something, say nothing, but don't promise a thing."

What I didn't say: *a cold river divides us*—cold currents, cold fish, cold limbs, so let's succumb to the darkness that glints beneath our inhumanness.

After which, I put my mother to bed.

If kissing is the mouth's elegy to itself, let me always mourn: at dawn, when sleep frosts the lips; at noon, when mouths are indiscreet as unlocked rooms, or at dusk—best, perhaps, midnight's kiss, like the one I gave my mother, redolent.

Always, the bitter plum of that last kiss, unknown until it's past—half kiss, sly kiss, floating back unexpectedly, like snapped water lilies—mouths cannot be tamed.

No kiss completes. Multiple as the self, they abate narrative. Lawless, we unfold.

As did I. The next day as I lay under that man in the woods, my mother collapsed on the couch, her shoes off like toy boats cast free.

I too left my body like a hammock, swinging low.

White as a toothache, her dry elbow skin and her crown of bones, a narwhal's tusk, though I've never seen one.

That night, as my mother's body was being taken away, like a small red bell eaten at the center, I ripped the sheets off her like a bandage, like a rush of birds.

I drank, pretended to need someone to soothe me—but didn't.

Instead, I huddled in my flesh as if in a stolen mink, stroked it, like a dilettante and considered the black hole my body's been.

The scent of my dead, which is somehow marsupial, is a cotillion of leathery brown gardens or those apocalyptic oranges whose entire peels fall on the plate, the weight of desertion, definitive.

Cherished by no one—not even the moon, which I want to see cloaked but won't because my fate is to continue despite, *until.*

AND THE REST IS A ROSE

It has snowed and the evening is blue. The trees look like buoys, like waders the water has gotten too deep around. Ringed by ice, branches clack like dentures.

In the half empty light and the room my husband just left, his smell grows so sweet, so strong, it could slice me open. It does.

I'm not the only one for whom love feels like bedsheets being ripped into prayer flags by the wind. Whenever I stand before Harry, I feel like I've been falling for decades.

In this bleakness, there's a starkness that's arresting and the idea of color terrifies.

Deep in the woods where my husband's draped in the snow's silk hemorrhage, he fondles the butt stock. Muffled lust needles Harry's cheeks as his craving for the sugared heat of the trigger intensifies.

Surrounded by crowns of unspent shells, he skewers chunks of Spam, drinks pink Walmart wine, and gazes idly on ammo and cakes of blood-frosted snow.

The doe is a swerve, a crooked yet regulated mark as her legs flex right down to her hooves, which are supinated claws. She holds one up, a cupcake, let's loose a minor moan.

The hoof dangles, a broken tooth, and the sound of her pain sets off a chain in so many other animals, each cry dissolves into the next grown louder.

Even if I were blind, I would know night by the noise it makes: our groaning bed, the mewling staircase, drapes that scrape against glass panes behind which stars rise, blue and silent.

But not even the stars are silent: their pale waves echo through space when Harry's gun lets loose its big expired grief and the doe goes down on the ice-escutcheoned ground.

Like a pickpocket, his hands work her. Brown, soft, and liable to melt, her wounds, as he lays down on top of her, to press the bile of desolation into every pore.

His weight, this I feel like a basket of cut throats. And the window within the doe's dead eye sees the creek with its snow-scummed broth. Then the broad silver river, shiny as a turnstile. Each strand of fur in Harry's hand, a slip of dead grass.

Attrition, dispersal, growth—a system unfastened to story, as though sight itself were beyond story, beyond any clear meaning. No one will let us through if we don't walk through our own sadness, no one.

But why this gust of alertness that comes every time any indication of the human passes—like a mirror, like to like?

Aren't we small in our suffering as Harry yells, "I'd rather be dead than share you with another" while he drags the deer into the barn?

What's left? His voice, like the war I was born toward; her skin, which he edits with his knife?

I hear the blade go in, go out, and when her nose bleeds a velvet collar, time slides through the flesh, turns my body into a bomb inside our well-built home.

The light that breaks out of her is red, and the rest, unlike the past, is a rose.

III.

And the rest, unlike the past, is a rose..

THE END WHICH ENVELOPED THE END,
A BRAMBLE, A ROSE

Lonely, like a coffee mug on the shelf, I slow roll into the empty spot on the bed where we shed the best skin of our lives. We were a thing of beauty, weren't we?

A thing of beauty, us, before that man—*not you!*—shoved my face into the weeds. I can still smell his sweat, the cleave of his breath like lice on my neck.

When he ordered me to pull down my tights, nylon-black like my mother's chador, I did what I was told. My spine, a grounded stake, lit with liquid brass and burning peaches.

He said, "I devour best with my mouth closed," but his teeth, these didn't sleep.

Under the soft sumac, cottonwood hard as my nipples. Exotic, my hair, thick as a rug, this he snatched at like newly acquired money.

I was alone. "Don't do this," I said because pain and

brightness are distributed in equal parts and only exist because of excess.

His boot heels were hooves as he pushed into me and left me sore, like a balloon full of glass. This left nothing in me but the wounded side of Jesus.

When I got up, a dead beetle stuck to my back. Catastrophe crowned me as I made my way across black humus, a loose bone floated in my foot.

I crawled until I was under the wide swatches of light which sliced between gray tree trunks, to where the air had the texture of drying moss and the birds of the forest sang of before and after: as musk from the mushrooms scalloped mold.

The birds sang from where there can't be an order, there in the dry leaves where something smelled like the past, which was stored in me, like an ever-widening abyss.

And the marred twines of cinquefoil, false strawberry, sumac—a low branch hung above a cave just the width of my shoulders.

As I crawled in, I remembered—the two of us walking hand-in-hand—both of us like an omen, smelling of oleander and oxalis, or ovals of dew on the pokeberry, yes, us walking over the bulbed phosphorescence of the roots, over ground covered by pliant green needles, their piney fronds.

Your eyes went soft like a child's drunken nipples. "Honey," I said.

We were too late. The gods moved us away from each other like waves greenly welcoming the sun, which poured over us like bracken and primrose, the color of taste or— should I say? —waste.

Once we walked in this forest, so strangely alike and

yet singular too, but the truth is—it is lost to us now and I am as far as the deepest sky between clouds, I am as far as cicadas and locusts, and you are as far as the cleanest arrow that has sewn the wind to the trees because I sent you there. I had to.

From the cave, I watched that man rub his eyes, then wander naked into the road. It was cold. His mouth steamed like torn bread. His voice shrieked in an ocean blind with ghosts.

When the semi slammed into him, I felt nothing, yet knew I would have to begin with the end and there were two endings: the end which enveloped the end, like a bramble, a rose. And then, nothing.

How to start again against the tightening. A knife can give up, but I could not—there was the miscarriage, and before that the months of waiting: like a basket filled with bright shapes.

And then what arrived: the forsaken event, the blood, the scrap, the enormous present collapsing, folding over, like a wave overtaking a grain of sand.

A tiny skull with bones so fragile, it flaked into dust— bones of water, bones of light, bones I asked for.

Once I climbed—*there was a bunch of us!*—to the top of a trestle bridge where I watched a bird drop, heavy as a stop watch. I watched its dark wings thrash. Then yield.

In water cold as pincers. Like a suicidal blackout. That I wanted what the bird had was my only truth. Beneath me: a river, a swollen river, river of star-hole, of harness, lichen river, river that we—*we were kids!*—wanted to velvet with our filth.

River of butter, river cracked open like an egg, or burst apart, unleashing its violent load. River of sound, river curved like a backbone.

River in which I wanted to particle, feathery and wet, lemony and loud, river that still smells, river I still wear tight on my hips. River I still dream about. River from the inside. River above which we shouted.

Septum river, bundle river, river of mercy edging far into night. All night river, burnt sugar river, we jumped, plummeted, our hands, the color of paw prints.

Into the river we went. River where my flesh belonged to me. Made softer somehow by its honey, its vaseline.

Brown river, black river, off the map river. I'm still there, snatching at the air as I fall.

And yelping, of course, like a dog.

The joy of it, the magic, the water somehow like Ophelia or an infant, gardenia-pale, floating, under and away, as far away as invention, as the scarlet wing of that suicidal bird, the one that plummeted, thrashed, then yielded, a halo, bright as the shock of a ruinous post-mortem rainbow.

IN A RAGA OF NIGHTINGALES

I watch my father cast out. Moments later, the fish twitches, a lit piece of tinder—artful, legendary, there on a hook so slender it looks vigilant.

In this landscape of pale knees, the wind howls at least thirty-three times an hour. Which is never cliche. Nor is the clownish yak of the chickadees.

It isn't me who kills the fish. A shaft of sun leans in to behold the scene, to assist the sacrifice by turning into a knife, shelling the fish, flake after flake.

The fish thrashes like a lamb. I think it's a lamb. A small one. A sincere sacrifice.

My father nods, granting its convulsion a gentle consent. After all, it's a clean doing. No blood. Only the white scales descend, like pear blossoms wafting.

Slowly, the fish ceases its futile tussle, gasping. Every breath an agony. The fish throbs intermittently the way a widowed man throbs when waking up suddenly in the middle of the night with the feeling of an unstoppable fall. That's how the lingchi was invented one thousand years ago by some wise Chinese. A sinner was put to death by slicing three thousand pieces of flesh from the body. This slow slicing was considered an indulgence to watch.

"There's an art to cooking the soup," says my father as we go back home.

In the kitchen, the soup's white. So white it's as if all our sins are washed when we drink it. The body of the fish intact.

It seems we've only borrowed the fish to produce this soup. And that it will come back as soon as I place it in the water again, but it is in water.

"Drink it hot," my father says, "the flesh is soft."

Indeed, the flesh is so soft that it melts on my tongue. Like butter or the archetype of a primitive desire.

The flesh's so tender that some old hunger dies in my mouth. I remember years ago, when my Buddhist mother took me to a religious ceremony to release the captive fish.

And there was one small fish, a kid-fish perhaps, who barely knew how to swim, lingering between my fingers as I stroked its scales and said, "Go."

It wiggled a few inches away, then back into my palms. I stroked it again.

Again and again. Until it learned everything about the water and everything about leaving.

Leaving, I heard the water thrashing behind me. The fish leapt out of the lamb-white water, like a gull, to give me a last glance, or perhaps allowing me to give it a last glance.

The water riffled like those white April flowers, or snow itself, falling and rising again.

I think of this while chewing the meat. Perhaps, it's that kid-fish in my mouth. It grew up. Grew larger. Like a child.

I think of it: the way the fish made me turn. The way its skin burned my hands like charred jade. How its eyes inhaled all the blueness of the pond.

Of sweetness my tongue drowns. In a raga of nightingales. Which is never cliché, nor is my father and I, for we are a contested border. In good faith.

One lamb receives the anvil with a quiver, the other with a bleat. When the animal is lessened into an ache, it makes it easier to watch the tendons uncouple.

In a corner of twilight, my father—is his the quiver of restraint tempered with vertigo and abandon, until it's not? How prolonged will the ache be?

The calligraphy of one man's discontent turns the flesh into a thousand failures. How tenuous the task, to name the trespasses against gravity, against grace.

But what to make of this—his hands scaling what's in his palms, flake after moth-mottled flake.

And the moon, pale, like a clock that says, now, *now,* is the moment for telling about the father who throbs when waking, suddenly, in the middle of the night. How that father is mine and I, the deep reader of the cracks in his worn down slippers.

His Bordeaux-soaked voice, how it murmurs below speech. That's when I touch every dead part, even his toes, black, and the farthest thing from God.

Even when I hide in the darkness of his body, I know that neither of us will last: we're a quiver of jelly, collapsing.

My mother, when she died, stole my father in his sleep.

Like a flayed fist of twitches, her tongue sliced three thousand pieces of flesh from his body. No, it scaled them from his soul.

It was considered an indulgence to watch. But I did. In the silence that is of lime and kraal stones. The silence that's not shadow but of what's buried under trees, hard as the symmetry of knives.

Then she leapt. Like that kid-like fish, out of the lamb-white water, like a gull, to give me one last glance or perhaps allowing me to give her one last glance.

The water riffled like those white April flowers, or the snow itself, falling and rising again. How her eyes inhaled all the blueness of the pond.

When I taste that fish. Of sweetness my tongue drowns. In a raga of nightingales, or a landscape where the wind howls, *howls*, at least thirty-three times an hour. Which is never cliché.

Nor is what dusts all the rooms of paradise, nor the velvet sunrise clothed in silences so accurate, they thwack me, like fog, or the sadness which is the force that breaks the body inevitable, until I storm in the memory of what first nailed me to the dark.

THE TORNADO'S SOLILOQUY

"You," you say, as if your words are lard from that woman's carcass.

This as we finish off the flimsy-skinned oranges slipped from the baggie her body imitated. Or the body a baggie resembled. To be shut that way and turned and shook such that nothing's wasted.

After the oranges, we eat salt. Slopes and slopes of it. The sea tires many a tiller and grays in the evening. So much fails to be hammered in.

The iron rainbow, or hearts made purposeful in what they mutilate.

As we smell the wet lindens, we heed the metallic sounds of that dead woman's curses; hard as horseshoes.

Spring rain and your eyes gray, like an oyster eaten between lust and madness.

Her mole was lush, carmine, hefty with spices, secret excesses. The flesh, that supreme study, can be mastered in many languages, all of them dead.

Spattered measure, her blood.

What beauty, sad world, all of this beauty: what of it, around the stately ugliness of her screams: O, said the dumb hanging world, lost in its bitterness.

Her face turned blue, blood came out in thick round drops. Now all that remains is a single copper splotch the size and shape of a pumpkin seed on the wall, just above the wainscoting.

Shouldn't she have kept her blood, strong under her skin?

"Nothing to see here," the officer said, binding the crime in tape, and still you stared, you who didn't feel, as children might, a bit of shame over what had been broken, like that woman's green shoe.

That you loved her, I know, like a cold light in a lonely office.

Everyone keeps telling us to leave. Even the deposition says so in its small melodic cursive.

Instead, I tell you how my father slapped me for something he thought I said—just what that was I didn't know—and as I looked up, confused, too young to understand that this was his birthright and my flesh its beneficiary, didn't he feel as though he was a part of something larger than himself?

Always too hard, the blow that christens a child. Out of nowhere. Just like that.

Always too much, the aftermath when a father knows he's wrong, and sees what the child does not, that the gods, being human, say nothing and keep on saying it.

While we stared into the grave we made for her, I lowered my face into the darkness and said, "I'm sorry, is anyone there? If so, can you hear me?"

And what I heard was something of the unspoken in all things. Like a tornado's soliloquy.

We understood nothing of the glasswork that is a human heart, the way it glistened, like the spit that sexed her screams.

Last night I dreamt about girls in chairs at the dark edge of the dance floor, and their shyness made me shy, a stranger in my skin, and I turned from them to the apple blossoms in the window.

And in the distance, more lovely still, more fierce in its skirt of trash: a great tornado, dark arms flailing, drawn this way.

So this is how a monk feels on the mountain path—only the parchment is on fire. And terror, the new sublimity, is what scales us down.

I was the new girl once. I sat at my desk as the winds blew our windows out, like candles, all at once, and our blouses shuddered.

"I see you," said the wind in the strange tongue of broken things.

I came before you and leave as such. Knowing I understand little about sacrifice and rage and the wicks that seek nothing from the flame.

"Move," said the wind. Then I heard nothing. Only stillness. Then my heart beat a little faster. And faster still.

THE SOLACE OF AMNESIA

When my brother Ed tells me that most mammals have the same number of heartbeats in a lifetime, our mother is lying on the garage floor, like an avocado about to slip from its skin.

He lifts her while I try to shout louder than her sobs. But it's her heart, a washable ink, which is her dark genius, how it moans slow enough to undo her. And her eyes, the size of thumbtacks punched through the sky's eyelid.

Ed also tells me about the orca who pushes her dead calf a thousand miles out to sea before she drops it, or it falls apart. The next day, she goes back to play with her pod.

All this disturbs my son, who starts to cry. When I go in, pick him up, he says, "The sad is so big I can't get it all out."

While clouds groan like thumbs, I take him out to the garden where a spider consumes her home, knowing she can reweave it tomorrow between citrus leaves and earth. Her heart, like a wet red sting, cleaves to the length of her body as I witness the birth of my son's grief, his own heart, a marvel I refuse to invade.

Who already knows what it is to be human. Who's thick and neckless. His head shaped like a gravestone. And his skin, theatrical, electrical, all edge. White that is red is pink, a hue, a glazed enormity, tangerine plush.

With him in my arms, the rising sun is a blistered apple, gold that molts the eye and boils animals in their caves.

While walking, I tell him how the ring finger of his grandmother's left hand had been cut, just above the knuckle, but not by whom—it was the one I held onto, there in the garage.

The nub, smooth as the velvet on a stag's horn—as I stroked it, there vibrated a plaintive itch, like fur rubbed the wrong way. If bumped, it throbbed, a newly bobbed tail.

To marvel in the missing—this attracts me. The way a glove reports a vacancy. The singing presence of a molecular echo, how can it not keep us attached to absence?

I tell my son that the light exploding in the air is love, the grass excreting green is love, and stones remembering the past is love, but he's too young—not for love, but for death—whose blink is slow as a camel's.

Still, while I pat his hands, I see death all around him—in the trees from which hang strange fruits like an implant in the brain—and the landscape is infinitesimal, like the structure of music, seamless, invisible.

What holds it together and what holds music together is faith—faith of the eye, faith of the ear. Or is it absence?

Nothing like that in the language. Yet, when the clouds chug from west to east like blossoms blown by the April wind, anything's possible.

And so, I tell my son the story of Hsuan Tsang. A Buddhist monk, he went from Xi'an to southern India and back—on horseback, on camel-back, on elephant-back, and on foot.

Ten thousand miles. It took him from 629 to 645. Mountains and deserts. In search of truth and all its attendant, inescapable suffering. And he found it.

Wang Wei, on the other hand, before he was thirty years old bought his famous estate on the Wang River just east of the east end of the Southern Mountains and lived there, off and on, for the rest of his life.

He never traveled the landscape but stayed inside it, a part of nature himself. And who would say anything to someone so bound up in solitude, in failure and suffering?

If landscape, as Wang Wei says, softens the sharp edges of isolation, then the future is an animal.

I tell this to my son as I look at things, not through them. With him, I sit down low, as far away from the sky as I can get, under the weeping cherry, which flushes coral, each blossom an anemone.

We stay until twilight, when everything starts to shine out, when the bats, like strange Christmas ornaments, skulk in the trees, their wings folded, their heads bowed.

Arising out of emptiness, that same emptiness wants to reignite the stars. April's celestial wordlessness, burning like the hope we live by.

What I don't say: in every kind of dream I'm the black wolf careening through a web. I am also the spider who eats the wolf and inhabits the wolf's body.

In another dream I marry the wolf and am very lonely. I would love to tell my son that all of this has a certain ending, but the most frightening stories are the ones with no endings at all.

The path goes on and on. The road keeps forking, splitting, like an endless atom, or a lip, and the globe is on fire.

It's been said, *In the beginning,* and that was the moral of the original and most important story. The story of one woman, one man. One story.

I lay my head against my son's shoulder and it's heavy. Hair sprouts through the skin, hair black and bending toward the grass.

The mind is a miraculous ember, but when I become the wolf again, I must run from the story that's faster than me—just as it catches my heels, I turn to love its hungry face, but it's my son's, cold as milk.

I now understand what happens with the years—in each one, my brother is further gone. He and I, we're not so different. We wear our sorrow, a costume, which tries to contain its glitter, like grotesques.

As a child, my brother's look was fenceless: coke bottle glasses, eyes wandering behind the rims like tropical fish.

I didn't notice the short frets of his spine, nor did I feel the rumbling of honeypot ants gathering crumbs down the length of my torso. I was just waiting for the next thing, which came later.

It was the day my mother reached inside me for something I didn't have—and, like pulling a fat shining trout from the river, she pulled the river out of me. The sound of it, an unearthed wave.

This was when I knew the way to be—blood-bellied, a child still slick with birth fat. My son.

Above us, a parish of bees, the mass of them, like an empty thought. Each a curled letter, its own striped flag.

Every word rounds error, stands in, badly, for something else; discrete the words of a language—then a small wind, the size of a wrist, woke us again, which may be all that's left of my brother and me.

Cold as aspirin, Ed's voice, or was it his face, blind as a dolphin's with its thumb in its mouth?

Which is why, when we find our mother in the garage, her hands strangely crossed, like knives and forks after supper, we break her buttons, blow air into her lungs, count heartbeats like limps, but her round soundlessness, it's a blot dark as a Rorschach.

She's wearing the beige dress where the dark gazelles have been stilled—her smell a bitter doll's. The sockets of her eyes, dry as thimbles, hold one wave hidden in another, just like my brother and me.

Holding onto her nub, like a doorknob, I scream.

Which is what awakens my son. I carry him out. Quiet his cries, under a sky like a staved-in crown whilst rosewater sluices his wrists.

Standing on the driveway, we stare into the garage, its open jaw. The baldness of my baby's head, so meek and smooth and bare, makes me long for the solace of amnesia, white as a cut apple.

Meanwhile there's the body, red, alien as a foreigner. "Move it," I say.

When Ed crutches her under the arms and drags her out of the garage, her body sounds like a dry zipper.

One hears everything in this landscape—it's a clean knife, slicing the mute, just like the cat wiping its face, or rain falling from the firs, heavy as books from a shelf.

In my brother's deaf ear, there's no such sound. While he kisses the hundred-fifty-pound body of our mother, I watch the loud animal bones in his face and smell the earth.

Kneeling, he takes his glasses off, lays them on the ground, a shining weapon. He then throws his t-shirt over her face, letting fat hang over his belt. I want to pinch that fat, make it a rosy cheek, but my brother's pulling a lemon out of his pocket, squeezing the juice all over our mother.

I'm a ripe woman. I could be happy, but the spiders, they're eating their young.

When my brother says, "something terrible has come to live in our house," we wash our faces in the wind, forget the strict shapes of affection. Let the dead woman, our mother, hold clay in her hands.

While my brother wills himself not to speak, I watch a worm raisin on the pavement, then look up to see a police car, blue light careening like a wailing angel, turn down the driveway. To bitter us.

Both of us become slowly-tearing-itself-apart clouds as our mother's body is loaded into the ambulance. We kiss her forehead, approach her from every angle.

When the doors whoosh shut, green birds, so exactly the color of the grass the grass itself seems to shriek, fly away. As does the ambulance.

In that shrieking grass, our mother's silver wig shimmers like a mackerel. When my son shimmies down and dons it, everything becomes a kind of bird. Some kind. Some not so kind.

My son. His honey-cured flesh is a pharaoh's. As he dances, the wig shimmers like the shell of decorator crab bedecked with silver polyps, knobs, and buds of algae.

As he wheels around on stubby legs, the three of us join hands, dance, our faces bland as the blind. Zigzagging, there's nothing paltry about our dance. It's as if every move invokes our desire to be conjoined. Eclectic, electric, flecked with death, nothing can be drab so long as the birds and angels storm us.

But heavenly ascension is slow-going—our mother knows this—as does the sky which spills over us with the vaporous colors of tea and milk.

Our bodies, these are red dragons, for this is when the sky opens—we laugh, are drenched, entombed by the splashy bowels of a golden chimera, which fills us like the strange idea of living.

IN THIS COUNTRY OF GHOSTS

The night I met Micah, the sky was so listless it scripted egrets into a swoop of gray. Wind wrinkled our foreheads as we watched a nebulae of emeralds. We didn't know when or if we'd ever see that tangerine blue again.

A youthful flush drubbed his cheeks. With him, there was a name to wake into and music to sleep through. His throat was a lighthouse.

Why he returned to a country that didn't want him only makes me want to retrieve our time from the men who stole the sweetness from his mouth.

Language minus a voice is still a man. I came to know of his capture in dreams where I feared what the dark tasted like.

Was he left in a room facedown in his own salt? Or was it in a field of almond trees in early spring? Maybe a guard's bullet did him in. Maybe.

How is a person's name peeled from the mouth? Can

metaphor console memory and what remains of a man's genitals thrown to the dogs?

Maybe his death was a replenishment. Who knows? What the body needs, the mind waters. His heart, was it cut into pieces?

Nonetheless. Nevertheless, I believe there are many kingdoms left.

Which is why I nestle him inside my brain with the word *distance* upon my tongue—it's a field of almond trees, sharp like the seams of the Kashmiri wind.

This country of ghosts leeches into the river, casts itself across couplets, leaves concentric circles in the Mughal miniature's watercolored garden above the bed.

It also takes five quills from the nightingales shrouded in the gold-leafed margins of the banyan trees among other birds rendered flightless, some falling into Persian blue, some surrendering to rock while winter holds its shape against bone, against tender, against a wish for the pastoral, which has a longer interlude than the white inside the snow.

Once, in twilight, two nightingales retrieved a ghazal from the lily of Shah Jahan's only water garden—from a sketch in watercolor, hers was the quiver of refusal sweetened with jasmine and his was the quiver of restraint tempered with vertigo and abandon.

When the veil of twilight parted, she was one half of the couplet and he was the proportion of wingspan, the gilded departure, what Rumi would have rendered had he ascended.

And what of this gesture—Micah's hands, which held me and the blind court poet crushing a nightingale in his palms?

When someone becomes ash, there's nothing you can do. About this, even diamonds do not lie.

The egret stands still as a glass of milk. And there are clouds of yellow dust along the road. I lean on the railing, watch my spirit fly away.

A white-skirted beauty, it turns into a fairy and the long flute carries a lasting note of sadness.

When I see the night creatures: the green-eyed dog upright on his throne, the winged lion, the woman whose third eye brightens the room, my hands tremble.

The woman is grinding lapis to paint the veins of her breast. Her nipples are coated with gold. It's true I rarely speak.

What I'm looking for is the unmarked door me and Micah walked through and this is what we wished for: a vision of love, which isn't just a manner of speaking, but it's hard to say why the dead feel harder than the living.

Yet he's so opaque, even brief moments of transparency seem fraudulent—windows in a Brutalist structure everyone admires.

"Eden," he said, "always disappears, but the sea which no one tends, is also a garden."

Forget that the two waters of heaven also drank from the garden, but still it springs and fruits beneath the fathoms—at night, I let my prayers rise, knighted by frost, while the air burns like alcohol across the mouth of every wound.

For too long I waited. As if Micah would reappear, a soft tassel of snakes.

So much forgiveness awaits us. Isn't it in the way fish accept the hook and how ice heals itself, but a weeping house, it's forever haunted.

How can I explain why I drown birdcages at low tide? Isn't it because what lives inside them is dark, songless, a short tablature of loss, a place where hell becomes what we're afraid of—even my mother, whom I need to cast out, knew that paradise is for those who bear the mark of suffering.

As a child, I wanted to be a cartographer. I bent maps from spheres into rectangles, noted the monstrous seas full of split-tongued mermaids and ruby-lipped whales, which could splinter ships and swallow sailors because who else dared the sublime?

I liked labeling rivers with silky ink, loved the known continental curves and how mystery could be formal, like the menacing tentacles between latitude and longitude. Or a mother and daughter.

I wanted to behold the elusive squid, the patience of eels, how barracudas appeared out of the blue with the panache of magicians.

Micah wasn't supposed to go back, but he said he belonged where the air thickens with heat, where pleasure is ruthless and words are sweet.

Before he left, he accused me of hiding inside beauty, but what a breathless place to vanish in, like this height, this mountain, these snowdrifts named for how they appear like ascetics on their knees.

I have asked a man to hurt me. "Do you like pain or humiliation more?"

"Neither," I replied, knowing there's no escaping the desire to be unmade. Even snow knows it's unclean, that each flake makes its geometry around dust, where everything begins.

No one knows why penitents face the sun, but I knew

why I did. To the man who asked me to choose, I said, "Let this be a penance, one that I've begged for."

When his hands candled my throat, the pain was intense because their smell reminded me of Micah's, like a ceremony of sand.

At the edges and shores, in the rooms of quiet, in the rooms of shouting, and the gorgeous unlikelihood of it all, I subjected myself to a stranger, whose hands, like my mother's, were the color of a matador's cape.

As she stood above me, she insisted that the heart is the organ that makes music, but I've never found the keys.

My mother. With her face slack as an umbilical cord, her dust-black hair and skeletal legs threaded pink, she pounded me. My mouth quiet as a dinner roll.

I can still feel the tender net between my shoulders and neck, the even more tender palace of my ears from which fell a necklace of blood.

She saw the blood and touched it. A red sound and its hammer.

I stayed that way for days while she puckered, a brown sack. I was the only one with such a mother who, like a theory about violence, was a furnace of tongues, a lace of burned fingers.

Like time never was, I still believe there are many kingdoms left.

And Micah, is he not a little lost, is he not pressed, as children often are against a dark that has no children in it?

A DOLL FOR THROWING

Stunned, I watch my uncle walk into a stream full of flickering clarinets, lopped-off heads, silk canvases, machines that throb quicker than the human heart. He stops under the sky, raises his clenched fists.

At first, I think it's a monstrance that shines, but those are his knuckles, Burt's sharp knuckles.

Not knowing what else to do, I look at the honey seeping from huge honeycombs: there's the throb of pianos, children's cries, the sound of a fingernail scraping down the skin.

This is the only landscape able to make me feel. I stare at Burt's egg-shaped head as he shoves his hair from his brow, then plants a big load of dynamite and is surprised when everything spouts up in an explosion which cuts the yellow buildings in two and crumbles the motley walls.

Like trash in a puddle, he observes the clouds and what's in them: globes, penal codes, dead cats floating on their backs, locomotives—below him, a banner the color of a romantic rose flutters and a long row of military trains crawl on the weed-covered tracks.

This is when the soul asks the body—*where will the dying begin, in him, or in me?*

This while my neighbor keeps a box of baby pigs in her kitchen all winter. They're motherless, sleepy creatures of blood and fog—a vapor of them wraps my house and the windows mist up with their warm breath, their moist snores.

They wear steamy gowns, watch her peel potatoes. She must be a Demeter to them, but like the weather, this box of pigs is the source of all my suffering.

They smell of invalids. Death is over there. When I look toward my neighbor's house, I see trouble looking back at me.

I start to dream their dreams. I dream my muzzle's pressed into the whiskered belly of my dead mother. No milk there.

I dream I slumber in a cardboard box in a human kitchen while a woman I don't love mushes corn for me in a dish.

In every kitchen in this country, there are goddesses and pigs, the sacred contagion of pity, of giving, of loss. I can't escape my neighbor's fuzzy lullabies as they drift in cloudy piglets across the lawn.

I dream my neighbor cuts one of them open and stars fall out and roll across the floor. It frightens me. I pray to God to forgive me, or her, whom I despise.

Of course, the pigs die. One by one. Afterward, I glimpse my neighbor's white bowls in the orderly cupboards filled with nothing.

The sound of applause in running water. The pantry full of lilies, and the recipes like confessions. The confessions like songs.

The sun. My uncle's bomb. The white bowls in the orderly cupboards filled with blood.

Her scissors. They lay on the kitchen table in the blue light. Did she cut the pigs' tails with them? Each a severed ear, or half a peach?

Unsure of who I am, I slip the scissors, like an axe pulled from bark, into my apron pocket—my breath, a pile of moths' heads.

I begin to notice scissors all over the house—in the pantry or filling up bowls in the cellar where there should be apples. They appear under rugs, lumpy places where I settle before the fire or suddenly shining in the sink at the bottom of soupy water.

I even find a pair in the garden, stuck in dirt among the new bulbs, and one night, under my pillow, I feel something like a cool long tooth and pull it out to lie next to me in the dark.

I long to throw them out, but how can I get rid of something that oddly feels like grace?

It occurs to me that I'm meant to use them. I resist a growing compulsion to cut Burt's hair, although in moments of great distraction, I think it's his eyes they want, or the soft belly.

I decide to trim his beard. I don't look at the wasp at the window, nor the cat's white hair matting the orange peel, nor do I listen to the train's green breath, its asthmatic clack upon the tracks.

No. I don't focus on the men walking the rails yelling, "Cerveja, Coca-cola, agua," men who disappear like motes of dust falling inside a sleeping child's mouth.

I keep all my attention on the hair on my uncle's chin, this man who once peeled oranges for me before placing each quartered wedge upon my tongue.

Between snips, kites drift down from the hills while the clouds, slew-footed, wade into the sky like drunken wasps.

"The kites," Burt says, "are suicide notes. Soon, I think, there will be gunfire, drugs and dead children head-to-foot along the paved and unpaved roads, leading in and out of town."

"Do they have this in America?" he goes on. Meaning kites, meaning children, meaning winter rain unable to flow into the gutters because of the bodies lining the streets.

I want to tell Burt that my dead are tucked into my apron. Instead, I show him a photograph of the police chief smoking a cigar as the ear of a dead child catches his ashes.

Why aren't I dropping orange slices into his mouth? Because there's a black car out there, burning beneath the highway and rising above it—not smoke, but something like the blur of horses, or sticks, or stones, or several plagues at once.

While I stand in the harnessed heat, I become what my uncle needs. When the scissors slice my thumb, I drop them—the water glass gets knocked onto the kitchen floor and in its shattering, there's a low laugh.

Looking up, I see no one but the old cat. She stretches, feigning indifference.

"Marla," I hear, "Marla," but the air's so thick with ghosts it's hard to breathe.

My uncle, who was a beautiful language, is gone. His

hair, like tin embroidery, litters the floor, smelling of oranges and blood.

While sweeping up the mess, I look out the window, watch the guards in their grub-colored uniforms clinging to blades of grass—worm on the leaf, worm in the dust, worm made of rust.

I laugh at these men with their boots and borrowed muscles, their long guns, the worm of their faces among the leftover leaves, yes, I laugh, *laugh* at the assassins on our roofs, for the time of the assassin is also the time of hysterical laughter.

When their trucks start humming like vacuum cleaners, I cinch Burt's belt tightly around my waist.

Uncle of mine, I pray, *please hold the loosened ends while telling me the name of the boy who died with ashes in his ear.*

As I walk out the door, I think, *one in six bombs falls into a bushel, a basket, a two o'clock casket,* as if reciting a nursery rhyme.

It's a warm day—glory of plums, glory of ferns on a dark platter. Glory of willows, glory of the stag beetles, glory of the long obedience of the kingfisher.

But everything has changed, the bomb my uncle planted a doll for throwing.

My feet go forward. There are roots. And a giant sun which focuses on the moiré morning.

Water, reeds, electric eel: one possibility. Sun, reeds, dust motes and mites: another. Whatever the conditions, it could always be worse.

Until it is. Then everything fails, leaving its mark. Sudden things happen inside a sudden frame.

A flame is lit. In that guard's hair. With its pathetic

squiggles, like those pigs' tails. An immeasurable distance sizzles between us. Then it doesn't.

Like an overly exposed photograph of a man, he becomes ashes to obsess with, like those hived inside that child's ear.

This happened in June. And I haven't heard the angels since.

CHATOYANT

There alongside the bed where Adam lay dying in sheets clean as a plot of daylight, the pillows thick as diapers, I pray.

While holding his peace-white hands, I wonder: has my rapist learned to slink unnoticed across the nights' sad meadows, leaving the asters alone in their clusters, evading the blackberries' thorns?

So much running: from the body slam, the knife in his sock, an earth streaky as polaroids.

He had a scar under one eye, hair lush as a puppy's. Touching him saved my life. Remembering him saves my life. His legs, slight ferns, but he has to be old now, maybe a little less mad.

Something about the squalid rattle deep in his ribs. It was only a cough. It was only a wolf's fury, the sum of his father's father's despair, and no more than that.

He had no shirt. He had no coat. His shoes were torn.

He was thirsty, his teeth the size of chapel doors and then, the splashy moon waded in, turned like a taller sibling, and left.

As the first stones grazed my shoulders, as all of the crop-less meadows woke up, acre by wind-torn acre, I went under.

Afterwards, while running, I slid down a slope, the dirt the color of found pennies. My sandals broke. One smelled like crushed chrysanthemums, the other a dust-blown note.

I fell onto a pile of horse skeletons, which had fossil-ized, a startling number, an acreage of bones prickly as cacti.

When I stood up, screaming, "Where am I? Belly, am I in the belly? In the intestines? In the hollows of my blood?" I was relieved by the sight of a man who looked harmless as thread.

"Take it out of my skull," I yelled, "I have the right to see myself."

"Adam," he said, as he walked over, took me by the hand and led me to his house. There he brought me choc-olates, dark chocolates shaped like tanks and fighter jets, milk chocolate tomahawks, a bonbon like a kirsch gre-nade, mint chocolate bayonets.

Even after we got married, he brought me boxes of truffles, missiles of semisweet dissolving on the tongue. He brought me Glocks and chocolate mines, a tiny transport plane, a bomb that looked delicious in its cello-phane.

He never asked and I never told him what happened that day, but the two men—my husband, my rapist—shared one mind, which like the world, was a fractured room.

And now that Adam is dying, our room is sunless as his bedpan. On the nightstand, the orchid-pink morphine is lined up in syringes like nervous girls at a dance.

Night after dry-mouthed night, I read aloud. The words forward-march like ants in a void while I guard his sleep, each leg and foot pale as magnolias.

One night, before his illness, Adam snapped his lighter shut, placed it beside the metronome on the nightstand. We'd just made love and I was sitting naked on the edge of the bed, watching the stars appear.

He told me my skin was chatoyant, like wet fiddleback maple. I asked what chatoyant meant.

Adam grinned and explained, "growth distortion." This meant it could pattern wood fibers into flames of alternating tones.

I told him that was nice and he said he could take me to the shop for a look. Show me what he was talking about. This is where he built musical instruments.

I rolled my eyes. It sounded so boring. But then he bit my thigh and pulled me out of bed.

He drove with both hands on the wheel and told me he thought of everyone as an instrument. He said his father was filled with knots, like a burl, and only good for music boxes, but his mother was quilted beneath her surface, like rippled river water.

Then he just stared ahead, kept quiet the rest of the way. When we got to the shop, he felt along the wall, flipped a switch, so I could see three white torsos, each with a headstock and fretboard attached to the sternum.

They were displayed on hangers like guitars. With a shaking hand, I covered my mouth, backed away, and ran out to the parking lot.

Adam stood at the door and watched me. The sky clouded over. As if the darkness had been sawn off a black walnut's trunk, then sliced into veneer. Which is why he was at the pit where I fell that day. For the wood, no, for the music in the wood.

When his last breath, music-less as a moth, shrinks the walls of our room, I open the window, let the large, frosty air enter, healthy as tragedy.

Human thoughts return as do human concerns, the misfortune of others, the saintliness of others. They converse softly, sternly.

"It's time to go," I say as I climb through that window onto the roof in order to jump, like ice into a glass of sleep.

But I don't. Instead, I watch as the yellow moon shifts behind the pines—below me, my dead husband squats like a bride, a yolk suspended in each open eye and in truth, he isn't dead. Or is he?

I wonder: did my rapist do what he did, pressing down upon my flayed kneecaps, just so he could imagine a time when he would be a human among the humans again?

Because my body was a cave, because he built a fire there and forgot to put it out, because the world got shoved up inside me, I kicked him, ran, and when I fell down the slope, I too turned into a moth before hitting bottom, where the horse's hooves left streaks of midnight in the sky.

I still can't say what happened. Silence writhes inside the walls of truth, like a fox thrashing in a hound's jaws, or a riled fly, frantic to escape the hand that carried it to safety. Adam's.

My grief. It wanders strange gray streets, knows that

no one can promise safety. No one. Especially not the body and I can't explain it in physical terms—what happens between two people in an ordinary bed, in an ordinary room.

Afterwards, we lay curled, two bass clefs facing this way, that. We talked. Sleep came later, a raft pushed out onto a starry sea.

The oak bed. In our room. There's nothing there now but me. In a dream, Adam's voice slices through me. "Come," he says, "walk with me on the water."

As it happens in dreams, we don't even know if the water has begun to freeze. I hope the lake is like glass and that I can sit on it and this desire is almost sexual.

He holds my hand as we step carefully onto the ice. "Don't worry," he says, "if we fall, it will be into a double paradise."

Like a god who has many lives, I step onto the ice and strike it with my heel, the sound of it, a dull cello.

As we fall through, the silence is the silence of a bandage wrapped tight around what's sunken. The depths. This is what my rapist left me with. The depths.

When he kissed me, I bit him—and the butterflies, millions of them, flapped their wings and the ampoules of Benzedrine, thousands of them, broke open, yellow as bullets or the forsythia.

Because he had the most face-splitting, beautiful smile and a voice like a washboard, I bit him again. What else can I say?

Or was he more like the horse skeletons at the bottom of the cliff I slid down, landing among the sunken, mummified hemlock and birds-eye maple—salvage logs kilned and carved into finely-grained instruments. By Adam.

Slight and thin, he looked at me as I screamed, his gaze

pointillist like a phantom frozen in its own headlights.

His hand, the color of a damp iris, took mine in his as he walked me to his house.

That night, while the moon like worried art hung over the roof, he described the math of cubed hollows, this as he touched my torso until it torqued, a red cello. Thrashed, drastic, with seemingly-silver sounds.

Heavy I was and the black wheels bent. The alders sagged over the powdery road-bank, as though they had borne, and it was all too much, the seed of the year beyond the year, the tight cleavage of the seasons.

But for the kilned logs and the mummified hemlocks, the salvage, the curly chatoyant, the wet fiddleback maple and the fetal spines curled in each yellow ring, bleating like a school of winter trees.

From Adam I came to understand how the wood, like a patterned fire, is altered when laced with strings thin as criminals—it makes a music so cold, it fractures. Like light traced with arsenic, or a piece of canvas in a dingy museum.

And the tones, the alternating tones, these are torpedoes fired in the depths we're all left with, like the tears we're tasked to shed, tight as hairs are to the head.

LIKE A CEREMONY
FOR THE DOORLESS WORLD

The scent of pigs is faint tonight as the lime trees hang their heads against gradations of blue.

I remember how I first felt my baby's limbs, like the gloves around which I turned, until I was that deep cave I once visited, as it tried to carve out one secret place and failed.

The ham flowers have veins and are rimmed in rind, each petal a little meat sunset. I deny all connection with these flowers and the barge floating by, and the white flagstones, like platelets in the blood-red road.

I put the calves in coats so the ravens can't gore them, bandage up the broken gate, and when the wind rustles its muscles, I gather wood.

But when I see the horse lying on the side of the road, I yell, "Get up! Here's your pasture flecked with snow, your oily river, your one and only barn!"

Lying there, she looks like an inside-out mermaid with greenish veins, the bits of fat at her belly, her small gray spleen.

Kneeling next to her, I tell her about the man I slept with, how the dark wept in the small of his back, and in the back of his knees, pale music.

He hovered, pumped into me, made me gasp; asked difficult questions, then left.

No need for bouquets or sad stories. He was just one more key I added to my collection—I dropped it in the basket alongside boxes of zippers with teeth of every imaginable size.

How much later was it when a sheet of geese short-sheeted the sky? The water tower, ten storms full? And the horse, back in the red barn?

In the hospital, I practiced drawing cubes—I squared away the house and the incubator with the baby.

Under its glass lid, he was akin to a square of cheese on a rented altar, or any other element of the imagination—a cough, dry as a hinge.

How can I say that the bed contained my body, but not the dreaming head? That this was where I became the creamy skin on his inner arms, his, entirely.

As I bent over the incubator, I told the baby not to collude with my inability to give or receive love. To collude, instead, with brief periods of intense sunlight striated with rose pink glitter.

Outside, the hay had been gathered into gold rolls in the field, the calves in concentric circles. Every other picket in the fence, a funeral pyre.

The papery poppies in the plastic cup. Just because I

threw them at the nurse, wasn't reason enough to condemn me. Who wouldn't object to what they did with babies when they turned gray?

It was a boy. I knew he would never come back, unlike the cats that walk into the next room in order to cry.

It's tempting to think that the lost return to the place where we found them: near a parliament of lamps, or the window I leave open enough for him to appear like the unthinkable, his name a white nightmare.

Lately I've been thinking that the boy loves the orange sky and doesn't know how to tell me and so I sing, my voice rich as the fabric he swims through, like a dark triangle in the wind-field. Handsome and then some.

His head pushed its way out, learned how to waver. Beautiful flaw, terrible ornament.

Upside-down in a spoon, I think I'm getting closer—blue windows everywhere, the sharp smell of keys in the air.

Was he the inevitable slap? I wonder this as I prop the storm windows against the side of the house: like twenty paintings of the sky: novelty, slaughter, snow.

One hour the same as the next, I held him the way I hold snow. Like a sculpture, forgetting or, perhaps, remembering everything.

Red wings in the snow, red thoughts ablaze and me with my fingers curling around a shard of glass—in order to forget holding his placenta-soft hand.

Everything I hate about the world, I hate about myself, as if this were a law of nature. Say there are deer in the snow, walking out the cold, the dark of their knees, a watermark.

Say I'm not the only one who saw or heard the trees,

their diffidence greater than my grief. Why must every winter grow colder and more sure?

My head is heavy with the cargo of childhood—in a dress bullet-holed with pearls, I hid in the root cellar, one hand flat against the trapdoor, the other hand knocking, *knocking.*

My mother with one hand, like an open eye, the other, closed: waited.

It was October. Moments before, our three horses had pawed the ground, turned snake necks while my father marked me.

The year went dark as did our flowers and fires and what we thought we were.

And yet, our faces opened to the whooping of coyotes at the canyon rim, how they threw their voices out, like starless veils over our still, stilled hearts.

Smelling the purple fennel in the root cellar, this hour became the bottom of my rank world.

Years later, when I heard what was inside me—a flock of sound flighted to be, I knew there were many earths inside the whirl.

Like the whirl of doctors around the bed, the baby's noiseless struggle.

Like a ceremony for the doorless world, I carry him into the same root cellar where the flies, six in a metallic pile, identical green, bristle, are gaud.

"Imagine," I say, "an orchestra playing to an opera house filled with three thousand plants. Rows and rows of plants. Canna lilies. The red of hibiscus, crinkled with the insignia of interiority. And the gold inside, cloistered."

Dirt, not copper, makes a color darker. It makes the shapes so heavy and every melody harder. Which is why I leave him like a carafe or blind glass or a single hurt color. There's nothing after that. But the music, it glazes the shattering while a colony of ants, each with a piece of chrysanthemum on their backs—begin to reassemble memory; the petals become the lining, but the shape of the flower is completely lost.

How much later do I find myself looking at the lone suitcase in the middle of the yard with a sense of solidarity? Almost forgotten. Under the lime trees.

When I pick it up, I don't look back. Everything's moving, pixilated, the yellow grass, the raw etiquette of the wind. And the smells: coal, plow, rust, century. All the layers like the ball of wax in my hand.

Because I can still feel his thumb—warm, burled—moving in my mouth, I turn back. His thumbnail, a flake of sugar he won't allow me to swallow.

I walk into the house, crawl back into bed where I work the wax in my hands, knowing that the heart, like a window, can only be broken once.

Somewhere, somehow that orchestra is playing to a concert hall full of plants, fingers rooting inside cellos as if to pull out the last notes, a gold wheel spinning.

And yet, he clasps my arms like a root, and his voice, it's slow and at peace while my kisses, happy as embers, fall upon his cheeks.

EMPYREAN

I'm fifteen when my mother leaves. I tent my sour girl body with boy-textured T-shirts from the could-have bins, become real in the flee.

When the man who takes me off the street orders me to hold his skull between my hands the way you'd hold a bag writhing with howling birds, I do what I'm told.

The head is thick, the room a cage door opening.

His beard, a collapsed country I refuge inside, his laugh a memory so liquid I hear it when I open the window to where lilac birds swirl like muslin.

Because I'm a wound I make and pass through, I need something awful done to my body. Careful as poison, he puts himself in me.

When we're done, Justin asks how many men I've slept with that month and haven't loved.

I don't answer. "Dance with me," I say, "it's getting late."

In light, like the twist of a tourniquet, I dance as if I have a morbid secret to disclose.

When I spot that rag-like, woody bump, which I know is very much alive, which I know is very much something to deal with, despite its refusal to scurry off, I get as close as I dare.

Its body goes bark, its slightly under-lit arms, serrated sticks, slow as the battens in dead flags.

A female, her head swings wildly above the long oval abdomen of her body.

She makes a sound like an old leaf as she drags herself across the floor, her tiny head like a dull jewel on a hinge, her open jaw into which the brainless male parts go, still operative, or operatic.

Is she now sated? So disoriented by the drag of desire, she'd crawl toward anything?

My arms feel like logs. Like a damper pedal, my breath presses down on Justin's chest, turns him noctilucent.

The business suit he wears is a subset for bunt, for bondage. Something he stubs himself into, like a tune, an autumn lust. His fingers, though, are pink as a baby's booties, a carded lace.

Is it heretical to expect things from this world? To want to live forever in the jeweled glut, the body opulent, a heaven squirming in each tight fist?

Does he call out my name, or is that the floorboard wheezing? The chandelier too full of brilliance to be indolent.

I tell him that I don't need rain to break into a rainbow. Nor snow with its six crutches in each crystal. Only inanimate things can sparkle without sweat—the threat of music in its depths.

While I sing to him, everything dies in the throat, becomes the spooky rift between itself and its intended. Even the mantis knows this.

Like a wishbone breaking. The little crutch inside is not a toy.

With Justin, the bed is a haunted preserve, the blanket rough as sailcloth. In it, I ask, "is the snow ever kind? With true undivided light and nothing flawed about it?"

Because my mother taught me that if a song goes wrong, one must dance, I make him get up and dance me with me again. Moment after moment, I let my body express how I've been moving, like a vein through the vastness of.

As any mammal knows, the little crutch inside is not a crutch. More like a steeple. Neither silver to be chased nor gold to be beaten. Like solitude, which aspires to want nothing.

When I was born, my mother was thirty-one. She was naming the one hundred ways she loved her life, until our likenesses made them one leukemic spill.

Even now, I hear her cry about how I weighed her down like a beast, how my wavy howls stripped her.

I find in these memories no borders or edges to grace. Sometimes, she set a pearl on my plate. Oil-hot, it floated upward like singing. Of course, I ate it.

Defeated by the body, slowly annihilated because of it, my mother left. Then came the darker sooner, the later lower.

And tell me what creature, what peril, crafted my cries that night? Already I understood there's no freedom when loss forces us to speak from organs other than the heart.

It was something about love. A far cry. It came to me

unmediated, *go to god lengths.*

My mother had shown me that. With a fur cross on her back.

I hoped my one and only heart, crass as orgy, would see me through the dusk ahead, the months gray as a donkey.

It didn't. When the madness overcame me; when my body sloshed like rubbery meat; when the night brought marching ants to my pillow and wailing teapots swarmed in the kitchen.

When a flock of birds erupted from my throat, leaving my mouth a clog of feathers, I paced the apartment, yowling.

Clinging to sanity's slipperiness—I swallowed my mother's meds, gripped the kitchen counter, and when the madness subsided, I left.

In the hallway, a little girl was cutting out dolls from tan paper, the kind attached at the hands. With crayons she gave life: blue eyes, red lips. Brown and black hair, yellow—expanded, her world of dolls held hands and sang. Collapsed, they were beached jellyfish.

She looked up at me, her eyes the color of milk. "Empyrean," she said.

"Empyrean," spilled from my lips, floated like hot ash, grew brighter, stung my eyes. I raised my hands, touched the slightly dimpled walls.

Wearing my face like a bathrobe, I went out, saw my heart: *beat, beating, beaten.*

When I found my mother, a needle in her arm, I lifted her hands, gentle as questions, and crossed them over her heart.

Above her, a swarm—terrible, not feathered, not exactly birds or angels, not cellular, but translucent, veined like dragonflies, a wing like a blade, like a sword hammered flat, thin as paper. One wing per wrong.

After leaving her, I wandered—living in my body as if though were a row house. Or: the tallest chalk hill. Or: nowhere at all.

When Justin's hand first covered my mouth, like a secret inside an envelope, I bit it. Its skin, thin as a door.

"Shit," he said as he slapped me, the air a silver tack.

Up into the room we went, where I scattered like watered bees. Sheets turned down, sleeves rolled up, the chain already on the door. His business suit a lost cause.

In a stench stout as chives, time collapsed, was captured. A pair of scars badgered his arms, resembling a heart and spade.

I loved his half rotten aroma, the bloodshot octave of his groans; I especially loved falling to the earth, a gutted balloon.

I said his name and here we were. Here we were. In the gut of aloneness and I quite liked it.

What I saw in his face: the elasticity of expression, the sashay between left and right eyebrow, the crease between his eyes like a riverbed or the lines of rapturous sentences searching for a period. The dimple in his chin.

Mostly, his eyes. And those wrinkles, the feel and color of wet driftwood.

In the middle of this—the pain stopped, and a certain clarity descended. In a sudden effortlessness of being, I could forget physicality. Mine, his.

I stayed perfectly still, caught up in wanting it to last, this unexpected innocence born of holiness, or loneliness, or both.

Minutes passed before the pain came back, rising, twisting. This time it was throwing me across the room. Was it the dark-gold wind coming through windows? No, it was Justin knocking me over like furniture that needs dumping.

Urgently. Like a bouquet of bloodroot, he kicked me down the stairs where I saw myself as a house, cold as lard, on which there's nothing left to lean.

But the snow, as it fell, was kind.

THE CAT HARPSICHORD

Like a dot, the ladybug landed on the quince berries as the man who grabbed me snorted. Trapped, weightless, I was drenched by his outline—a man whose face merged with mine, and the dark idea of God descended.

The night noosed me, a turtleneck. His arms were cannons, his eye color a soft summer dress slipped on slowly.

"Please," I said, "when my husband sings, I fall to my knees."

With my breasts smelling like cigars, he sparrowed into me—and the moon was a spider tracking its whiteness across the sky. Orange blossoms opened like red peppers in the courtyard. Everywhere, blue rooftops.

I was both here and gone, but the lemon bushes, these overflowed with the patter of mole paws, the scythe, in its rosary of raindrops, gleamed.

I should know better than to believe my own body, but hasn't this story already changed because I told it?

His fist. The earth that shattered like burnt sugar.

When I woke up, I went back to the house, said nothing to my husband, and then out of nowhere, after months of silence, my senses were graced with an odor filled with earth.

It was like rain in a troubled breast, sweet as air that arrives too suddenly and vanishes.

All passions were swept aside. And in their wake, the fragrance of the lemon trees embittered me.

One day through the open gate, amid the green luxuriance of the yard—the gardens fired and my heart melted, and golden songs poured into my breast from the raised cornets of the sun.

An eerie emptiness. And the thunder parroted itself. Oh, wounded day with its spectacle of blossoms, wily as swastikas.

For my husband, I dressed like stone, gray and submerged, ready to be pitched, skin the precise tint of a pomegranate. Among the natives, I told him, I love the Aztecs most because of the way they lit fires in the gouged chests of men to keep the world spinning.

I wanted the miracle that would make me ordinary, to be the thing that buried me.

Instead, the television glittered, a glamorous fish. A woman in a red, red dress drank a glass of champagne sparkling with small explosions. "Don't," I yelled, "don't."

Just then, the storm clapped hail onto the stiff leaves of the magnolia tree; the sounds of shaking crystals startled my husband and the gold on the backs of books flared like a grain of sugar under the eyelids.

The lightning that blanched the trees and walls froze

them into images on a negative, a benediction and a destruction I carried within, a condemnation that bound me stronger than any love.

And then the tearing crash, the jangling sistrum, and some gesture blindly groping as when, turning around, and sweeping clear his forehead of its hair, my husband swung at me—and entered the dark.

I wanted to tell him that even dark things yearn for clarity, that bodies fade and exhaust themselves in a flood of colors as colors do in music, but I didn't.

Dizzy as a newborn shadow is how I left, a thousand unfinished threads unraveling. The promise of a new beginning like a severed wrist.

As I walked, rain strayed into the marrow and bogs, into clay and brine, sapped the gaunt light. As it did, I felt a murmur pelt inside my womb and the taste on my tongue was a gunshot of synapses, warm and light like butter.

When I crossed a rutted field and saw a barn, I flung open its doors, climbed the ladder to the loft. I wanted to jump, to be splayed and broken as the weeds that bladed the soil.

But when I heard the chickens singing from their coop, jostling each other like refugees on a train, I stole their eggs.

I went into a stall, ate them. After a clap or two of pain, my body became a slick whale—what slithered out was a jellied sack of she-ness, warm as paraffin, monstrous as a fetal eye.

Because no one would take this balmy baulk from me, I went into the next stall, placed it between the mare's legs. They lay in tandem, a pact between bodies—soundless as dew, the mare licked her clean, neat as a paperclip.

Here, where all love ended, I mouthed the wrong words for the stillborn I just pushed out. A barbaric abstraction, I kissed her slick forehead, blue eyelids, feeling how quickly honey cools to stone.

An atmosphere she was, her eyes an elegy in bone. In me, she was less than a butterfly, something that barely stirred, a curvature that could neither enter nor leave the world.

Someone I didn't know left her in the barn, an ingot of violet energy. The mare's lips, gestural as a dance.

Knowing that suffering is faithful work, I didn't look back. Out in the field, I knelt, my mouth closer to the ground and began the dutiful act of drowning everything that's been lost.

Into the woods I went, the emerald trees big as pill bottles. Here my memories spilled onto the forest floor like ruby-red seeds rough as a cat's tongue.

Silence awaited me, a pit hidden at the center of my own flesh. Night dark as a wolf's throat. And frightening.

I imagined the perplexity of beings born with a soul of paper—the woodworms, spiders, mites, creatures which sucked the blood out of cellulose.

The fetus was one such being. Like a pomegranate, she stained my fingers that pensive, murky color, the color time won't clot—the open color of memory.

Full-moon night. The leaves were falling, three beats, three somersaults in the air before losing their equilibrium and slipping out of the wind's taut cord.

Who wouldn't want to dismantle them, piece by piece—to transport them into another less painful dimension where it wasn't necessary to begin over every year, to repeat the same gestures, to sweep away the leaves, calendars, griefs?

Like a secret secluded in my warm, silent mouth—that child.

Sorrow is not that far away from sordid, nor is mortality from marble, nor leaves from lead, which made them fall beyond all meaning.

How to order disorder when the silence is immense: within it everything fit and was lost.

It could be just that. It could be that God goes around pouring salt into human beings until they sink, heavy as a sandbag. The way I did in that barn, and long before, under that man, and now under these trees, like Bengal tigers.

Luminous as an oil slick she was, and I almost swallowed her, an angel slimed with seaweed, wrack, or a snake on a raven's back, but for the mare, who picked her up gently, her black nose beating like a heart.

Carnal, marvelous, her paradisiacal Miltonic keening—fragmented, green, pawed through, shambling, kept.

Daintily scorched, these sounds were scented by cardamon, star anise, cinnamon, hyssop. As if minted in a marble bowl, the one that feels like a day in this one lifetime, if a day could feel.

Huge and awake, the death I left, a feather on the mare's tongue. Black and white and quick—her inner sanctum, an injured plot.

As I went back home, the cliffs offered caramels of granite. Sparrows big as hens sang so loudly, they briefly struck me deaf, their eyes, old lemons.

In the cool moonshine where grass and flowers were grey, but the scent green, I climbed up the slope in the color-blind night.

And before me, the house with its still surf of weed, pagodas of weed, an unfurling body of Upanishads weed, a Viking fleet of weed, dragon heads, lances, an empire of weed.

The cat harpsichord. It worked like this: the tails of two cats were attached to the strings of the instrument, then pulled by different notes, and the difference between the way the cats cried was the music.

I wanted to be the cry muscled to the bone—there are those who touch a body and leave it graceful; I'm not one of them. Because her mouth tasted of bitter almonds and smelled like a bracken of broken ferns.

In lunar fog, I stood at the edge of the world, mouth screwed shut.

The bones of our house, the house of our bones was in a sudden blur of wind and wings, where our voices still throbbed and palpitated like an occasion of owls.

Did I say, "When my husband sings, I fall to my knees?" If so, I meant it.

An obsidian sky betrayed me. Every serrated shadow flayed me. Soon enough, the crows will caw. The cock will crow. The door will close. I'm not going back, no, not until after the wet hours of grief relent.

In thirty years I might forget. Precisely how tonight's pain felt. And in whose black house I dwelt.

DUST OF THE FALLEN

It's predictable, the logic of dreams. Long ago I lived in heaven because I wanted to. The night my mother died, I fell to earth. I knew the way.

Still, it took years. Upon landing, the ground embraced me with the gentleness of someone delivering tragic news to a child.

I was that child.

All alone, I studied the deranged forms about me: the road, the upper pasture, glassy fronds of cut moonlight—there were vultures like mile markers over the icy river and a red-shouldered hawk that reeled and veered in the wind and beyond it, a purple gallinule with its candy corn beak.

In it: a catch, a hold, a possession. My mother's last word: *always*. Disappear, be born. Amiss? Arise.

Her death made me quiet and I remembered when she locked me out—I was five, maybe six—I went to the willow tree, wrapped myself in its whips, stroked its many sharp eyebrows with my hands.

This was when she went to the hospital to give birth, then returned without the baby.

"Where is it?" we asked. Did she shrug? She was the kind of woman who liked to shrug; deep within her was an everlasting shrug. Did she give birth to a shadow?

That didn't seem like death. Yet my mother never slept. She moved, slowly, like the dust of the fallen. She rarely spoke. A dose of death occupied her—in the cold rain, the gleam of grief.

Brittle as a paper mask was the skin of things stretched between my mother and father. I saw streaks of tiny particulars in pained relation and understood—*every childhood is terrible, you choke it down, until you choke it up.*

When I returned home from school one day, I saw my father sitting on the steps of the front porch. He had a look that was unfamiliar; it was flooded, leaking.

I climbed the steps as far away from him as I could get. He was breaking, or broken. Or, to be more precise, he looked to me like someone understanding his loneliness for the first time. "Your mother is dead," he said.

In that moment, I held myself back until nothing was left but the dissolving blues of metaphor.

Difficult to pinpoint the fear. Was it my mother's specter, unstrung? Which left my body open for the moon to break into, unspooling.

He took me inside where slashed pillows belched feathers across the mattress and floors: what was an oriental rug, was now cut into strip steaks, gone-astray socks rolled like tumbleweeds.

What was I to do? Slash the vivid tethers to my

mother? Throw everything away? Margarine containers like plastic ducks? Expired sardine tins? Dozens of receipts, their honeymoon photo?

I took in the spew, pabulum that a bird feeds its nestlings.

In this palace of grief, my father's footsteps approached: on the tip of his tongue—the bloodshot, the struck, the sorry, the senseless.

He dragged me outside. "Bury it," he said, as he handed me a mason jar. In it, floated a husk, eyeless, deranged.

When he left me there, I didn't say a word. Instead, I let the doves do the calling for me. Storm clouds, brackish as eels, slithered across the sky.

Not wanting to feel the snow brush my knees, as if wading for the first time into the ocean and myself insisting, be anything, buzzing with blood or wings, anything alive, including grief, because isn't this what my mother wanted?

When I went back to the house, my father had locked me out. I pounded on the door, "you have to let me in," trying to understand someone who shifted like a gale that hurricanes.

From the front stoop, I watched the living death of the sun, high above the shoulders of the stricken moment. His voice coming through the door, it was a gray bite.

And the night grew, from nothing to nothing—grew and sang, fragrant, shaken. Nothing changes. Everything's just as it is.

White as the meat within the shell, the wind settled in my body as I exhaled, a variable absence.

When my father finally let me in, I understood that

everything and anyone will do anything in order to depart its fate. A consonant will depart its sentence before being shamed. As a daughter will her father.

I wondered: *What do her ashes know?* That her death started in the living room. That for bonsai she used pliers the size of a nail clipper, spools of wire and a fist-sized rock. One bore a petite pomegranate, never to eat, nor to touch.

No, her death began with the baseball bat. She smoked cigarettes. She'd light up and blow smoke out the apoplectic window. On the stereo, a bluesman cried, "I need my ashes hauled!"

In the vineyard, my father secured the strongest cane from training stake to fruiting wire. Pruning with handsaw and loppers. He always left a spur for the next season. My mother.

After her death, my father barred everyone from the house and the yard where, at night, long red worms slithered from the ground.

Then I understood: her ashes knew how the lamp flickered, a displaced sound, when he came up behind me, said, "If you were a star, you'd be called 'Forgive me.'"

To which I replied, "Or not." And the air we moved in was a monk's in a meditative year.

"And when I say honey," he said, "it means I'm going to graft her sweetness onto you."

"No," I replied, "you won't."

He shrugged. Just like she did.

I cradled the bat, its honeyed wood. The weight of it a boat, hard as a hillside. I hefted it, swung, arose, amiss.

I was never warned about these things: that we hobble wreckage down stair after bricky stair. That once we leave home—its gaseous oven—that once we walk down our own front steps, we're the murk we blow to cool. The slop we curse. The hum of incandescence.

As I ran, I grabbed my mother's braid, which smelled of black cherries and old pianos, went out past the hazy-as-sandbags junipers.

I raised my father's shotgun by its metrical butt; my skirt, a prison of iron verse and when I fired, the braid flew up, as if suffering from whiplash, and hunks of it flayed, *flayed,* like a black scorpion's tail, and then I took the baseball bat to its remnants, until it mortared, pestled.

Dust of the fallen. Like a lawless pantoum, no one warned me about these things: the forever-hush, the vulgar peal of morgues, that time just runs itself out.

BETWEEN THE TWO WORLDS

I begin to fathom the brittle intricacy of the river's icy scrim. For years, I managed without memory—stalled, un-numbered, abridged—no more alive than a dismembered saint enthroned in two hundred reliquaries.

Now, it's hard to say I don't remember, hard, in fact, not to remember. In the sleet-lacquered gullies and scored rock, fractures of the myth.

Here in the woods where the river cracks its knuckles in every crevasse and every bird the right color is invisible, no one should be this alone—not the pines in their prepo-tent verticals, nor me.

This is where my brother Denny's hands went around my neck, while my heart closed, a snake, its mouth, a beaded cuff, as if to behold the prize at the bottom of twenty-four.

How unstable the moment of suffering: one does not

turn to the rose for shade, nor the charred song of the red-wing for solace. In a single day: a retrospective of weathers while what we were floated between the two worlds.

My body, a lozenge, his tongue clammy as the rumor of morels and snow mingling where it fell, a spring of cold profusion.

Which is what I was under trees dark as cathedrals, a scrappy squint of sky, foreign as ice caves, or the self one seeks, its crenellated deeps, exotic as stamps while the crocus blades refused the crush of snow.

Because desire is long and beyond logic and *here* just a part of the soul, when Denny's body shoved into mine, a curtain dropped. This made the past glacial, a memory seen through to.

Until that moment, we were of one mind and all the quiet afternoons childhood offered us, lit gray like a cat, or blue, and cursed with an early moon, these were ours.

Because my brother's touch tore me shut and seeping, like a swollen organ, with no vastness or marvel to hide in, I used a rock, then shoved him, still as a piece of pie, into the river while the crotchety ground hog, like a dignitary, watched him sink.

This was after Father wore an apron and crept around like a bear. After we screamed. We were still children, but lost like thimbles.

Nothing is so gone. His record player and the channel that forked a distant year into us, like a slow magnet. Things were happening. I lay a stick on the white note my brother left on the desk. I lay a stain on the clean note.

Things were happening. Orange and purple things. Rivers flooding at dusk, wheels threading the roads like strangers.

When he went away, the clock in my thigh was ticking. Somewhere a body was being lowered into the ground. Our father's.

Somewhere, yes, and I was counting. The clean note with its numbers. I remembered. The road ended in the flooding river. At dusk.

Where I found Denny. In the white bed. Why here is the river. On the thigh. Remember what we did?

The trees stamped our minds like trauma. Filleted trees in the frozen sky. Holding each other and threading thighs, I lay a stain on the white bed. Remember what things we did?

The mind ends everything. Denny was and is my brother, even as he moves from the river to the sea.

In this hour, everything is lit—the difference between light and shadow, the sun, hard as a bottle cap that glints in the silt. Some heavyweight leaves, and in the why, just this: *the strangeness strangely passes.*

And evening mounts. There is no glamour, but if I return, I'll find some in remembering how I once looked for Denny, like Latin roots in the satin of things: the difference between something and nothing, which is nothing.

The gravel lies, like dust on the water. I find a quartz, milked clear: I couldn't hear it if it sang, no matter what.

If I lifted it, would it be heavy as a dead hand?

The shape of things fit between us in a certain way, not waiting or filling, its weight in the hour's damp—what can be taken presents its face, what can't: baroque as a lacewing.

I was deep, blank as the river when my brother's body skunked mine—and the small oracles of our flesh, these moved forward into some finite but lengthening story, this as desire folded itself into an unspeakable future and slipped into my arms, and was also lost, as were we, who once dragged our toys along until the last door opened and we passed into it like a charm or a storm.

IV.

*Until the last door opened and we passed through it
like a charm or a storm. . .*

EVERYONE NEEDS A PLACE

My lover George lies to me about the smallest things. Now he's dying and I'm trying to forgive him and everyone else while painting objects.

I keep saying I've never been in love. That's not quite true, but I keep describing the same things differently, as sailboats through the locks of reversed rivers or as streaks of red across the sky, visible only in one eye.

I forget who I am and wake up exhausted. I once had a teacher who died. It was as if she removed herself into the forest where I scatter leaves to read them, like pages, as if she's speaking. She was in love.

I'm choosing between two trees with two hollows. One begins breaking as I step inside while trying to sleep. I find a feather and have a thought, there must be an object. The field is empty, sloshed with gold, a hayfield thick with sunshine.

The man I love, he's easy to desire since there's not

much to him, just light bouncing off skin thin as a peanut shell. He's vague and smeary in his hospital johnny, which is tucked under his chin, a green bib.

Forget about his insides, his plumbing and his furnaces—put a thing in his hand and be done with it. No one wants to know what's in his head. It should be enough. To make something beautiful should be enough, but it isn't. It should be.

The smear of his head—I paint it in, paint it out again like a whisper of ashes that says, *We were born before we were born.*

I paint it in, paint it out again. A blur of forces. Why take more than we need? Because we can.

Deep footprint, it leaves a hole. I'd break George's heart to make it bigger. I'd even crack his skull to make his mind swell into a thought larger than his own head.

"You're dying," I say, "so why not do something?"

When he doesn't answer but dozes off, my mind moves forward—the paint layers up: glop, glop, and shellac. I shovel color into his face, shovel his face into me.

From the apple green hospital room, I see a bird and find it beautiful. The bird has a song inside and feathers.

I feel like the bird and I feel like a stone—solid, inevitable—but mostly, I feel like the bird, or that there's a bird inside me, or that something inside me is like a bird fluttering. This goes on for a long time.

I see the bird and want to paint it. The problem, if there is one, is simply a problem with the question. *Why paint a bird? Why do anything at all?* Not how, because the hows are easy—series or sequence, one foot after the other—but existentially, why bother, what does it solve?

And just because I want to paint a bird—I mean, I actually do want to paint a bird—it doesn't mean I've accomplished anything. Who gets to measure the distance between experience and its representation? Who controls the lines of inquiry? We do.

"Blackbird," says George. So be it, but he isn't a bird, he's a man in a bird suit, blue shoulders instead of feathers. Besides, he isn't looking at a bird, a real bird, as I paint, he's looking at his heart, which is impossible.

Unless George's heart is a metaphor, silent and upright, which it is as it stands in profile against the green wall, until looking at the paint is like looking at a bird that isn't there, with a song in its throat that he doesn't hear, but I paint it anyway.

The hand is a voice that can sing what the voice will not and because my hand wants to do something useful, I think about a sable radiance where gloom foregathers, and the stern winds brood.

Before George started dying, we looked at the walls in a cave that different men had painted in torchlight: red mostly, sometimes black—mammoth, lion, horse, bear—things on a wall, in profile or superimposed, dynamic, alert.

They weren't animals, but they looked like animals, enough like animals to make it confusing—this meant something but the meaning was slippery: it looked like the thing but wasn't the thing—was a second thing, following a second set of rules—and it was too late: their power was no longer absolute.

What is alive and what isn't and what should we do about it? Theories: about the nature of the thing. And of the soul. Because people die. *The fear: nothing survives.*

The greater fear: something does.

The night sky is vast and wide. In the hospital bed, we cuddle close, shoulder to shoulder, paint ourselves as a herd of two, together and apart from the rest.

We look at the sky and the stars. This goes on for a long time. To be a bird or a flock of birds doing something together, one or many, starling or murmuration. To be standing on a hill as half a woman or half a man, shivering in the flock of himself. These are some choices.

The night sky is vast and wide. My lover has two birds in his head—not in his throat, not in his chest—and the birds sing all day never stopping. Because they are dying. That's what makes the singing. The dying.

When George says, "One of these birds is not my bird," I agree. The lines my eyes cast braid me to his skin until I know I'm a thing that can take itself away—refined, resolved to curving inward.

Screaming isn't looking—when my mother died, I folded time into my mouth, as if to flee into private chambers only to find an uninvited thought whispering, *It's easier to unmake everything.*

Come morning, my paintbrush takes yellow from the pewter sky while I wonder about all the rooms the sky makes and about George's body, which is a sheet of sand and snow.

"A boy hung a dog in the playground today," I start, "right there under the dark leaves where the birds go."

Sharp sweet dung smell. The yelps almost digital. Above the dog, faint blue expanse, and won't I always be closer to the falling away of George's gaze than anyone else?

With my hands on his chest, I set the scene. When grief

comes, I'll bite through it as though it were his soft hands, these I'll bite through as if into the bright white light of summer.

I leave George's room and go to the playground. By the jungle gym I find the dog the boy hung. Its neck looks like a U-turn. I stop, pick him up.

Everyone needs a place. You need it for the moment you need it, then you leave and move on. Who does this? Everyone. But the dog, I carry him like a wine bag into the woods.

I look at all the trees and don't know what to do. A box made out of leaves? What else is in the woods? A heart, closing. Always and nevertheless.

Everyone needs a place. It shouldn't be inside someone else. I keep my mind on the moon. Old moon, long nights, moon.

From the landscape: a sense of scale. From the dead: a sense of scale.

Because everything casts a shadow. Even or especially the dog. Which doesn't sing. Still it finds its way out, leaving behind it the future, dead and entirely, ours.

I go back to George, whose body is like wheat. Nothing will release us from the death of the dog, which I diapered with leaves. Unleashed into us now, the yelps that blazed from his lungs.

We are meant to ward off the desolation that bores into our blood, but what will we do without this aching chord, without the bright morning that tore the parched dirt from the dog's throat?

I hold George's hand, which is lamb-soft. How can I live without the dictionary of his face? How can I accept the certainty of his quiet grave?

Beneath the hospital window, girls walk past, hair fluttering like commas. And their dreams are musk, or water gently falling on smooth, warm stones. This is what George's dying looks like. Musk, water falling on smooth, warm stones. Something I'll carry around like a baby.

My eyelids droop and fall, heavy with sky. Going up slowly is how George dies. His body exerts a last pull that drags like a match across sandpaper, then ceases.

In the phone booth, which is caulked with soggy directories, I call all the people we hardly know while watching the morning spell his name on the cracked glass.

The sound of his mother's dial tone smells like fire, like the sun projecting simple stories, and I wonder if I know I'm melting, if what I feel is more than empty space.

Because death sets me apart, I see George as a small boy, digging a hole so big he can't see the other side.

This is where his mother laid out his dog, where she made George eat his organs like cabbages. Lonely as manure, the bones—these soiled his gums, until she tossed them into the starless hole.

It's the hole, of course. In earth that is mink-lined.

This is place we all go back to—the color of its bones we do not know, but all of us are stationed before it, like glass sheets; we see right into it, into the dirt and dregs.

Now, both of us understand what heaven is, that it's the surround of the living: *bliss, loss, trembling, compulsion*—a lesson wiped off a chalk board.

MURKY AS THE EYE OF GOD

I'm out on the back patio of the restaurant swatting bees the first time Pete and Mack catch my attention. It's late summer. My thick braid swishes every time I spin around and snap the towel at the slightest buzzing sound.

When I look up, both Pete and Mack are sitting back in their chairs, staring. It's hard enough to be looked at by one man, let alone two. I get hot in the face and go after another bee. Then I turn around, put both hands on my hips, laugh.

Pete smiles. I walk over to them, wipe my rag across their table, as if to clean it up. Although I haven't met these men before, I know they are both vets. They are also best friends.

"How was your meal?" I ask.

Mack flicks his cigarette ash onto his plate. He winks. "You tell the cook she's got something here."

"You mean me," I say, as if I don't know he knows it's

ELIZABETH KIRSCHNER

me. Mack then asks me some questions about myself.

"That's for me to know and you to find out," I say, more to Pete than him. Pete's hair and eyes are dark. He wears a sleeveless undershirt with the tiny ribbing in it that moves when he breathes. I shift one hip toward him and smile. Mack sees this, grows agitated, and complains about the heat.

Pete's way with me is wordless. He comes in once or twice after that by himself and hangs out while I close up. I briefly brush against him whenever I have the chance. One time, I slip my hand in his and feel his breath come down upon my neck. Getting close to Pete is like stepping into a parlor I don't want to leave.

Pete moves in with me in under a month. Our time together is quiet and deeply private. It seems slow too, like the procession of rainy autumn days. Leaves fall, are brown monuments. The air is fragrant brandy.

We hold each other a lot without knowing why. His arms hold broken rooms, tiny as toys. They are warm, mortal.

In December, Pete—who's a carpenter—falls off a ladder at work and breaks his knee. Away at the time, I'm vain enough to believe he fell because he missed me.

While he's laid up, I nurse him. I give him meals and sponge baths. The headboard on the bed has dark walnut eyes, like Pete's.

Being laid up is hard for him. He sleeps a lot and when awake, he's despondent. Only Mack, who comes by regularly, can snap him out of it.

Sometimes we play cribbage on the kitchen table. The walls are green slime. The pegs move like darts thrown into the back of a bird, one which doesn't bear the gift of flight.

The day Pete gets his cast off, he moves out. This is in the early spring. The micro leaves on the trees are hard as an eye blink. When I come home from work, the keys are on the bureau. Mack says Pete resented his dependence on me.

"He had no choice," I reply.

"Exactly," goes Mack. When he sees my eyes blur with tears, he adds, "Look, you know he can only live in the moment."

"Bullshit, I don't believe you're on his side."

"Listen, I didn't tell him to move out. I just helped him with his stuff."

"Leave," I say, "I can't work with you here."

Maybe it's because Mack tells the truth that I can't stand the sight of him. I want things put more gently or not at all. Pete's muteness allowed me to invent how it was between us. Moments like light coming through a cracked door.

Once Pete's gone, my breath becomes a dear pale flutter. I sit at the table, drink and while I drink, tiny deaths occur. Each death helps me understand that life can only be understood backwards because I already know I can't live forward.

One musky, haunted day, I watch a neighbor take down a tree. Limbs fall, gleaming, are the dark torsos of mares. Even horses know how to grieve. Teeth like yellow dice are rubbed against the fence rails. Whinnies snap, are pick-up sticks.

My reaction to Pete's leaving is to hide. I even change jobs so he won't come in anymore. In the new place, I'm afraid to leave the kitchen.

When I bring an order out, the men at the bar turn on their stools. I feel lukewarm, mammalian, and wish I wasn't a blonde. The rough tenderness of my walk betrays my feelings.

Come summer, Mack comes in. He wears work boots and cut-offs split so high, his grayish underwear show underneath. I bring out a bowl of pea soup, sit down in the high-backed wooden booth.

"What are you doing here?" he asks. I don't answer but spread my fingers on the checks in the red-and-white checked tablecloth. They feel firecracker-hot.

Mack finishes his soup, grabs the little American flag stuck in the napkin holder for the Fourth of July. He snaps it in half and uses it to clean his teeth.

"Old Frank wants you back," he says, referring to my boss at the old restaurant. "There's a raise in it for you."

"Now, listen: Pete won't bother you, he's too much in love," he goes on in a tone meant to make me see reason.

"Pete can screw," I say as I pick up Mack's soup bowl and stuff the oyster cracker wrappers in my pocket. I try hard to look unaffected, but once back in the kitchen I go down cellar and cry.

Back at the old restaurant, Mack comes in often. Once he brings his dog Cookie with him. She's a Husky with one brown eye and one blue. Her toenails click, are romantic stalks.

When I sit down with Mack, his eyes go all over my breasts. I'm suddenly tired of being in a body and rub my eyes until they redden. The lids are chapped.

"Are you over him yet?" he asks, "or are you going to take this one to the grave?"

I ignore his question because it's too personal. "Here,

Cookie," I say. When the animal comes to me, I lift its head by the jaws, am the id examining the odd.

"What weird eyes," I remark, as I peer into them as if into two worlds. Does each tinted eye see things differently?

"All right," he says, "have it your way."

I look into Mack's face. His eyes are blue, worn, salted. Toughness and cruelty worm in them. Mine are brown. This explains everything.

Mack gets up, drops his keys on the table. "For you," he says, "when you want it."

The *it* perturbs. Nonetheless, I go over to the development where he lives. The buildings were once used for military housing.

Once inside, Cookie jumps all over me. I hug her. The black ruff around her neck feels like a queen's. Only dogs create what the created destroy.

A sheet with butterflies on it is tacked over the sliding glass doors before the frozen bed that's Mack's garden. On one wall there's a photograph of him and Pete standing by their motorcycles grinning like idiots. Seeing Pete feels like a scratch across my eyes.

When Mack comes home, his smile is a knot in a nest. We hang out on the couch, then go into his room. In bed, Mack looks at me dead on, then touches my ankles.

I run my hand behind his ear, then pinch the gold earring. He has a scar below his ribs. It's an inch long and protrudes, like a cocoon beneath the skin. Is it a prophecy and like God's breath, does it rise and fall like fiction?

I feel it as he rubs me, this man whom I do not like and never will. Still and why not, I let him have me, let his will be done.

When we get ready for sleep, Mack swats me away as he reaches for a smoke. The tobacco crumbs get all over our naked chests. He lays on his back, stiff as a board. I watch his chest rise and fall in the dark. When I get up to pee, he startles and a look of panic crosses his face.

"Where are you going?" he asks.

"Nowhere," I reply because in being nowhere no one can find me, not even me.

Come morning, Mack wakes up talking as if his voice alone carries him forward into action. I drag myself out of bed, but once I'm at the kitchen table and get some hot coffee in me, things begin to look better.

Turquoise bandannas with white butterflies on them are pinned to the windows as curtains. Stiff as football pennants, they flutter in the draft. It's bitter cold out.

I shiver, hug myself while Mack jabbers away about safety glasses and free lotion provided by the job. At best, the two of us will have sex. This doesn't seem to be a problem.

His button collection. It's stuck to a cork board. There's over three hundred of them. "Tits," "Miss Piggy for President," and "Devo" are a few. In the center is Mack's Purple Heart.

We become a bad habit. One morning, Frank joins us for coffee. I become invisible while the men talk.

"Jesus," says Frank, "a nine-second hand grenade." He goes on while tugging on his dark, fleshy, upper lip. "If you're an accurate throw and get it near your man, he's got four more seconds to throw it back and watch it explode over your head. Got to have a four-second hand grenade. If you want to survive, you snip the fuse."

I'm at the sink. I finish the dishes, then wipe my hands.

The tag on the dish rag says, *Make Lasting Friends*. Is this my Chinese fortune cookie message, the one, which—like me and Mack—is on automatic repeat?

I look at the two men. Their eyes are glued together. "Fuck," says Frank, "those years were shit." His face looks sick and gray.

"Easy, old man," goes Mack. I leave, feel like the dot on the *i* blown off by the top of a dandelion.

Mack and I see each other all winter. Eventually, snow melts into a stale mess of luminescence. Spring turns a trick or two, then summer comes. Seeing Mack only increases the degree of unpleasantness in my life.

By midsummer, the heat in the kitchen is so bad, it jells in my head. Fly strips hang like parachutes. I watch flies wriggle themselves to death. Some days I run a tally on how many I swat.

But Christ, they crawl over everything. When I see maggots in the trash, I realize they are the larvae of flies. It makes my stomach turn.

One night, when I go home, Mack is there. "Pete's getting married," he says while sticking his hand between my legs. I squeeze them together, a vise.

"Fuck you," I say. Fuchsia blooms strung on porch ropes turn like lollipops in the unquiet breeze as I bring Mack inside.

Even though my bed is sacred, a place I swore no man would lie in ever again, save the one who loves me, I let Mack into it.

When he's done with what he does, he drops right off, but the neighbor's electronic bug zapper keeps me awake—it sings, snaps, its purple light murky as the eye of God.

I try to pick the flowers off my peach bedspread. To pick one would disturb the stars, but even stars, like fruit, rot from the inside out, just like a woman's body.

I turn to look at Mack. Beyond him, armies of insects fly toward their destruction while I kiss his rigid, irreducible scar.

THE SONG OF MUD

The June bugs, fat as pinto beans, glisten on the carrots' spidery neon tops. Behind them, the hills looked flat, like in a real bad landscape painting.

This is when all the colors of the trees come to me, like some commercial for dying, above which a blur of birds make kid-like laughs.

Light too is a presence I turn around to face, lean into, and join as I bend, pluck bugs hard as tacks. The swaddled leaves, green in the season's infancy, have me thinking about my husband.

While the breeze, pale as the taste of pears, reminds me that I comprehend nothing more than loss and fragility and the fleeing of flesh, I go inside where Moe's hands, having endured the apes, move like mud as though I were a kilt of dirty, brown leaves.

After he's done, even my arms feel bloated, like an infant spread over a plaque of water.

"Your face," he demands, "straighten it," his own, a slate onto which light scribbles, what? A dark joke, an elegant equation, garbled grief?

While the seam of his mouth glues shut and sleep seeps in, a coldness sets in, a cold-bloodedness. There's no heartache when I place my hand over his mouth, no heartache, just my breath, soft as smoke-gray gloves.

I release my hand. It is now, it is not. Precisely pointless is what I think. *Precisely.*

In time intensified and time intolerable, in sweetness raveling rot, I look out at the apple tree. The branches sound like an oar in an oarlock.

The smell of grated ginger. Warm socks and my mother, her precision a ceremony. She thundered over me—everything I dreaded, all I couldn't bear—dissolved and, like a needle slipped into my veins, left me with a nugget of pain.

I suckled it, cradling it on my tongue like a slick, red pomegranate seed. Lifting it tenderly as an animal might carry a small one in the private cave of its mouth.

That pain felt ordinary. The baby does not. The way mud covers a hole, she's an enormity that collapsed.

Incomprehensible, the unmaking of the irreplaceable— her body, which I held onto until it entered death, fell into complete darkness from all points of itself, this I cannot forgive.

But the love that I felt for her unearned, inadmissible beauty, so much like zinnias spraying this way or that, a court jester's hat, or sunlight on the river.

Something akin to the kiss I lay on her cheek, sleepy as koi coloring the water.

When I touched the slur and flange of her ears, like

melted coral, and her jaw—didn't it resemble mine, which was not particularly radiant or splendid in the hospital room where our bodies drew on each other like song.

The baby was like a willow when summer is over, a yellow willow by the river from which no leaf has fallen, nor yet been bitten by a sun turned orange, turned crimson.

Like leaves, she clung and grew paler, clung and grew paler, there in the swirling pond of my lap, as if loathe to let go—she was drunk with the swirl of the wind and of the river, with my milk, pale as an orchid.

At the moment of her death, I held her like pictures of the field—or fields—or an infinite field.

I wanted the baby to stay this way. Rhythmless as ribbon, I carried her down the hospital hallway, then down the stairs at last, my body, burdened, and erroneous, a dead weight.

Outside, Moe waited for me, took me and the dead baby home.

From the bedroom, I look out and see that the horizon is hum-drummed with haze while the quiet repetition of everything catches me, an annihilation. But such are my observations, which are bathed in a daze of grief.

There was no definite reason. Only the sense of peril. Why I stash away the umbilical cord I cannot say, but grief is a tether of fleshy petals.

When she was inside me, her presence jelled. I was overjoyed, in-orbed, coiled, loyal to her tangle and tendrils which were held captive in me.

Intoxicated, I relished her ingrown, ambrosial implosion. Binding, bound, she was my solitary bushel, island, self-world, whirl.

Swelling, cellular-like as if in a molecular thrall, she was born imperfect, pink, ruddy-pink, pink-gut-yellow: beautiful but imperfect.

Like an exit into the void, her life was arrested, stilled. As I carry her to the hole Moe has dug, there exists only this: the inevitability of a scarred life, the pulse, the breath, *go on, go on.*

I place her into the dirt from which we are formed and crushed and formed again—and make myself empty while the pines, tall as fashion models, shake their bleary heads and rub their great noise into the spangled dark.

Pike-faced, pernicious as gangrene, Moe comes up behind me. "Let me look at your face," he says, "to see if you're worth having," then he cinches my throat. With the baby's cord.

"You," he goes on, and his eyes look like begging. The scar on his arm, its sad music gives me the audacity to bite him. The moon doesn't care. It shows its teeth anyway.

"When I don't have any teeth left," I scream. "When you have the bite marks to prove it."

As I chew through the cord, which tastes like the chlorophyll dying inside a star, there isn't an exact moment, I just know.

I stand on the cliff of our marriage and look down. I stand, become a cliff.

"Fall off," I hiss.

He hands me a fistful of rocks. We wrestle to the ground where our want horrifies us. I hold him like we've never disappointed each other. The rocks, desiccated grapes.

The fog rising from the tall grass isn't the breath of God. There's no romance in what we do.

I cup my hands around Moe's face, drink in the blues and whites of his bruises. The sky so brittle, the moon so grown.

Tasked with naming the baby, I take one last pull from the wine bottle. The rain starts its descent. Though we don't know it yet, Moe's heart will soon unwind from the body, like a murmuration of starlings.

Naming her. I do it with my lips closed. Everything bears witness to this—the moon which looks medieval, which this place is—cold, open as noon, this place in time and out at once, the hills' chiseled risers: the sky, slick as a tomb too slick for script in this bright shriven hour.

I've been told grief ebbs, but my bones have to stop screaming, the end of which ends in a song of mud where the secretarial heron stabs her khaki beak.

As the heron steps, a dented helmet, in clear, chill currents which are cold and unfeeling, my thoughts spread, as does my mother's voice.

She who was a cold river rising, glistened as shoved me into a hole, the dirt red as bite marks.

The heron steps with a sound austere as sharks in eel grass. Her hesitancy undoes me. Her secret, mine: humiliation is a stab in the mud, the beautiful, golden mud, the holes where memory is fixed.

A hole so deep it's on fire, imagined endless, like the first glimpse of absolute loss—my mother in the kitchen, her hands, snapping open the scarlet runner beans, which were shaped like a viola, then she sliced the trout—its bones lined up like pews.

But to be held fiercely, a wave: *be still.*

Absolute loss. From the mire, everything. Sunlight, my undertaking. The ashes. In a song of mud.

Rain, certainly, but from where I stand, I'll never see my child racing through the warm excess of the day's soft decline, so I place my hands flat on the weeping branches of my hips.

Earth mixed with quell and the peal of the heron, like a bright shock, as she lifts her legs, a red scratch, her wings, vehement.

While I wonder what invented us, Moe comes to find me. "Wait here," I say while I decide which sprigs of blossoming heartbreak to bring into the house.

Gladiolas with their chaotic buds of flame? Dahlias like a fortune-teller's sign? Horrible, how we carry on, horrible.

Precisely pointless is all that's left, the sky, cartilage soft as a child's nose.

Leaves tremble, fall, as absolute loss wraps around me, an old fur.

Still, I think about my life. The way Moe holds me until I choke. Startled, my breath bolts to where the horizon rasps against a green cloud which seems both desperate and sincere.

And somehow I have come to terms with death while I wish the god of this place would put me in his mouth until I dissolve, until the field doesn't end and I am broken open like a shotgun swabbed clean.

AN ORDINARY PALACE

My grandmother's voice is silky. It lacks gutturals and registers in that sleepy spot just below my hearing.

"Freya," she says, "wake up." I'm napping on the sofa, the one my mother sprawled on, luminous as bladed cream. At the end, darkness was in her everywhere. It conveyed gravitas.

Grandmother nudges me again, "Freya," she whispers, as she gently pries my pinky finger out of my navel where it has burrowed. Her tone is a muffled cloud.

My navel is raw and red like a crab from sticking my finger in deeply. Hasn't it been there since Mom's death?

When I sit up, my growing pains sound like an attic groaning under the weight of old photo albums.

"Tea," says Grandmother, as she sets down the tray. Her face, isn't it a gray mare's with lavender eyes? As we dip biscuits into our tea, the wind flattens the grasses.

Darkness hovers, a stranger who threatens to become intimate.

Mom sinks in me, a stone. Once she locked me in the dog's crate, the steel door, a trap. She wanted a puppy, but got me instead, a booby prize.

"You need to be safe," she said while wrapping the cage in a heavy quilt, her hands, heavy cement shoes. My breath, it was a sack.

She was gone then, but not the yellow spots on the wall. Dented and devil—my tears, thick as snot, were smudged white fingerprints. Her voice rose in the walls. It withdrew from my body and spoke as if it had never been there.

In the psych ward, she crawled in and out of the holes in her face, which burst into a psychedelic mess—*it takes so long for the human to become human!* In the psych ward, Mom's mind took off like migrating birds. But many. Shot down. By rocks detailed as toys.

"She was gorgeous," Grandma says, her pinky lifted, a sprig. "Even after she shaved her head that one time."

The garage. I smell it. A mashed clove. Manic at the time. I haven't gone in there since. Why would I?

Outside, the trees look elegant, as if filled with evil purpose. Oh, how I long to pet Mom's thick, luxurious fox pelt, but like her, it is gone.

All of fifteen, I wear her Levi's, lacy T-shirts. We always slept together, snuggling in a ton of pillows, soft as a Claude painting. Dreams soaked us, like the convulsive asylum of plants. Her moans, weren't they a form of violence?

In the garage. In her white overalls and nothing else.

Carbon monoxide. Was it quiet? Like the inside of an orange?

Happy memories, I have them. Like when I shaved my legs for the first time. I stepped out of the bathroom and there was Mom, sitting on the sofa. I walked over to her, lifted my nightgown, which was pale as a bunny's ears.

Her eyes grew wide, as if they were museums of sadness. Then she smiled broadly, her teeth opalescent. White as a nun's wimple.

She patted the sofa, motioned for me to sit down next to her. I did. One leg had a nick. I laid it across her lap, which was a despondent minx.

Gorgeous. Like I said. A platinum bob that day. One never knew. She took a finger, swabbed the blood off my leg, brought her finger to her mouth, then licked it. It was as though she dipped it into a jar of honey.

Even the light had a honeyed radiance, or maybe it was just the light around her, like a mannequin without bones. Everything that evening went from noir to gold. She was my Midas as she wiped the blood off my leg, lingering over the honeyed taste, as though it were my birth blood all over again. My Midas, but gorgeous.

When she popped her finger like a lollipop out of her mouth, she laughed. Hearty, hale, kind of like applesauce and strong enough to push the storm clouds in her black eyes out to sea. For the moment only.

Sure, she had her dark times, but who doesn't? Mostly, I don't remember, or at least not yet.

But damn, she could be fun, like when she bought a whole wardrobe in maybe a minute just to change her look. Once she even bought me a pet rat, Charlie, as if that's all I ever wanted. White as a snowflake, Charlie was.

We put him in a banana box to carry home.

On the way, Mom cried, "Books, we need books!" This as she careened into the parking lot, only to slam into the library's drop box. Not that she cared.

She was dressed the day she bought me Charlie. In a wide-waisted, softly pleated skirt, but the fabric was stiff, as if starched. Heavily embroidered with black and white flowers cross-stitched. Downright Hungarian, that skirt. Her hair, like a bent orbit, bristled down her back. A real head turner.

Under a sky bluer than Charlie's eyes, we marched right into the library heedless of the No Pets sign.

Hidden in a head scarf, Mom held Charlie pressed against her chest. Held him gently while she talked up the head librarian. There was an edge to her voice, like a nail scraping through it.

That's when I saw Charlie's tail hanging out of her old hippie scarf, like a tampon string. Before I erupted into laughter, or she into darkness thicker than oil paint, I tugged on Mom's skirt to hurry her, but she was especially talky that day.

She went on in a blue streak. I heard a swallowed scream at the bottom of her voice, the beginning of a howl.

"You know," she started, "I'm more than happy to give a talk about the benefits of breastfeeding. It's even good for the house plants. Just put the milk in the spritzer and talk real soft."

The librarian looked up, her face masochistic as a nun's as Mom added, "And be sure to put sachets of breast milk in the freezer for date night."

"I could also read to the little ones. Would you like that? Start them out easy?" She winked, "or a sing-along?"

By now, the librarian looked ready to push the eject button. I tugged Mom's skirt even harder, but her feet were strong as a soldier's as she sang, "Round and round the mulberry bush."

My fear jolted like lightning tearing through the sky. Would Mom pull out a knife: let the knife nick like a bite to the soul? If interrupted, would she come at me, her nails ridged, a headless saint?

In that moment, I knew Mom. Her smallness. The softness of her belly, how it doubled over, puckered like me, ugly when I cry.

Which I was ready to do. Cry, that is, but for Charlie's tail, and my fingers, tiny as tots, gripping the wide universe of her skirt, pale as the pathos of hostas.

Charlie's tail. Slender as a rhyme. And wagging just a bit. When Mom got to, "Pop, goes the weasel!" the rat's scraggly little head darted out of the hippie scarf. White as a ghost, the librarian jumped about a foot.

I snorted, then dropped my jaw. Charlie was clawing his way up to Mom's nipple, which was salmon-skin crispy. He latched on. She was bra-less, of course.

We guffawed our way out of the library. Got into the car, as if for a getaway.

Mom drove, a race car driver, laughing as though her belly was full of funny little demons. The smart aleck-y kind.

"Your father," she hooted, "picked his whiskers. Like this." Her hand went to her face where she pretended to pluck out whiskers tiny as spider legs. "Then he ate them. One by one."

Intrinsically fuzzy the sound of the pavement as she

continued, "hunger," she mumbled, like a prisoner, blue and dreamless, "his, mine. Dangerous. Even when dead, I'll burn in hell. With him and his damn whiskers."

"Madness," she went on, "it's like sticky glue. It belongs to us like nothing else on earth."

Mom. That day in the car. She had cocoon eyes, wooly, awful. Hellbent on destruction, she yanked the wheel, this way, then that.

As she bombed into the driveway, I clutched Charlie like those pale, skeletal seahorses I ordered out of the back of my comic books. They came in a test tube, goopy as glue. D.O.A., those seahorses were.

When Mom crashed into the tree under which the seahorses were buried, along with the puppy we never got, I was still hanging onto Charlie. For dear life.

This while her arm karate-chopped my chest in an effort to keep my head from slamming into the dashboard.

It didn't work. Like a crash dummy, my head hit the glove compartment. It crackled, an empty box of Cracker Jacks. A tooth flew out, light as a wrench.

"Charlie," I cried. Wrapped up tight as a mummy in my arms. His shriek, catastrophic, was almost heavenly.

Mom ran into the house. Came back out with two things. A Hashish brownie. "For the pain," she whispered.

She also held a Gerber daisy. Brighter than the rings of Saturn, that dazzle-headed flower. This she affixed to the busted bumper with duct tape.

"Kind of classy, ain't it?" She asked while handing me her hippie scarf to staunch the blood blooming bright as violets in my mouth. She then snatched up Charlie and my loose tooth.

Brownie crumbs bibbed me as I staggered out of the

car. Dressed to the nines she was, and I was smashed on her, absolutely smashed. Her hair, brilliant as a helmet, but for Charlie.

She held him, snug as a gun.

"My rat," I whispered, "my rat," as I pried him from her arms the way Grandmother did my pinky finger from my navel after my naps, gently, ever so gently.

Cold as a hamburger, he was. Mom could have killed him that day because her edge was way too sharp. Way too sharp. It cut me. Cut and cut. But the daisy, the damn daisy saved him, me, us like a goodnight story. For the moment, only.

After Mom taped the daisy to the bumper, I carried Charlie into the house where I wrapped a bandage around his head and fed him bits of Hashish brownie. His eyes rolled up into his head, two smiling clouds.

I sang to him, placed my lost tooth under my pillow. Mom was downstairs where her fingers gripped her martini glass like a trigger. Her drinking allowed me to forget who I was while Charlie and I slipped into sleep.

The wind, this spelled its music, eager as saltwater or my nightgown, which smelled of peaches.

Downstairs, Mom talked to herself, "hope, smote, boat, coat." Her voice went down the wrong horizon while thunder ignited the sky.

I ran down to her. "What was that?" I asked.

Her voice, bald as a queen, replied, "Just a storm," then cut itself out while her hands snatched Charlie out of my arms. I smelled egg yolks as she, like the end of the storm, stole away.

Come morning, the land, old, leathery, rose up to meet

me. In damp grasses, roosters, ethereal as crushed fire-flies, mourned daybreak.

As I walked into the kitchen, my breath was sharp as a fade. Charlie's name was on the tip of my tongue, like the click of a cocked gun.

"I am who I am," Mom announced. She was holding a can of hairspray in one hand, spritzing the cherry she had placed on top of her hot fudge sundae. "Extra hold," she snapped.

"Mom," I started, then stopped. She was dancing around the kitchen, a spinning top, spraying hairspray as though it were pepper spray.

"In case your Dad comes," she said. "Now be a good girl and put the ice cream away."

"Okay," I replied, as I put the lid on the container. Hot fudge sundaes were her standard breakfast.

When I opened the freezer door, the sachets of breast-milk were still in there, like little pots of gold. I shoved the ice cream in, only to see a bunch of ziplock bags, sealed, numbered, like body parts.

"Mom?" I asked. "Where's Charlie?"

She just stood there real quiet like an onion. Then I saw the knife, plus the string it cut.

"Mom," I asked again, "the rat, my rat, what have you done with him?" Even then, I understood that there's little distinction between beauty, violence and utility.

I grabbed a ziplock bag. "What's in here?" I demanded. Organs, white as a snapper's belly, but mute as suffocated doves, bones thin as the breath?

"Charlie," she replied, "I saved him for you, in case you get hungry."

"Saved him?" I asked, as I threw the bag at Mom, hard

as candy corn. This is when I knew I was one kind of alive and it wasn't the good kind.

She screamed as she reached for ammo. Out of her handbag she pulled keys, a cigarette case she hurled like a missile. Out came the mace. This she squirted every which way.

"Saved him?" I yelled, "or yourself?" This as she yanked out my hair, warm as a biscuit.

Behind Mom's head, I saw a doe tongue her fawn. They were out in the yard under the elm tree. The doe's bulging face pressed into my memory, like a corpse in a crawlspace.

Because Mom and I failed to quiet the animal inside us, we grew vicious. Like two swans locked, fighting, a wing of sweat opened between us, yet the second her cries became an arsenal in my mouth, I stopped, tried to hold what wasn't there, but her body, like her mind, was in thrall.

When she hit the floor, violence too went down. At least for the moment.

Outside the kitchen window, the two deer ambled into ferns high as my thighs. A bird crooked her tongue like a dirty finger, repeated what Mom's flat bright eyes denied until she got up, a boxer, still flinging punches.

"Your ice cream," I said, "it's melting."

"Then grab a spoon," she said, "we can eat it together."

And so we did, holding hands quietly like a daisy chain.

That night, I danced with her in the garage like a surfer without a board, decked out in black boots, black leather jacket, black jeans—hip-hop music played while I pulled her hips to mine.

She was humming louder than the radio, along with the mosquitos. Out of the garage she went, stripping, her body curvy as a Coke bottle.

Eyes like concrete needles, she twirled in a yard no bigger than a barroom, naked, a purple-furred orchid, but golden. My Midas.

"There will never be another night like this," she cried while reaching for her breast, the way the gods do.

"Never," she repeated, "another night. Never."

She was right. How fibrous and incidental it seemed. The tiny leather jackets we wore then shed like vernix on a plant. What was it that I longed for from her?

Loping around, her hair stood out. Ears of wind rushed through the many trees.

Dancing, we wept, laughed, held each other's blood in our eyes. With our hands interlaced, we twirled and twirled, faster, faster.

A kind of thrill it was for her to lie out on the road and flatten herself, like the fledging that never makes it from the nest.

Mom did this whenever she felt threatened. Lay motionless. An animal. When headlights swept over her, she whooped, a Homecoming Queen. "Let them come for what's left," she cried.

And so I did. Watched her that is. Cars sped by, fast as dynamite. They swerved. Honked.

When I could bear it no longer, I ran to her, hauled her off the road. Into a ditch we rolled, heavy as luggage. We breathed, our hearts pillows of fat. I licked her the way a mother cat would her kitten, wanting to carry her away in my teeth.

But we stayed in that ditch, hopeless as wrecked dolls. When something breathed and it wasn't us, I shuddered. There, alongside us was a dead doe, the one I watched hover over her fawn when Mom and I fought over Charlie. The hair inside that deer's ears wavered, delicate as an oyster's. Between the doe's legs, there streamed maggots, like strange new butterflies, yet nestled by her side, no, practically under her belly, was her fawn. She quivered, shuddered onto piano-thin legs, used her nose to nudge a nipple, shoehorn hard.

"She needs milk," came Mom's whisper. "In the freezer. Go."

"This isn't *Bambi*," I cried, but still I ran and in running became something more than the moment when I was conceived. Or was it something less?

I wondered, *How good could fifteen year old breast-milk be?* as I snatched a bag out of the freezer. Now I knew Charlie was in there, fossilized, like a cat in a pyramid. Intricate, bent bones angled into impossible triangles.

On one ziplock, Mom wrote, *It's all paid for.* I shoved it way back. When I did, I found the Mr. and Mrs. wedding cake toppers, stiff as Punch and Judy dolls. Their arms and legs were tied up.

I put the milk in the microwave. Watched Mom, in the rosy dark, lead the fawn into the kitchen. I handed her the ratty robe Dad once wore, more holes in it than Swiss cheese.

"Get an eyedropper," she said as she put the robe on. Her face by now looked like a gilded insect, hard as armor but still golden. "In the medicine cabinet."

I did as I was told. Used a funnel to get the milk into the dropper, carried it over to Mom, who held the fawn like a bassinet. Her limbs looked like wicker. Her white spots, custard.

Over to the sofa we went. Mom put the fawn in my lap.

If I could get ecstatic, I would have then. The fawn's weight, this was creamed gold.

When her lips, plump as a vulva, tugged on the eyedropper, Mom whispered, "The minute you flew out of me, I brought you to my breast, but unlike Charlie, you wouldn't latch. You were all curled up. Colostrum which smelled like grass and time and the planets, bubbled on my nipples, which by then were nail-hard."

Mom sat there. The pines in her eyes glittered around the relics of her sorrow. "Your dad," she continued, "held the placenta up, like a purple saddlebag. As if it were his."

The fawn stirred, then folded inward, a knapsack. "Because you refused to nurse, I put my pinky in your mouth. That's when I told you there was room for you to cry in my mouth."

"The nurse swept in, snatched you from me. I screamed bloody hell, bloody hell, I tell you."

Mom paused, tapped her forehead, as if a wasp were inside it. "This was before. This was when all I wanted to do was hide you, your face a miraculous swarm."

The fawn was quiet. Her tugging sounds were silk stocking soft.

"Once we were home, you latched on. For good. Like a tugboat, you pulled and pulled until my nipple about popped off. The right one got so hard, it cracked. It even bled. The pain was so bad, I had to wear a nipple protector. My plastic shield. Had to be sanitized each time I used it."

"You'd think I could take a shower. On Christmas Eve. I asked your dad to boil the nipple guard. Easy-peasy, but when I stepped out of the bathroom, barrels of smoke barreled into me. He boiled the damn thing dry."

"The smell, good God, and him holding you like a claw.

Tried to stick his pinky in your mouth, but you spit it out. Sort of like sucking on canvas, wasn't it, honey?"

I nodded, dumbly, blindly. Like I remembered.

"Made him go out in a blizzard to get me another nipple guard. On Christmas."

Mom pulled out a cigarette, lit it. "Years later, when I heard your Dad grunt, like a bull, then saw his fingers probe you, well, you can imagine what happened next."

Because I couldn't, I went silent, pet the fawn so hard I thought her skin might split, a melon.

"His hands," Mom continued, "these I pounded, hard as a meat hammer, until his mouth opened into a scream so naked all was sucked down, like pulled teeth—and all that could be broken, broke while I pulled on you like the cord you began with."

The lump in my throat, rare as the Hope diamond, this felt like the bottle left in the garage all winter, the one holding the silver body and wing dust of a dead moth. Or my mother.

"Not much changes, I tell you, not much, but your dad, never again, even if he did have me locked up." She paused, sucked on her cigarette. "This is when I had Grandma move back in. With her shotgun and the teacups with the sprigs on them."

The room floated back, an ordinary palace. In it, a smear of yellow, the fawn, Mom, me. In it, ordinary sweetness, lit by an eyedropper of milk. The fawn emptied it, pulled away. Her eyes, these mooned me.

"No need to sparkle," Mom whispered, "no need." Just then, she placed her pinky in my mouth.

I wanted to hold her like she held when she touched my lip, called it a Cupid's cusp. Copying her, I placed my pinky in the fawn's mouth, which was a green cloud, desperate and sincere.

We sat there. In a kind of peace. Not a big peace, nor a little one. Just peace. Pure and simple.

The quiet. This was remarkable. And the darkness. All of it a good night story. But without the happily ever after. No need for that. None. No need for anything but Mom saying, real soft, nothing, nothing at all.

TENANTS OF THE LITTLE BOX

Me and Brian and Woody. Throwing the ball on a cool-as-a-glass spring evening up on the baseball field.

Twilight turned, a rose on a spit. It was time to leave. Time to make supper, I suppose. Brian's sneakers. Red Keds. Grass stains on them, a milky green fire.

I leashed Woody. Mangy, his coat, soft as syrup, his mouth. He pulled, hard, as we went down the cement steps. I fell, somersaulted, released him. His barks. Loud, shrill.

As I went down, my forehead smacked concrete. The woods flushed, red shadows licking up the trees, breathed.

In between my eyes, an ice pick. With my mouth half open, I jerked, spasmed, went out.

The sirens. That screech with razor teeth. *Was someone dead? The dog? My son? Me?*

As I was strapped to the gurney, then shoved into the

ambulance, my mouth was in two pieces, my eyes split pistachios. The EMTs laughed as my consciousness faded, bland as a paper bag.

In the ER, the blankets were warm as hot cross buns. I wanted to hold my son. Instead, my clothes were cut off with shears, hard as a dinosaur's jaws. Into trash bags they went. The sound, a river sawed in two.

While my heart trembled, I wanted to tell Brian, *there will never be one like you,* but a needle went into me. Long as the pin in a grenade.

My body became heavy as a glove. Paralyzed, I couldn't move, but once inside the MRI, I knew why. I was meant to be paste on a popsicle stick.

In and out of the machine I went. Everything tasted like copper. Or foxes. Or dogs.

The ICU. This was where I woke up. A breathing tube shoved down my throat.

My husband was there. His face, a fallen box. How to be the name uttered, but not the burden of being the name said? To not breathe anymore, to be the thing. To be the thing that did or did not breathe. To be already dead.

I didn't want to make my pain Peter's. Holding his hand, why would I? Didn't ghosts already bump between us?

His face was never warm. His mouth, glutted with flurries, opened, shut.

Then he went away. Quietly. And so did I. The voice that once called him to me, packed up, light as twine. With absolute ease I shut down.

I remained in the ICU, behind a curtain outmoded as paraffin. A nurse came in, removed the breathing tube. It had gotten rubbery, like the sheath inside a calla lily.

"Breathe," she said. I tried, but my tongue felt like an eraser, my throat tight as woodwork.

Burnt almonds. That's what she smelled like as she handed me water, *burnt almonds.*

She slipped away. This was when my terror became blue as the capillaries bursting in my eyes, blue as the vein under a razor, blue as skin beaten so badly, it breaks into the sound of blood.

The doctors came in, muttering like motors. "Your seizures," they said.

"My son," I answered. I wanted to tell them how a magnolia warbler, sky-sprung, had landed on our doorstep, dropping like a blossom suckled by song. Sun-yellow underside streaked with black, she too was charred with scar.

I wanted to tell them how my son approached her, wishing all his life to pet a wild bird. She didn't move when his fingers brushed the blown light of her feathers, nor did I. Flying in and out of the house, he set out a bowl of milk, as if for a lost kitten, but we were lost, so lost before her quizzical visit.

Did those yellow tears of light bibbing her breast smear away the black aura of nights caused by my brain seizures which seized mother from son? Whistled through the space made by his missing front teeth, bird words from sweet lips soothed forth.

Exhausted from wing-sweeping sky after sky, the magnolia warbler sipped Brian's liquid sounds. Clutches of buds brooded on the branches as he mothered her into air white with bride signs.

Principled by the wild, she lit away the fear blinkered in our eyes—even my scarred veins were carried like string to build a nest—gifts god us and then our god is gone.

The manual neurology test, "Look right, look left. Put a finger to your nose."

My eyes, these banged open. After the doctors left, I retreated into a place of spruce and fading light—tears, like small stubborn gods, started to fall.

My husband took me home. In the car, his voice was shattered glass. The kind that breaks soundlessly. And the gall in his throat, the boil it's prized for, this told me that I was losing him. The air between us was pared down by diamonds, like the ones in my wedding ring.

Even as we drove, I missed him. I missed him the way I missed our happiness.

Here we were not talking about how I might not survive. Here we were not talking about how my eyes were bruised rocks, or how badly our hearts were hurt, once again, by an illness hard as a hunter.

Like the tenants of a little box, we lugged the trash bag full of my cut up clothes into the house—what does one do with half a coat, half a shirt, half a pair of pants?

Once inside, walls the color of mint, exuded bile while I tested the air for doneness, my finger a meat thermometer.

My coming home wasn't special, but the hurt coming out from my mouth, this could open a grave.

"Brian," I called, "where are you?" He bounded up the stairs, leapfrogged into my arms.

"Mom," he said, "I just found a chunk of amethyst with a face inside it. Come look, it's in my room."

We went on down. As we passed by the master bedroom, I saw Peter toss my bag of clothes onto my side of the bed. Woody barked once, lifted his leg, peed on my pillow. I was home.

In Brian's room, we studied the amethyst. It was willing to wait for its scream to come out. *Was I?*

Let that be a lesson, I wanted to say but didn't. *Hadn't we all suffered too much in the space of a single night?*

Brian looked at my eyes, kissed them. His lips, delicate, like sails crossing wind.

He pulled away, stood up on the bed, jumped, a Mexican jumping bean. "The Mash, Mom, let's do the Monster Mash."

I joined him. We danced, screwing our toes into the bedding. Screaming, we jumped up and down in the urine-colored light. "The Mash, let's do the Monster Mash."

My throat hurt. Badly. Being intubated had left it raw.

Like water finding the lowest place, gravity pulled us down onto the bed, so I tucked Brian in. His cheeks bloomed in a pink profusion, namelessly complete. They looked like small hippos, but the night sky, it was a blood page. Unreadable.

Woody jumped onto the bottom of the bed. The night, saltined with stars, was neoned with spectacular globes of light, a dozen moons instead of the one. Still, I had to let them go—boy and dog. They were groggy as wet eggs.

As I got undressed, my face in the mirror was a belt cinched tight, one that knew about what disappeared and never returned. In the mirror was the face of an animal meant to lure another animal into shooting range.

In bed, Peter's kiss was light as a tap on the kneecap. It built a boundary out of our skin. Even in the dark, his eyes were a bull's, his mouth a goal. Salty as a nut, his bare back, the shallow of it pink with ache. This was our dramatic arc—to be immoveable as sand in a trap.

Come morning, Peter rattled his newspaper like a sword over breakfast. Behind which he disappeared. After he left for work, Woody and I walked Brian to school. The yards we passed through were stiff as commuters.

As my son entered the building, I remembered how a butterfly once mistook his strawberry hair for a flower. Light as pollen it was. A monarch landed there, a bright idea.

When the dog and I walked back into the house, the phone was ringing. My head ached, as did my eyes. Every seizure gutted me like a little box, which had no insides, no outsides, not even a world to call its own.

My sister-in-law was on the phone. "You fell," she said. "I did," I replied. "But the doctors. They've finally agreed to start weaning me off my meds. This should help. I may be able to eat again."

I was down to ninety-three pounds, weighed less than the bird's nest Brian recently found, bird bones flecked with frost.

"You," started Lynn, her voice red, thin as a bass's gill, clean, bloodless, "are nothing but a drug addict. I've watched you fall down the stairs, then smack right into the walls."

As she spoke, the air opened, a raw egg. "Clearly, your so-called seizures are the side effects of all the drugs you take. How can you do this to us?"

Everything steered against the curb of her voice. When a bird hit the kitchen window, stunned, like a theory about the future, the sound of its fall, was of a sick dog.

Lynn began to rave. "Believe me, I'm only trying to

help. Come on. Do us all a favor. Get yourself committed."

The phone, I threw it against the wall, fell to my knees, and wept. A drug addict.

The weeping went on, long as a rope that strips off its own skin. I couldn't stop. Like a bag of crumpled laundry, that's how Peter found me, conked out on the kitchen floor.

"What the hell's wrong with you?" he asked, his forehead, bowling pin pale. The strike-out, I heard it.

"Your sister," I blurted as I got up, "wants to have me committed. She thinks I'm a drug addict."

Peter took a giant step away from me. "When it comes to you and Lynn," he started, "I want nothing to do with it. The two of you have to work it out."

"But," I yelled, "wasn't I the one who stormed out of the neurologist's office when he insisted that all he could do was prescribe medication? Wasn't I the one who slammed out the door, leaving you with your briefcase on your knees, like a tidy TV tray?"

I had walked home in a fury. My illness, like a weird kind of wizardry, struck me as I entered the house, kiting me into a cruel geometry that defied the body's ability to survive.

I downed my meds, the ones stored in the ID bracelet Peter had saved from high school, the one I wore on my left wrist, like a sweetheart's corsage.

"If I'm so crazy," I continued, "why don't you just dump me at the nuthouse like you would laundry at the dry cleaners?"

In that moment, the space between Peter and I quadrupled, ugly as a rectangle, as his obscenely neat, obscenely cool mouth closed, a surgeon's.

What we didn't know then almost killed us—my husband would have to drive me to the nuthouse because, after the seizures stopped, the madness came in, turning me into a dust baby. And dust babies, of course, had to be put in a psych ward.

But in that moment, Brian's guitar. Useless to silence it. Impossible to silence it. It wept, as water weeps, as I had all day, I who was the elephantine shadow of my tears.

As Peter artfully left the kitchen, I wanted to tell him how much I needed him, but like the god who didn't gift us, he was gone.

This is when Brian walked in holding a drawing in his hands. Drawn with black crayons, many black crayons, crayons taken out of a little box.

"Your brain," he said, with a voice pure as a drop of water pinging on a glass. In the drawing, marks of a claw and a thunderstorm, a headless shoe, gray sponges, angry ants with the tails of white scorpions. In the drawing, my brain, with its knife edge of snow, my brain, a little box, vivid in its isolation.

"Wonderful," I said, as I stuck the drawing on the refrigerator with a magnet. Wasn't I that stick figure, face down, in the corner with a belly full of mice and nails?

Brian went down into his room, came back with both hands behind his back. "Guess which hand?" he asked.

"The right?"

"Yep!" In his outstretched hand a roll of duct tape. "Fixes everything," he said, "even your brain."

I brought out construction paper, scissors, crayons. Together we made boxes, lots of boxes. In one, we put a bunch of stars. Another had a hole in its forehead. Still another didn't have a heart or soul. Little boxes, we believed, didn't need hearts or souls.

The duct tape boxed up the little boxes. Each one had its little width, little length, little emptiness. How, we wondered, could we get out of them?

That night, I went for a walk. As I wandered, gravity told its story—had falling helped me learn how to stand, find what's there?

While walking, memory lifted the gray folds of my brain to get at the pink parts, which knew how to deaden, until even my own screams, abstract as an overture, left me balled up, tight as a pin curl, my arms a hot electric fence.

Lynn's voice, like the skin on a fist, haunted me as I climbed up the concrete steps, breadbox hard, where I had fallen, not long before, my throat rusted shut.

Upon returning home, another seizure hit, pulling me out of the world by its mean little teeth into a self the color of a beat-up door. It was as if I had been bitten by a red spider, a spider no bigger than my fingernail.

It was Brian who heard me fall, Brian who held my head, fed me the meds, then gathered pillows, as if to build a fort.

He brought out his guitar, played. Peter dropped a quarter inside its silky case, like a tip for a musician in a subway station, then placed his hand on my forehead as if to take my temperature.

They knew my heart was clapping, *clapping*, despite the red spider's bite, I who was that stick figure, my brain, with its knife edge of snow, a little box, vivid in its isolation.

BECAUSE THE SKY IS
A THOUSAND SOFT HURTS

"Donny," I call out, "let's get that trellis up."

He pokes it into the ground, an A frame, there where the plants are spreading, each part like a part of our own bodies, sacrosanct, edible.

While the leaves, feverish with bees, leer and scrape, a fingernail down my skin and the ways I can be hurt, so faraway in myself, already going missing, already bored by pain, smiling green as a seedling, gleaming in the silence I've gathered in this brief enactment of darkness.

Terrifying as it is, forever is a solid, as is the dark fugue of foreboding, which like the flood that begins and mounts and streams and cheats and grows in rain that falls until it's thinner than disquiet.

Which breaks us off as we pick apricots, whose flesh gets caught under our nails like old leather.

Our hands are sticky and an emptiness fills us—this is

the hardest scene when I think the whole sad thing has to end.

In the failing light, our dusty roosters mourn the twilight as we walk out of the garden where the ropy zucchinis are hard as mannequins and now we share a bed in the garish light, against the yellow wall, in the cold which smells like burnt sugar.

This is the moment when my body rebels—it would gladly escape, like rats from a sinking ship, or try to vanish, descending, slow as a diver.

I have come here many times, gone many times—who isn't bruised around the edges, peaches poured into the truck bed and here I am, kissing Donny like a nervous cat until I'm the story of every woman, or country, or house where everyone knows her place.

Because the sky is a thousand soft hurts, his eyes go feral—I don't skirt his battering, not now, not ever. Needles knit my lower back while every sound sours.

Suddenly, it's the middle of the night and suddenly, this is something I'll tell no one: how I, sober as a banker, cut my husband into segments, the knife poised, a ballerina. At which point, I grew old.

And so I sit among the garden weeds, pulling them from the roots without touching the wild trillium, then tie knots in the daffodil stalks, watching the firs scatter their birds, the tree itself under which I buried Donny, now and no more, but the green woods, these darken, oceanic and deep.

The green woods. A scroll worth returning to, one which tells me to love the way water does: wildly, like the meticulous architect of these woods or the black fog trapped inside them, so thoroughly combed, so thoroughly trapped, yet willing to shine on me.

All this as I remember the house I lived in one summer with a widower, his wife's fabric samples left draped over the arm of an unfinished chair, how I could feel her eyes in my own when I tried to choose between them, as if the sun in the alcove hadn't faded them, the dust and his arms worn as worms.

The sky stark as the first sheet laid down on her body. And this is the hardest scene—how the bones beneath Donny's eyes were shattered, like mussels brined in cold china.

IT'S A BRIEF DEATH, A BRIEF DEATH

When they drag the body out of the sea, her skirt shimmers with red sequins and tiny bows. And in this night that is not night, each word is a shape that body aches to fill.

As I watch the men, they defy gravity as they drag out the body. I hear the mad slap of its landing in sand.

The hours flow in place, marking what once was. Not just the voices scraping against the sea, nor the hands nudging the body, fingers like blind puppies, palms empty, echoing.

And I hate to do it. To set myself among them. Not now as they pretend the body is a myth, a parable for what even language can't move quickly enough to name.

A pulse is felt for through her garments. As I lean into the blow of loss after loss, it carries me further, to the road, the sea, dark hair, dolor and a question bigger than myself.

One day I too want to dive in and drift, legs and arms

wracked with danger. Like that woman whose body is now a skinny red cow with a humped back, a livid head, red receded eyes—which the men slobber over.

It doesn't look like anything I've seen before. When people gather, one of the women greets me. "I love you," she says. She doesn't even know me, but I believe her, and a terrible ache rolls over in my chest like a room where the drapes have been swept back.

"I love you, I love you," she continues. Each word heavy as a pillar.

The mother next to her holds a child, says to her, gently, "It's a brief death. This woman has gone on a brief death. She'll be back."

A man is on his knees, wailing at the sea. He slaps his hand on the wet sand and rough-cut stones the way one might a brother. He grabs a shirt of sand—the stones here carry the island's low cry inside them.

They say the man's a newlywed. Now his vows are inside the water. He claws at the sand. He wails: "Ocean, you owe me a body. Ocean, give me back my wife."

The silence that follows is the silence of what's dappled by a body that's no longer human but not yet a ghost. The silence, like boiled noise, has lodged in my throat.

The silence is the silence of broken ribs. The silence is the silence of the sunken head, of what's fallen inside the broken gait of that head.

It's also the holiness of her untied shoe, its entropy, or the jellyfish easing from the bottom like spores, purple clouds, some dead, all rising. Where it's easy to say good-bye because you forget to.

This woman walked to the edge of a sea, stepped into its darkness. Don't say infinite sadness, *don't*.

And here we are, faces pinched as peach pits. Here in this place under the old fallow eyes of heaven, a sultry, watery place, crawling with insects and birds where small things loom large: a salt-and-saliva-stained boy riding on his mother's back.

Standing at the water's edge, the moment is like ice in a champagne bucket—dolphins scissor the open water as if this is all God wanted.

There's no need to check for a pulse, nor hold a hand mirror for breath, but they do anyway. I know the woman is no longer there. No longer anywhere.

But the hair still spins the cowlick. The neck still cranes as if to listen.

Now comes the part where the body does not rise. Now comes the part where the moon is a broken ostrich egg, the sea defeated metal, and everything is a holy thing, useless as a dandelion puff in a savage wind.

So much of being missed depends on being gone. When they take away the body, there's the song of what's left, the song of the way we weather, like a low passion.

Then everyone scatters. Leaving me alone. Lightning zags the sky, enough friction to make the whole world shake with color.

On the sand, a few watery hairs like a peace symbol, and my tendency is to thread what pulls back to nothing, *nothing.*

It's almost dawn when I find a baby shark on the beach. Seagulls have eaten its eyes. Lying on an arc of shells, it looks smaller than it is. The ocean has scraped its insides clean.

When I poke its stomach, darkness rises up like black water. Just then, I see a boy beckoning from a dune.

Like me, he's alone. Something tumbles between us—not quite a feeling. I can see the pink interior flesh of his eyes.

"I got lost. Where am I?" he asks like a debt owed to death.

Already, I'm pressing my hand to his. Barefooted, pale as a storm of cherry blossoms, he looks like a divine coroner.

"Come along," I say, "stretch your feet out under the blanket. Rest, don't be afraid."

I lay him down while part of me goes to a place where I'm no longer a body but something more, a place where everything slides off: even my mortal self, which like a beetle irrigating a rose, turns my red thoughts into a red shade.

The quietness where the boy is feels fragile. Doesn't the world grow in him, as does the eloquence of before and after?

Next to him, my flesh forms a knot in on itself. When it comes, the rain is a broken piano playing the same note over and over.

When I get up, I pinch a mole on my skin, pull it off, like a bead of seaweed—for a moment, as I take out my knife, I'm precise as a bird's breath.

Shouldn't it ache, this slit into the sweet, salt mix of my blood? One drop, like a red gland no bigger than a seed of trout roe—this I ease open with my knife, as if anything can be eased with a knife.

Nothing could be so roughly handled and yet I feel so little—what in me could be so precious I'd cleave to another to keep it close? The boy? That woman whose body is a flaccid handshake?

I want to say I'm sorry, but the words like moist fingers appear before me, then run away to a narrow black room that's always dark, where they're silent, elegant like antique gold, devouring the thing I feel.

The boy, awakened, has turned his finger into a gun. "Bang," he says, as fish shimmy into the too-bright air, then plop down again, revolving their shapes into a hiss of light.

"Bang," he repeats. His finger points and points. At me. As I fall, play dead, I say, "it's a brief death, a brief death I tell you. I'll be back."

The boy, he looks at me a moment. His eyes are a flash of green, of gold. While he walks away, in the cold rain, we're juxtaposed in the juxtaposed: like the sand-soft husks of a walnut.

Even when I die, I don't think I'll go. No, not even then. The boy, he understands, and the night is infused with violets.

A CRY IS NOT A DESCRIPTION

As I put the garden to bed, the dirt under my shoes is old
as the meat of memory—about suffering, the Old Masters
weren't wrong: how well they understood its human position; how it takes place while someone else is eating or
opening a window or just walking dully along.
Which is what my husband Tuck does. *Dully.*
He's not like entering a mirror, nor like closing a door,
no, what he gives me is the happiness of refusing happiness and the joy of refusing joy—and so, I watch the heron
like a dignitary write glimmerings, small as flakes of
sugar, on the water's candied exoskeleton.
Glimmerings, this while the leaves' watery text is
strewn upon the river's roof like suspended thoughts—
only: here, or here, inside this settling, a hint of shade, almost like memory: I'm reminded what it's like to slide my
left hand beneath my son's back, my right one under his
knees, and then carry him up the long flight of stairs to

bed.

I can still feel his bones, the little ridge of the spine, the tiny smooth stone of the elbow. His sleeping body was so slight, the whole catastrophic world fell away.

Had I forgotten how easily a child can turn back into a glistening butterfish or finch or firefly? And they do, just like that.

The throbbing in my bones reminds me how quickly the sky rent apart as it roared and swallowed every socket, every thorn, every pebble. In a single gulp the boy's bed swirled down the tornado's funnel. Green it was, like an upside down tree.

The dust was blinding. It separated the three of us as we scrambled, ran, plummeted. We heard no screams, none, though we saw the spitting ink—the shadows of clouds.

In our ears, the ringing didn't stop. When I found Tuck, we were silent but for the piercing shrill inside our heads.

Then, we saw it: a firefly—an actual firefly, beautiful among the ruins, rising from the tornado's debris, a flicker, a flash, a wink of vital breath. The firefly faded, but its ghost remained, a pale wand—we, the ephemeral, inherit this.

But our son. Because he vanished, only the gallant strain of a pilfered ant makes sense—its tiny muscles flex in grit that feels like a slap.

Nightly, I crawl beneath the sheets that once trussed my boy's bed. When Tuck enters without knocking—I take off my slip. Liquid alignment of fabric and outer thigh. *Slip.* This is when I see myself inside the amber of my son's eyeballs, suspended, a prehistoric fly.

Dropping my heart down my throat like a stone, I watch Tuck put hooks on his caress as he unstitches every seam along my thigh, my side, my armpit, my belly, which is thick as a callus.

How else can I be the boy's? Be his treasure box: a trove of marbles and stones, the ding of coins cascading through his fingers.

Under Tuck, I feel the moisture in my mouth, its crown of teeth that sparkle with silver or gold until they begin to decay.

After which, I go back into the garden. In its wet, incestuous plot, the green sheen of my son's skin still clings to me like algae.

Doesn't it smell like everything that kills as if I'd reached for something too little, too late or held onto something too long?

Here where every tree takes root and drops its fruit at eye level, leaf is against leaf without malice or forethought, a manifold murmuring. No harm intended, there never is.

It's the same with fault because the fault's in nature, which will without explanation make permanent havoc.

The boy was nine when the tornado impaled him against a barn, a bicycle wheel, spinning.

The world knows harsher things, but this one broke me. When did the EMTs bring him home? Was the bag burlap or sisal? Jute. They hadn't so much as cut out eyeholes.

Not long before, I had stood in the heart of the matter holding an egg, which was monotonous as a season.

While Tuck beat our son, I recorded everything. Everything. How his hands were ghost stories or those of a surgeon's, how they didn't sleepwalk or release fireflies, rather they tightened around the boy's throat until the space got smaller.

Because a cry is not a description, I didn't want to drop the egg. A cry which cannot be called a description is like a silver needle. In the eyes.

This while the soft coal broke in the stove of my heart— his bright wailing took on a brutal pull, stubborn as the moon. He was being beaten.

If I dropped the egg, would it break the spell? That someone can utter a cry does not mean that someone else can describe its nature.

Even though a cry is not an image, it is something. Against the skin. Fins out of water. The boy.

A cry, which is more primitive than a description, is nevertheless a description. But the body dies throughout our lives, thousands of cells every second. So everything should be clear.

To the cardinal attacking his reflection in the window, I ask, "Is this your very self?"

He, of course, cannot hear me as the quick coin of his breath disappears on the glass: air feeds his bones their portion as willingly as it feeds mine.

Is this my boy? If so, why does he spend his time here, *here,* besieged by the dull birds which gather and whom he cannot touch, his own feathers, red as wrought blood, he whose wings are backlit, beating—delicate cruciform, hollow feather, hollow bone?

I make voices for him: insistent, strong, strange. Maybe he knows it's spring. I don't. Slung in the sky like a tiny wine sack, doesn't he click his beak twice as if in warning?

When he throws the bright dime of his life against the

glass, is it to make sure it wasn't feather against feather that hurt him? Even though it had.

The Buddhists say that the front of a piece of paper cannot exist without the back. Because there is a there, there is a here. It's okay if we hurt one another. We have to. That's why his father did what he did.

The day the sky ripped apart, the clothesline snapped like a branch, loud as a warning shot. Which can be understood in any language. Any. Like the mouth of a skull without eyeholes.

It's as if the earth mistook us for part of itself, our limbs its own settling, like we had sunk into the mud that would orphan us.

It seems simple: how we harden into dense shapes and are settling—sediment, shadow, us, from the spaces where we lived.

Silence settling who we thought we were, are, in this all-consuming lack. Nothing settling but a choke around the circumference of light.

We no longer know if our eyes are open, only settling: where the boy sank in his pillow—his hair—and us somewhere too, though we're yielding to this loss, we who once lived what we could bear.

Now there's a weight so true, we could die in its lightness: it exiles us into formless terror—no blanket, no bed, but this settling where the ghost of a woman is tucking the ghost of her son into bed—and the weight of her kiss as it passes through his head: absence collapsing into absence.

WE CLIMB MOUNTAINS

While driving a bunch of juvenile delinquents up to the White Mountains for mountain climbing camp, one boy, Timmy, opens the hard, bitten suitcase propped on his knees. He jams packs of cigarettes into the silky worn pockets and then pulls out a light blue velour shirt. He holds the shirt up gingerly by the shoulders.

"This cost me fifty dollars." His eyes slam open like lenses. He's showing me his worth.

Patrick is also in the car. At twelve, he's already been arrested for pulling a knife on a little kid. Patrick's cheeks are apples. He breaks Timmy's cigarettes every time he tries to light one. The tobacco is a brown bib on Timmy's chest.

"Motor gut," he yells, "what's your malfunction?" Then he slugs him.

On the way to the campsite, I let the kids crank the radio. The windows are open. The hard sound drives into our chests and presses out our pain. We are in the moment, only.

As we set up camp, I blow my whistle. I have to keep these kids alive. They don't even know how to make Kool-Aid. The can opener mystifies.

We pitch tents. The head counselor Richard says, "You know, Sally, kids are our best renewable resource."

I snort. "Maybe your kids are. These kids just chuck a lot of rocks."

While cooking dinner, I look up, see Patrick whirling a burning stick around Timmy. They're running all over the campground. I take after them, catch Patrick by the back of the neck, which I swear I want to break as I throw him in his tent.

I then slice potatoes which fall softly onto the table. I don't like how the knife slips through them so easily.

While Patrick is in his time-out, one of the boys grabs the meat knife and slams it into the picnic table. He talks about slamming machetes into people's necks.

A newbie, his name is Chris. He climbs onto a rock where he carves a club out of a hunk of wood. He strokes the blonde club while dusk favors our faces. He wears sweatpants with a white stripe ribboning through the twilight.

At dinner, he makes us pick a number. This is the order we are to be killed in. He says, "if you don't pick a number, you go first."

"Uh-oh," says Mary, "spaghettios."

When the light shrinks from the mountains, I feel it go from my eyelids back into my head where it remains like a drop of blood. The mountains have turned into misshapen humps in the shrunken light.

The kids hunch together on the picnic bench. They won't sit near the fire because they're worried. They tell stories. Chris brings up one girl who was in the Beauty School when she got murdered with tufts of hair shoved down her throat.

These juvies huddle on the picnic bench, chew their hair, suck their thumbs. Already broken action toys, they know how to live-in-the-body, but-not-of-it.

Patrick mewls from inside his tent, "Can I come out now?"

"Sure," I reply. All the other kids are making s'mores, so why not let him? The s'mores get smeared all over their faces. Mostly their eyes shine.

I look up. Space satellites slide across the sky, like graphics on screens in arcades. The same bright graphics climb through the kids' eyes. They make the stars look like they're falling, so we make a lot of useless wishes.

"Hold up the flashlight," I snap at Patrick, "so I can wash the dishes." When he complains it makes his arms ache, I make him hold it up higher. I have to have good light.

The black on the pots grits my fingernails. I scrub. I'm reminded of children's drawings that are covered with black tempera. *You have to scratch for the beautiful colors underneath.*

Our children come from homes where the closed curtains are blank, cadaverous television screens. Strewn with open cans of cat food and garbage, the moms and dads make sure these kids are nobodies nobody wants. *Nobody.*

I hear laugher, see Timmy and another boy squatting on the ground. They cast shadow dances through the flashlight planted in the dirt. The obscene dances flit on the girls' tent across the way. A giggle comes from deep within.

Tina Norton stands by the fire smoking cigarettes. She's lost in the smoke because she's so small. She's eleven and a shoplifter. Richard takes her by the hand and walks around the campground with her in her red and white Dr. Denton pajamas. They flash like candy canes, then get duller.

Later that night, Richard and I sit at the picnic table facing the lantern. Flames leap, are heartbreaking, beautiful fish.

"There's incest in Mary's past," I say as I poke the fire with a stick.

Richard smirks. "Incest is best," he says, "it's all in the family."

I kick him hard.

Inside her tent, Mary carefully rolls out her sleeping bag so her head faces the door. There are big cats on her comforter. Mary's breasts sink into the bellies of cats as she rests. I see her watching us. She keeps her shoes on.

Richard and I make up a children's story. I have the idea of a little girl in a tent swept down river by a deluge. She passes by other tents. In one tent there is a cow. The girl wants to milk her, but she doesn't have a bucket. In another is a player piano. She puts on a waltz so she can dream of dancing off with the man of her dreams.

Richard doesn't see the story that way. He sees different tents floating down the river: square tents, red tents, hexagon tents. I say, "but the mystery's what's inside."

I creep into my tent, into my own mystery. Wind beats up the mountains. The storm bursts while I doze. When I wake up, the boys' tent has blown down. I know Richard is out there by how hard the stakes are being pounded into the ground. He uses a rock.

Chris says, "I want to pound these stakes into the chests of vampires." His voice vibrates through rifts of rain. I listen to the wind wind up and come slamming down the notch.

Tina screams in her sleep, "Mommy says I'm just a little punching bag. Just a little punching bag."

The wind gets ready. There's a lapse, like when you know what's coming, and then the wind hits. The tent rocks. It rocks like a taut blanket held by two parents who are tossing the baby. They like tossing the baby. Maybe they'll flip it onto the ground. From the direction of the campers, I hear a squeal turn into a scream.

The wind punches the tent walls. The aluminum poles buckle—the tent drops to its knees. I feel like I have had the wind knocked out of me.

Next morning, we head over to the Glen Boulder Trail. We touch cairns as we pass by. We touch something doomed. The cairns are on a crooked and colorless trail like gumdrops on the road to Candyland.

We play a game while we creep up the trail. We describe ourselves with a word beginning with the same letter as our names. In the chamber of woods, our names break on our tongues like fate, like the sun breaking on the leaves of trees already gutted with the initials of those gone before us.

Timmy wanders off trail and we bay for him up the hillside. As he comes out of the brush, he flushes a pheasant in the golden leaves. We know we belong to a species. Which one?

We go up the mountain. We flash in the gaps between trees. Sweat breaks on our faces and soon the trees are gone. As we go up, we heft ourselves onto the rocks and out of the big, heavy beds of our families where the other members still lie in dirty, inherited darkness.

Up on one ridge, we look down into the valleys where we live most of our lives, where we will climb back down, sullen and exhausted.

Richard points to the scrappy pines and says, "Look, the branches only grow on one side. They're called Krumholz. Blown and stunted growth is characteristic of these mountains."

We crawl up Boot Spur. It's windy and cold. The kids' words blur into chorals and their mouths are perfect dark Os.

As we climb, it's a wall of people. The wall of people rises vertically, poised to crumble.

The trail is short and steep until the light gets crisp at the brown crown of the tree line. There's a chimney—a brief, vertical ascent with ledges of stones and roots stitched tight as sorrow.

We shove Patrick up the chimney. As he stands, he bobbles his head. "Look at that old man. He's as old as the crust in your underwear." The old man's doing fine.

At the top, he whips his nun chucks around in the cold wind. The nun chucks clatter. Then he shows me his knife. Behind the boulder, he jabs at his shadow, flinching as he thrusts. He is the woman he throws knives at.

Over on Bigelow's Lawn, one kid cries because his hands are too numb to pull up his pant zipper. I yell, "You dumb shit," and yank it up. I must have gotten him from the way he yelps.

When Timmy emerges, his boxy frame pack is a flying contraption doomed to crash to earth.

He wanted to get to the top and has. There's a cafeteria and a gift shop where he buys a postcard and writes his mom saying he's made it. She's an alcoholic. She probably doesn't know where he is.

Richard and I get giddy like we do every time we climb above tree line. We dance over the rocks in the highland wind. Tiny Alpine flowers break through the craggy rocks. We toss out songs the way a magician pulls scarves. There is no sun.

We walk through the Alpine gardens, the acres of low-lying balsam. We go out to Lion's Head. The sheer ridge juts.

The wind is a cold, textured carpet seeded and knotted with ice in designs that move before our eyes. I wonder what we can see. I lean back so I won't blow over. We are on the ridge where a young woman has been killed.

Richard has already told us to throw away our aluminum frame packs if there's any lightning, then sit on the soft packs to absorb the shock. I can see that woman in the braces of her aluminum frame pack, her bones gold stays of light turning in the sky like a beautiful box kite.

I feel her arms come from behind me, *how to be held without actually being held?*

The wind rolls the carpet down our backs and the shapes of animals, plants and minerals form around our vague, heavily clothed bodies. We are lifted through the auricles of the world, that huge, gray walled organ, with the winds screaming into larger winds until the moment we will be dashed onto the rocks.

We realize Mary is gone. She's bolted. Why? Because

to be safe is to be nowhere to be found.

"Mary," we cry, "M-a-r-r-y!"

I'm the one who finds her. She's lying in the woods in a cloud of pale sunlight. She has taken her shoes off and stuffed the socks inside, like birdies in a nest. Her hair floats on a rock. She's half asleep—a flaccid hydrangea crushed a little more each year into the attar of herself. Pallid. Incapable.

All around, the mountains soar with the energy of what I feel is the free, female mind. Perhaps Mary will become a tall green goddess, a woman in a country of phenomenal women. Perhaps.

As we descend, the green thickens and the air is dense. I feel as though I have climbed out of a dream and back in.

Mount Washington has its own microclimate. Thunderheads can form in less than twenty minutes. Clouds slither over the ridges like skinny amoebas. While foliage collects in the trees, the woods get crowded with our chattering voices as more and more leaves plug out daylight.

Back at camp, Richard drives us over to Pinkham Notch to take showers because we're gritty and bored. He gives me a bunch of quarters. We have to double up in the girls' room, so I take a shower with Mary. Every few minutes the water fizzles and I have to put in another quarter.

Mary talks a lot. Her breasts bobble, fleshy baubles.

She tells me about her mom and her sisters and her golden retriever who's going to have puppies. She describes her room to me with the Garfield the cat posters all over the walls while we sit on a bench outside the clammy shower.

She french braids my hair. We talk. I know it's all a lie.

All these kids lie. They have to. No kid from the projects has a golden.

During the drive home, we drive past several old resorts. The windows are slammed out in the huge, sinking yellow buildings. I see into the decayed ballrooms where men and women once held each other, where love was grand.

Mary says, "Everything I remember is bad, like swimming." For once she is telling the truth.

A huge truck barrels down the highway. I read the bumper sticker—WATCH EVERY CHILD—then look at Mary and Tina Norton. They are singing to the radio. Cigarette smoke trenches them.

Tina is sitting on the hump between Mary and me. She doesn't stop talking.

I can't stand to look at her. Last night, she yanked out all her eyelashes. Her blank lids flutter up and down, open and shut as she talks about her favorite band, her china horse collection and about sleeping in the same room as her mom when the weather gets cold.

MUSTH

I never thought I'd love a man who has a room full of skulls. In one, fur still clings to its ear where Christian hasn't finished cleaning it. He tells me when he killed this one, and how.

Amazing how many methods there are for only one outcome. He lifts a gun longer than a cobra and blacker than burnt shrapnel from its glass case.

"This one," he says, "was my father's." His arms strain with the beloved weight, the weapon as heavy as I am in the morning when I want him to take me home and he won't.

"This one," he says, with a skeletal chuckle while pulling a petite piece of chrome from the bottom drawer, "is for you."

Christian's first gift. The pink handle, the color of a scalloped bedskirt, with grooves designed for smaller hands. If I hold my fist loose enough, barely tickle the delicate trigger, the grip fits perfectly, the gun dangling like an afterthought from my flimsy wrist.

I move against his chest, draw a heart on his sternum with its tip. He smiles, "You get it."

And I do. Each stark, immaculate and gray thought is a shanty violence among the cosmic squander that filths the zilch we're ensouled with.

Under his rum-sledged gaze, I follow him down to the sea where his tongue, happy as a louse, laps the long milk from the canal of my spine.

The sermon of the ocean: nothing lasts that I wish dead and a light so clear it feels like wind, like an undertow we could drown in.

I watch how the breaking waves strip the shore of its first skin, dragging its cage across whatever has worked hard to crawl into the choking, foamy groan of high tide.

His laughter slaps against my skin, a signal that I too should be happy. Of course the sea has teeth. Of course we lie beside it like a dare, starfish in our blood, limbs that won't regrow, his hands at my throat—*isn't this romantic, isn't this what I want?*

I crawl into the deep grooves of a sandy abyss. With Christian's hand up my skirt and his thumbs pressed into my eyelids, his lust is a tiny pink slug in a pigeon's beak, hotting up the air—and I remember, the doe's body around his neck, an upside down flag.

And his laughter, his toothy laughter like a trophy behind the glass case of his pupils. Four or five sand flies juking the beach.

His shirt buttons, fraught haloes at which I pick while two patrolling birds thrush out sand that looks like a coffin slab.

Suddenly, he starts putting things in his mouth—dead seaweed, the slow pulp of clouds, deadweight sacks of jellyfish. He can't stop.

He tells me how he once woke up with his mouth full of bees, their dead crunch still stinging his gums. "Break it," he yells.

Because pleasure is fanged, I take both my hands, pry his jaws open, fill it with lead-stained sand. I've never seen anything like it—his teeth, his gums, the impacted tooth with its psychedelic blues and greens, the stretch mark of his smile.

Of course, I bite it as if to weld it shut. Christian's tulip-gasp, fringed with blood. "Beautiful, beautiful!"

And somehow I get out of there, although a part of me is still growing darker beside that ocean.

When I grapple with the thought of having grappled, the whole of him is a hole in me.

A sadness certainly, yet something about him was so consolingly formal and devastatingly irrelevant, it was as if some immense idiocy had to complete its fruition in him, like a century plant which flowers once a lifetime and fouls the air with its ironic resplendence, its skunk stalk.

And the skulls, the creepy skulls that held the sad panache and fluent gloom of something gone wrong. It was a feeling that swirled inside me, a dark congruence, a tempest of the blood pulsing enough, *enough*. And so, I let the ache that feels like acid rising in my chest be just that.

When I go back to the sea, the sand flushes with an almost innocent heat. The beige shifting of the breezes are almost imperceptible, a gloved noise.

As I walk along the shore's edge, and rub the sand I

stuffed into Christian's mouth, I feel his vision. Stark. The skulls, like dumbbells, their deadweight laid out in increments of hardship, increasing as hardship will, like desolate businessmen.

I walk past the wet breathing ribcage of the horizon. At my back, basalt cliffs; and underfoot, beneath the wet bearded opals of old shells, stinking piles of washed-in seaweed.

I go on, bird after bird are utterly still; longstanding lichens scour boulders—there are soft holes in the trail and everywhere, burrows filled with skulls, conical as party hats.

The skulls. Raw as sirens, aren't they just a showcase for the mouth?

Yet when I hear the word, *aim,* I do, but the pitch of the slope is too steep—my boots slip, and just beyond that, a carcass: desiccated muscle, tail like a broken watchband.

It looks like an abrupt little dinosaur, lying under a snit of junked junipers which smell like fennel, bones, and leather. The rare cinnamon possum? With its underwater mouth?

I stare at its whisks, the color of aged tea, then kick its mouth, which looks like a bloated wasp.

Among hummocks shaped like saddlebags, I sit, rest. In this wilderness, hours pass—when I think of what happened, I see Christian's scrotum like a shipwreck, the two balls bald as virgins.

What's left lives lashed to the ribs of his mouth, a song like sorrel but pitch-black.

And still, the forecastle of his skull. And still, the quiet copulation of his guns, the holes in each barrel, oily and transportive like a trapdoor in the ocean.

But his mouth, this was soft as toad skin, which silence shaped from the inside-out, a mouth like mold, or mushrooms, or musth.

That word for when bull elephants are straight-up crazy to smash, fuck, and kill, their penises longer than yardsticks and erect for months at a time, a stream of urine dribbling a trail of stench, sludge of hormones leaking from their temples and into their mouths.

With trumpet, stomp, and stink, they tell the truth. The spell lasts only days because then they're chained, starved, and held in solitary. Or shot.

Weakening the body weakens the frenzy. What else can be done? There's no realm vast enough for such delirium. Musth. In the mouth. Like music, botched and wounded.

Because there was a child howling inside Christian's mouth, he screamed, "Please, please," and so, I chopped off his tongue.

A beheaded hen, it danced on sheer nerve until it fell through the trapdoor in the ocean, sinking, sunk among the golden kelp, a baffled wallet.

And still I hear how silence throated him. How I wear it like loneliness, or an ode to that which I do not know, for it, like absence, is something buzzing, or gold.

LIKE A SMALL DOOR IN FOG

The men who took Henry were a plague of blackbirds. Just as the sun collapsed behind clouds black as headlines.

The bellowing elk like a dowser's wand, and there I was, living in a frozen violence, an eye paralyzed mid-blink.

The sunset was a vial of lighter fluid—the colors not of this world, peaches dripping opium, pandemonium of tangerines, inferno of irises, Plutonian emeralds, all swirling and churning, swabbing like it was playing with me, like I was nothing, just a skein of light corkscrewing, red on red, a prisoner's wall.

And when it was finally over: the ocean generalized my tears, like candle drippings on a silk floor, and the men moved on like sordid doves in a wet motion, in a violent shade, this is when I went to him.

Henry's body, slick with blood, ottered. My shirt

started crying: it detached from me right there in the vanishing light and rose up, a great moth.

I went home, emptied a tall glass of whiskey like a long swim. My mouth, it was a mute skeleton. Larvae congregated on the last gasp of the lamp like ink frying in an old, elaborate alphabet.

His voice woke me in the near dark. It flickered near my window where his face peered in, asked questions I couldn't answer. The unrequited distance, a lesser monster.

Nothing but life dares dying. My memory, another obituary. My memory, a cross. Face down. Like Henry. A whistle in high grass. A shadow pouring down the sill of calamity.

The next day was a dark passage during which I began to fathom the brittle intricacy of the human body: *what can it keep, what can it bear?*

When I went to Henry a second time, his face was glazed with blood, his body, clay at the marrow—lifeless, slumped, tangled in a tarp.

I let my skirt fall, the hem splashing on the ground like urine, tucked it under him. Jade moss on the tree trunk intensified. Oh, how I wanted to bury my hands in the small of his back.

Two leafless trees held up the sky's leaden weight. Autumn? Winter? No wind to sway the upright trees.

All moss and lichen-ridden, woodpecker-pecked, antler-scraped, bark rubbed bare—hard to tell the living from the dead, the dead from the almost dead.

Even the gods misuse the unfolding blue. Even they misread the windflower's nod toward sunlight as a consent to consume and a promise to grow where Henry's blood drips, his bones wilting in the air's sour mash—forgiveness, which is a small door in the fog, I don't think so.

Not for the men who lynched Henry. I don't think so.

Why I want to string Henry back up the tree, return his skin to coal dust and blaze, then let his blood muddy mine I cannot say. I just don't know how to survive his floating discharge—flecks, tittles, smithereens.

And if I mention the wounds imposed upon him, which I finger as if to push them back in like a navel, will they become erotic?

Thinking of the men, I re-knot the pallid rope, try to yank him back up into the tree with the word "again" spelled out on his neck.

Beneath him, stunted grass, and like a ghostly horse, I keep yanking.

It's a tragedy. Still, if I could just get his body back up: lynched, Orphic, a scarlet message, then not just this tree, but all the trees could be themselves again, all sound.

And then, I could tell him how I loved him, even if he was born in a room a short distance from the rats.

A GHAZAL
OF THE NOT-SO-BRIGHT BODY

My mother can't move. Which is to say that her casket jumps around in my head, like something burnt down in the genesis of a struck flame and the range of her suffering, these are dark horses running inside their own dark horses.

Which means I'm holding her absence. Still, I carry a faded slip of paper where she wrote my father's name with a pencil, then crossed it out.

How awful to have had that final wonder—it opened beneath my mother's face at the last moment. As if she was a small girl kneeling in a puddle and looking at her face for the first time, her fingers gripping the loud, wet rim of the universe.

There's silence inside the house and in her garden—catmint, salvia, lavender and beyond that a cluster of sun-colored petals huddled together like families bound by a hospital-bright morning.

I too am leaving. Silence in the trees and the scent of cedar whenever I dream that I was born in a caul of music.

And isn't that the plot? First the palpitations, then the pain flowering upon her lips like a rattler's. Incurably, my mother.

Still deep and silent within life's secrets—dandelions, purslane, moon-grass, the shadows of grapevines and hawthorns and dark is the direction of darkness, like an unlit cross.

Seeing the body. Not hers ever again. Still, it was the one my own body pulled through like a long window, the gold cord in its wake.

That first morning, when I get up, all the windows are closed. I open the blinds. The light is specific.

Last night they dragged me howling from her room, which had a name, a number, in the cardiac wing.

In the room, I saw her winged shape leave, rise, forgive the vessel that fled her. I stared into myself—behind my eyes, a dead woman looked back at me with no trace of recognition. *Mother,* I said, and my own feral mouth opened. Closed.

At the moment of her death, I saw a headless woman hurrying after her like a jaguar. She pried her mouth off, an empty ash tray or a slapped moth.

My mother didn't need to tell me about the shovel. I saw it for myself. Blunt-nosed. And my father raising it above her, heavy as a bridge.

Waiting inside, I could barely make out the mound of her eyes, the blank expression as she ran toward me. "It's your turn," she said, "your turn."

I didn't go out. Instead, I picked her up and like a child

made out of longing, she clasped my neck. Iridescent, lovely, the famine in her mind, which wrapped itself, a tourniquet around me.

Longing to undo myself in her, I held my mother and like hers, my breasts were two weeping eyes. The naked trees leaned into the ocean. Did the ocean release us? Did the opal waves blow our cries to shore?

Last night, I bunched the bedsheet in one hand, like a nosegay. My nightgown was the shape of a waterfall. Through its fabric, I saw a cloud turning into a horse and a planet that could be a star—a star that might be a planet.

Grave and slender, the hours dishonor themselves, stair by stair. C minor, E flat, F sharp: all vanish. My mother has erased them.

As the months pass, the light wakes and finds the music of brooms—it pulls the grief from my hands and my heart is sawdust-clean and when I see a woman walking down the street holding her mind like a leather belt, I pick up this pencil like a flute and blow myself away from my mother's death.

A Venus flytrap can count to five. Crows and bees recognize faces. Mice suffer when seeing a mouse who is known to them suffer.

The intricacies of this life astound me as I go through the rooms where my mother dwelled when I was still naked and formless as a seal, sensitive to the tides of her body.

I came too early. The great lids of her eyes peeled back to see I was not yet whole. Her tongue washed that which still clung to me from the other side. I was dipped, sponged, cut free and delivered.

She built me bone by bone, counting the hairs that

would one day thatch my crown. When my father crossed the room to touch the spot where my skull was still soft, he set down his stylus, inked a bruise.

The bargain my mother made without my consent has left me here to ponder the meadow below the house—boggy in parts—the pollard willows sipping from frost-speckled pools, the turkeys scratching under trees dying back yet another year, littering the ground with mute, papery tongues.

My mother is easier to see when the world is denuded. And here she is, flashing in the shallow water, parting the willow fronds in order to gaze at my face like an oil stain on a map.

As she goes deeper into dust, it's harder to bring forth her features. Still, my day will be spent here in the middle of things, feeding logs into the stove, cats coiling through rooms as sleet ticks at the windows' double panes.

I read a book with snow in its center in a forest lost inside a forest, the sun, an afterthought, in the darkest days of the year.

When I look up, deer peer from a ragged curtain of trees. Hunger pulls them into the field where they dip their heads, hold forked hooves above the field, and turn furred ears to scoop from the wind the sounds of hounds or hunters.

They lap at a sprinkling of grain, pull timid mouthfuls from a stray bale. The smallest is lame, with a leg healed at angles, and a fused knob where a joint once bent.

It picks, skids its sickening limbs across a dark platter of ice. The sound of it is a dead leaf shaped like a Magritte heart, or a sad valentine posted to the wounded world.

When the body drifts off, losses accumulate—here's

one and it's deadly and beautiful and then the sky is flowering with her pink ghost.

When the body goes, there's no voice to draw it back. Its name is lost, its places float, anonymous as a metaphor—anonymous, that is, until my father returns.

He drags me outside where I use my mother's shawl, the soft bits like rain, to muffle his blows. I decide to seek hard things in order to keep my body safe.

To beat down the brown grasses in the pitted field. To seek bone, its murderous clank. Feign being air—maneuver between star and dirt. Reel hard from the wound. Err, find safety in the wind. Flick on the snow for light. Sit still with falling things.

Like the tree under which my skin is scaffolded against the bark.

After he leaves, I hear the songs of extinct birds: the pagan reed-warbler, honeycreeper, the bishop's *oo*.

When I come to, the head of that lame deer is in my lap. I hold it the way I'd hold a feather, turning it to view each side.

This is when I finally feel the whole ownership of myself, only after every part of me is undone, flightless, rent apart.

I carry that head home. Grab the shovel, which smells like acorns. The blood on me, slick, slippery as minnows. But the head. This I drop in the yard, a knapsack.

Like those extinct birds, I start singing. A ghazal of the not-so-bright body. Lit by the flint-flash grit in my voice, my father comes toward me.

But for the shovel's descent, the blade, curved like a tiger-lily's stalk. As it strikes him, his body, it hits the ground, a mess of melons.

As I grab him by the shoulders, gripping him like the bathroom door he once tore from its hinges because my mother was on the other side, I know a great strangeness will come like that other-handed music written for one who has lost an arm. Or a mother. Or worse.

AN ODE TO NOT

Already in my padded snowsuit, I walk in on my parents one morning, amid the shattering, wanting to know if I can go outside.

Instead, I ask, "Where do you keep the dark?" The wreckage of their smells, their mutterings—ice on the windows, like a verdict.

My mother's perpendicular intelligence, coupled by my father's vinegary eloquence shadowed our world—it was what one cast onto the other like a tapeworm.

"Your brother," they yell, "where the hell is he?"

In that moment, everything collapses. Which is why they throw me into the closet where I bounce off its walls. Bullied by the hour, I'm akin to a piece of furniture in a monstrous dollhouse.

Even now, I want to be free of that stricken moment, to crossover into the years before: airy afternoons licking the wooden spoon, pouring soft blades of grass from a shoe while listening to the gentle lilt of my brother's voice.

Instead I remember what got saved—not him, but the pears.

Swathed in socks to protect them from birds, they ripened during those bulbous multicolored days when I felt safe before I knew the word for it. But how to fossilize a feeling, or sustain it in the pears' amber?

They are things we wept to have and wept to lose. That summer, my brother and I plucked a shell from the broad, bleak beach and listened close while humming a word between us like sugar, butter, milk, chocolate.

Yes, we slept in sheets the color of sea glass and awoke with the taste of salt in our mouths.

Because happiness is devastating in the past tense, I lay these memories on the cutting board. Slice them open and the deepest blue spills, like numbness, or a wall of night and day.

He only wanted a Toblerone bar for his birthday, to eat alone in his room away from the violence.

They tell me he was too at pain with himself. Was this why he chose what he chose?

My brother. And I think but never say: the dryness of God; and yet I remember what he spoke about in five different gardens, how there's a filmic beauty to the people we've lost, like a husk on a broken morning.

I counter this: his hair was very brave. Maybe, he was too at pain with us—for a moment, he was winged: Wally hung himself. And in that moment, my womb curdled.

So clear and glassy, his eyes with their amethyst irises. Why, then, am I still full of blood circling inside me like watermelon quartz?

I want to stay awash in this blood, like an empty room,

red in every direction. Plenty of space for nothing to happen: just the circling, the dying off.

Sometimes I wear my favorite sundress dotted in flowers like a thousand mouths. My brother said it made me look like a pond full of thrushes and wet leaves.

What if I just said *no*. To Wally hanging on a rope, to green summer melons and peach crabs and the beach accruing sleepily on the shore? Would that make anything any better?

Why not just be this corrugated skin or that which spools from cerise hibiscus flowers and red vespers in the rain or a puddle the moon passes over?

No more laughing like the waves. No more ocean of words to drink from.

Only an effulgent grist, the sour taste of lemons against a metal teaspoon.

He said, "That's exactly it, they're the violence and we must break them."

"With what?" I asked, "With silence?"

"No," he said, "With utterance. With Hwæt!" Then he turned to let me know the conversation was over.

Was this what he meant when a bouquet skipped over his grave like a strange elation? Or when words fell out of me like warm water while the heat assaulted us?

The birds, like tyranny, alighted on the icons and the toxic halos of figureheads, which knew that the human body is a great mystery.

When the bottle broke in my handbag, everything became flammable, very flammable. I told no one.

Yet, when I found myself caught against my father's chest as he shoved me up the stairs, I thought, why wait any longer?

His shirt was pressed, but his hands, smirched with the greasy smoke of grief, were swallowed up, disappearing.

While my mouth closed, his steely eyes went rainbow but with gray inside them like the bottle I crowned him with.

The inelegant machine of his body bent over, sinister like sentience itself—it caused a disordering of my senses, a disgust filled with disuse and unease.

The bottle stopped him. Suffice to say that there was sufficient blood. Suffice to say, I clung to one of my brother's socks as if it alone could preserve the cosmic order.

Downstairs, our mother was consumed by a forest of saltshakers, as though each were an obstinate puzzle—I was afraid I'd inherited a considerable amount of her darkness because I already knew how to achieve the maximum intensity with the minimum of means.

When night fell, I slept in drenched intervals. My hands smelled like pastries or the insides of my father's gloves.

Wally could see our home and the frail walls of our conscience. He heard our moot conversations droning on like sewing machines—oh, how I wanted him to save me, to tear me from sleep, from amnesia.

Why is death, which takes the place of ripeness, endless, a prayer which makes the lips harden? And why does childhood only take place in the transience of things—the rustling of near misses, lovely and foreboding?

My brother who hid like a bullfinch in the rowans saw the whites of our eyes.

Like a falcon in the clouds' warm stockings, he

opened boxes full of song, the blood that pulses in aortas of animals and stones, then lit the lanterns in our back gardens.

When I left, the green hills trembled in the mist and rose sorrow-slung—the rope, I took it with me, a bungled braid. And the sock.

In order to praise the mutilated world, I remember the moments when we were together in a white room where the white curtains fluttered.

To return to where we gathered acorns, to where the leaves eddied over the earth's scars, and the gray feather a thrush lost, and the gentle light that strayed and vanished and returned.

I live on calmly, humbly—and still I seek the image, the final form of who we were between inexplicable fits of despair, as if Wally was still with me, always asking questions, always unhappy with the answers—exacting and perfect in their own ways.

V.

And always unhappy with the answers,
exacting and perfect in their own ways. . .

ONLY THE DEAD SUFFER BUTTER

I.

Sterno. This was what made me stare. At the man by the burn barrel. We all used them back then, but when he put a can of Sterno on the fire, well, I thought, maybe he was making s'mores.

But there were no graham crackers. No marshmallows, no chocolate; no, he gargled the Sterno, drank it straight down. I wanted to warm my hands up, so I went over to him. The day after Christmas, was it? Or the one after it?

"Dirt Bag" he said, in a voice green as lust, "just call me Dirt Bag." Reptiles, each a shape to fill the body with ache, dragged the night in their tails, lived by the dark.

Because even the trees perform sorrow, they capped the sky. A rage of wind and then this man gave me the last swallow, which was a reservoir of small, furious music. I knew it would cure nothing, yet everything at once.

Mom. She must've seen me talking to Dirt Bag, a stranger. When I came in, she punished me by locking me in the clothes dryer. The Sterno, hot in my belly, solidified like glue.

The dryer. It was a space made not for me but for what my family wore, a place of heat and turning—to be curled into oneself for so long the scent between the thighs is the same as the mouth.

My knees were at my neck. Crying and banging on the walls was too easy. Of course, it didn't work—God rarely rewards the hysterical, it's the quiet sufferers God likes to keep alive.

There was no light in that ridged steel round, no light— I began to believe I was not a victim, that I had locked myself in there, the way a baby's head is strapped into a helmet.

My body was dry, pitiless. It was oceans of bone, a machine whose teeth would shred all that was not me.

Later, who knew how much later, the chair slid away from the door and the door opened—light like a cracked tooth, and my mother was hysterical, could not hold me as the dryer had.

"Shh," I told her, "shh."

That night, I watched Dirt Bag from my room as he cursed under a symposium of stars. I felt it—the Sterno being swilled, his head bobbing, like a ghost without a body. Did he want to give up his brain, its clumsy meditations, its hell-bound thoughts?

I felt it. The sting in the nose, then the eyes where a furnace flared to hollow the face. How long would it be before he wintered in his own makeshift grave? How long before his vomit hardened the earthen floor?

I couldn't help but sneak Dirt Bag in, a stray. Why, I wasn't sure, but he screamed in his sleep, thrashed like a dead shark held in the arms of a living girl.

He was both the shark and the man, which impressed me. Nothing scared me like that.

Sweating, he woke up and walked away, his mouth, a blind spot.

Over a shallow bowl of strawberry milk, I watched my mother take my spoon, lift it up to the light where she broke it, a hollow harp.

I sat still, gentle as a rock sinking to the bottom of the river, and thought, *When I die, I want someone lift me like that. I want to be considered before being broken again.*

Next time I saw Dirt Bag, it was in the A&P. Swigging vanilla right off the shelf before moving onto the cough syrup. He winked at me, "Good stuff," he whispered.

At eight years old, I knew everybody had a story—even this man with his beard slapping around his ankles, rats in his shoulders, hair down his back, an octopus lifted out of the murk.

While hiding behind my mother, whose skirt was a brick wall, heavy and impenetrable, my childhood, which was many ages at once, became an intoxication, wrung and wrung.

What Mom didn't see was me tossing cans of Sterno into the grocery cart. The thunk, like disabused tools. Graham crackers went in, marshmallows puffy as a fish's cheek. Hershey chocolate bars, flat as boards.

That night, I wrapped cans in bandanas, each a tiny Hobo sack. It was time to go. Me and Dirt Bag. Every child needs a friend. Dirt Bag was mine.

For years I thought I could art my way back home. Where the cat sang of rosy dawns.

Until then, me and Dirt Bag, we loved each other. Or at least some parts of us did. And the rest remains: beauty, terror, and that country known as life.

II.

They call me Pit. Because I looked like one when I was born. Wrinkly. Hard. A walnut pit, but tart. Nothing anyone would want to suck on. Except my father.

"Better than a whiskey sour," he said as he smacked his lips, then mine, "that's my Pit."

As he snuck out of my bedroom, I curled up, a smacked pearl smothered by its own shell. Night pared its nails on me.

Not long after that, me and Dirt Bag ran away. We rode the rails, huddled in the dank corners of box cars like blind puppies.

My ears screeched with the chugging of the rails on their silver tracks: the clack and rumble, our fingers snapping like tambourines, our roar of applause whenever Dirt Bag and me hopped on or off a train.

We both liked looking at the sky, hunt for supernovas while contemplating things that are endless, like heaven and, maybe, love.

Under one such sky, I gave him my locket, which was filled with dirt. That made it the rare thing, the treasured thing. Nothing anyone can save for—I watched as Dirt Bag fingered it like a yoke of honey cooling in a glass of milk before putting it around his neck. He then blessed it three times.

So much was possible, but as the sky grew blacker, I wondered: who's allowed to hold the ones they wish to hold, who can reach into the night, who can press his or her own ear against another's chest and listen to a heartbeat telling stories in the dark.

More than anything, I needed the girl I was. I needed her questions, electric as honeybees, and the deer's tawny listening at the water's edge, shy antlers in pooling, green light while Dirt Bag and me considered fox prints etched in clay.

I saw that the deer had large teeth and no horns and wasn't afraid. Then came the softer animals, the snake in its trapezoidal skirt, how its face was a Freudian cartoon as it crawled through bursts of air, an innocuous slinky in colorful garb.

I watched this animal sidewind, slinking along—it was an escape artist, sneaking out of cracks and holes, plotting big adventures just like me.

What magnitude, those watery galaxies—not fixed in stunned suspension, but waiting in the dazzle to wrestle and whoop in the brightness of it—I needed the world to bear it.

Until it did, we sat in a mineral hush while Dirt Bag, whose face was a broken down shed, reached with hands the color of orange peels into the braided current. His curls shone like lodestone and his brain was a soft gray cage, empty, rattling.

Restless and lanky, I was that child for whom each moment opened, for whom the attention I invested in each frazzled seed or heartbeat told me that the world gives us second chances.

This, as Dirt Bag tugged on my arm, said, "Look, Pit, if you want to be like a wolf, then everyone has to fear you."

"Okay," I replied as I clawed the air with a howl in my throat.

"Now, Pit," Dirt Bag went on, "what are you afraid of?" This as he fingered the locket, like the scraping of metal because sorrow is regal, golden, irreplaceable.

"Everything," I said. By which I meant my father.

When I heard birdsong, I understood the notes as a singular missive—begging, flirting, fussing, each companion's call and alarm as sharp with desire and fear as my own.

I pricked my ears—within the hammering of the woodpecker was a tongue unwinding like a tape measure from inside his pileated head, darting tepid worms from the pine's soft bark.

This as I watched a spider birth a filament of silk and fly it to the next branch; under which was a log with moss on it in bursts of hell-green flames where the dark thing was visible and just beyond, a mink cracked open a mussel's shell and with her mouth full of gray meat, yawned.

These were great things, weren't they? Weren't they akin to the hush a dandelion's face made when it went to seed, akin to my own breath as I wished and blew, proud as a cat, that perfect globe away?

Because we couldn't help it, me and Dirt Bag leaned our exhausted weight into each other and slept like a cut gone wrong in five different places.

Sad sacks. Just a couple of big, old sad sacks. Under a night sky raw as a rubbed heel, we curled up like babies— I dreamt of minnows swimming through my ears, minnows smelling of wishbones, their bodies, little nothings, popping like a cap gun.

Come daybreak, my body had grown cold like the stripped fields; now there was only the soul, cautious and wary, with the sense it was being tested.

"Dirt Bag," I said, "we've got to go. I'm hungry."

The day was exceptionally still. The long shadows of the maples nearly mauve on the gravel paths. It does no good to be good to me now; violence has changed me.

"Look, Pit," Dirt Bag said, "what we have has no future."

I wouldn't believe him, nor did I believe I was living; no, I didn't believe him because I already grown to love the steady sound of so many kinds of caving in, the way a body gives itself away like a sullen bride.

"But," I replied, "I can already see time past. It's like seeing—no, smelling—stories."

"C'mon," I said. I was standing in my wool coat as if in a kind of bright portal—I can finally say long ago.

Pools of cold light formed in the gutters as we stood in the doorway of the A&P, ridiculous as it now seems. The light had changed; middle C was tuned darker now. And the songs of morning sounded over-rehearsed.

The light of winter, indigent and jinxed: *we were not spared.*

The songs had changed; the unspeakable had entered them. I strained, I suffered, I wasn't delivered. This is everybody's story, an allegory of waste.

But still, life burned in us like a fever. Or not like a fever, like a second heart.

I was young. I was hungry. I wore my green knapsack with the Smiley face on it.

Up and down the aisles I went. Cranky as an infant's,

my father's eyes followed me, he who had grabbed me with his mouth, his teeth ringing my nipples like soft bells.

Held like a beach ball, I was much too small—his muscles, boat ropes in a hard wind and so, I hardened as a stone sets hard its heart while his words, a dark narcotic, dripped.

Dirt Bag was busy tucking nips into his giant coat, nips like fish flies, shiny, murderous, but me, well, I fancied the fancy franks until I remembered what Dad did with them. *You will not be spared, nor will what you love be spared.*

Apples, then, oranges, potatoes, the color of my sweatshirt. These grew horns, nubby as a snake's.

When I saw Mom, I ducked, then broadsided her, smacking into her like a Mack truck, so I could swipe her handbag, black as a Bible.

She was stupefied. I ran out of the store clutching that handbag like an unopened Christmas present, just like the ones she took from us kids and hid in the attic.

Outside, the songs had changed, but still they were quite beautiful. They had been concentrated into a smaller space, the space of the mind. They were dark now with desolation and anguish.

And yet the notes recurred. They hovered oddly, in anticipation of the wind, which came and went, taking apart the mind; or was it the soul; it left in its wake a strange lucidity.

The bland misery of the world bound me to Dirt Bag more than anything else. In an alley lined with trees; we were companions, not speaking, each with our own thoughts; somehow deserted, abandoned.

In bitter disgrace, something had ended. I knew this as

we pillaged Mom's handbag.

We tossed out her compact, tight as a seashell. The mascara wand, like the spine of a fetal mouse that'll be drowned before waking. Dollars rolled up tight as Kazoos, these we tucked in our boot tops.

I was young. With Dirt Bag, I rode the rails as though to defend myself against the world. In each dark tunnel, the brightness of the day became the brightness of the night; the earth was bitter; bitter or weary, it was hard to say.

Something had ended. As we rode the rails, some of my ghosts rode with us. Not bright, not young, they spiraled deep in the dusk of my body as saucers or moons, wearing belts of colored dust, my mother among them, neither angry nor kind as she hummed down the hallway on curved fins sad as seahorses.

III.

There were things I wanted to tell Dirt Bag, how I bit the crisp apple of my father's throat and his slaps, they murmured a mountain.

I clenched my fists, my teeth, said nothing.

Homeless—this was childhood. Like family, it was a lullaby with an exit sign.

But the bear. Neither Dirt Bag nor me could have foreseen the bear. We were camped in a tent, which was a tarp with a cardboard door. The tarp, this was scratchy, blue.

Curled up, Dirt Bag turned his face, jagged, indecorous and roomy toward the wall while the wind, which was rife with iron and blood, slapped the tent until we thought it would collapse.

With Mom's handbag under my head, I dozed. Asleep, I heard my mother click her teeth twice, in warning—suddenly, I was back in my bed, which was cold as a locker.

My mother, carious, mangy, she needed me like ice needs the mountain on which it breeds. Like print needs the page.

Through walls thin as lint, my father's groans smelled like cigar smoke—he tasted me the way the claws of a pigeon tasted the window-ledge on which it sat, the way water tastes rust in the pipes it shuttles through.

With a laugh that sounded like knotted oil my mother struck me, her hands petty traumas—I twisted away, my checkered cries empty as a jock strap.

Everyone has a heart, don't they?

Dirt Bag did, this I'm sure of because when my fists struck him the way my mother's did me, he sat right up and said, with a voice that didn't suffer butter, "You're not alone."

I whimpered, offered my hands, like a pair of handcuffs, knowing that my heart was just a muscle made of mutters and little shoots of bone, a resting place where no one ever comes home, especially not little girls like me.

Dirt Bag, he patted my hands, as though they were kittens, then handed me his nip.

"The handbag," he said, "where's your mother's handbag?"

It was gone. I was scared, but Dirt Bag looked at me and said, "It's okay, Pit, let's just keep going."

And so we did, stepping over nuts grainy as soap cakes and mushrooms akin to malformed hooves. When a farmer said he saw someone lay Mom's purse in the middle of the road, we went after it.

But there was nothing. Just the road and beyond it, fields hard as the wood paneling in our family room.

We kept on walking, our boot soles thick as the ends of bread, but when a gun went off, my heart slammed into my chest.

I jumped onto Dirt Bag's back, which collapsed. Once we hit ground, our heads tilted up and we were careful not to look at each other. We got up, brushed ourselves off, stumbled on.

Into a clearing. Where blood bristled the ground, as if spray painted, and a bear, all sprawled out, dead as could be, with my mother's handbag clutched in his teeth, a baby's rattle.

While Dirt Bag's hands patted down the bear, as if he were the sand in an hourglass, he started to cry. His tenderness, a forgotten kiss, and his face, this was a diary of leaves.

All around us—the valley oaks, the ponderosas, the bark and leaves and hooves and hair and bones, the final cries: so many particular, precious, irreplaceable lives that, despite ourselves, were vanishing.

"I was born," Dirt Bag whispered, "on a day when the peaches were splitting from so much rain. I was born when the slick smell of fresh tar steamed off the cracked parking lot and I was strong enough—even as a baby—to clutch a fistful of thistle and the sun itself was proud to light up my teeth when they first swelled and pushed up from my gums."

He paused, "And this is how I'll always remember it: my momma, pale mica flecks on her shoulders, standing there, as if lit up by my own smile."

"It was brief, I tell you, brief, so sticky, so warm, so full of light, my momma, and then she was gone."

I wanted to say something about the grass alongside the bear, or the red rock rising behind him, covered by a lacy kind of scrub juniper, yellow-green in afternoon light, dotted here and there up the broken slope and walls scraped sheer, the red striated with bars of gold and brown.

I wanted to say something about the two ravens which startled from their perch, how they made a raucous noise in the slot canyon. Their cries bounced upward while my boots raised puffs of fine red dust as I yanked Mom's purse out of the bear's jaws.

It made a sound like popcorn, and why I put lipstick on the bear's lips, overblown like a tire, and why I rouged his cheeks, I don't know, but I should mention that the aspen leaves were golden and vivid, that the clouds quickly overtook the sun, that before I saw the bear, I was unbearably lonely and I might as well confess how acutely I miss him and Dirt Bag, but to give myself up in the supremacy of that moment, this I could not do, so I clutched the bear's paw, big as a boxing glove, and cried like the little girl I was.

Me and Dirt Bag, we burned the bear's carcass and when we moved away from the fire, surfacing from death, like beautiful swimmers, everything was so detailed, we knew no part of us was simple or meaningless.

Such roaring and so many fires in my head. That bear, its teacup nostrils. My mother's pocketbook, it cackled as it burned, bristly as a hairbrush.

This is when we understood that no one would forgive

us for being thrown off true, for the ashes we scattered as we walked away, our footfalls quiet as Amens.

This was our journey—sad, unheroic, unlikely, but it was ours, a possession like the locket that was strung round Dirt Bag's neck—worthless, pitiful, but still precious like the inside of a secret.

As we wandered, we still had a long way to go through such desolate space and why, we didn't know.

In the sky, a star gleamed with utter insatiability. It couldn't be taught a thing. Like the wilderness, like me: I couldn't get around it.

"No more trains," I announced, my voice hard as a headbanger's.

"Okay," said Dirt Bag. The veins in his neck. I wanted to pop them.

"And no more stealing," I insisted. "Or burning bear."

"Well," he replied, "if I need a drink, I need a drink."

"Fair enough."

We were broke. We were used to that, but I was beginning to miss things like flush toilets and clean bedsheets, but still I had faith in our nights, nights which made me and Dirt Bag a binary star.

This meant we were actually two stars, circling each other but never touching—hundreds of light years away, they were edged in two colors, one blue, one gold, which told me forever is now, was never, was just the future occluded or dreaming.

Wherever we went, I saw us: stark, brutish, the very same selves, after all, and at long last, we found a houseboat.

"C'mon," I yelled, "let's climb aboard."

Dainty as dancers, me and Dirt Bag stepped onto the

dilapidated boat. About the size of a soiled dinner napkin, one which slid down the chest of some decrepit old man whose drool was lunar and green, we pushed off.

Drifting, slow as a cow, the slur of the world fell away like spray from the bow. As we moved across vaults of black water, absence declared its blunt self.

I couldn't believe the extent of our luck. Somehow like violets in a bath of lukewarm water. The blue of the water was the blue of the world.

A finite number of concentric rings pushed us out into space where, like a tedious fabric, we moved through time without malice while the water closed its one good eye.

Immured in mist, in fibrous whispers, trees thick as a man's wrist—what becomes of the girl no longer a girl?

The houseboat puttered in water thick as gravy. While we fished, I remembered my father's fingers—these were drawn, a magnet to my body, while his ears twitched, a crooked TV antennae, as he held me, a Lazy-Susan upon his lap.

Under shrubs round as rain barrels, a rabbit, with ears like a peace sign, saw how my father made home my first grave, he who pulled my name from his mouth like meat—and my crotch was calm as the odor of infants.

From the stern of the boat, I threw his soul like bait into the river and when it flew back into me—a silver fish—I devoured it clean to the bone. I was through.

And when the sky darkened, again, I thought it was over, but then he became the water, so I closed my eyes, swallowed him, let him swallow me too, and because I knew finally I would never be through, I asked Dirt Bag to forgive me.

For what, I wasn't sure, but I knew I needed him, for

his was the warmblooded body I sea-horsed into night after night, my tailbone, meek as a sheep's.

Because the unknown was stalking us, we drifted. We drifted while reaching for the brute, churning surfaces of the world left hanging on the bare branches like the threads on our ratty shirt sleeves.

Some might say this was hell and some just another, bolder paradise and some, a dark wilderness where we ached, like rainwater—it was extraordinary, like the fish we caught, then ate, like tiny figurines.

Leaning over the side of the boat, I saw how time embalmed the river's desolate curves while the sky shrank and a burst of rain wrapped me and Dirt Bag in soft, ashy hugs.

The light was there if we wanted it, but did we?

We were drinking. I was drunk. I was eight years old as I watched a long plastic sheet be blown like a shroud around the elm trees.

Because my mind sounded like someone suffocating in the meanest deep, I knew that when death came, a skinless cage, as it did for the bear—it would be hard as the smack of a trap.

While Dirt Bag and I drifted up and down the river, I dragged my fingers in the water, which felt like feathers. Velvety, thick. And my mouth, it ran, a bath tap.

This is when we heard it. A cry, like a tiny cut: thin, reedy.

We went toward it, the way sweethearts do toward heartbreak. Straight. Unerring. Our voices light as calipers.

Trolling into the wind, we hit the muddied riverbank.

In a little clearing edged with twigs, the darkness descended, seized us in its burly arms. Under a tree the color of exhaustion, we found a box.

From it came the sounds we imagined an empty womb might make. Like a smashed stone. White as God's own ribs.

Of course, we looked inside. Like the embers of a fallen angel, there was an infant. Her face, the wound inside the corridors of shells.

And this: the rare double curve of her lip while a pattern of burst blood vessels spread across her cheeks—the fingers boney, bowing, with knuckles where the skin bunched like roses puckered on fabric.

Her cries, wobbly as a loose tooth, pierced us while our hands reached for her, knowing that heaven has its discards, and this little baby was one of them. As were we, like rain in a tin can.

I touched the garnet of her wrist, said, "here I am," while her head, like an egg, dumbly bowed.

When I picked her up, her face was a pear laced with a needle, or a storm, an infinite storm, so I kissed her. And because you can only unwrap a child once, I made this orphan mine.

If, in that moment, someone had tried to seize her from me, I would have shrieked. Instead, me and Dirt Bag carried her like a graveyard back to the boat.

"Who," I asked, "would leave a baby like this? In nothing but a box, no milk, no nothing."

Dirt Bag, he shrugged. "You don't want to know, but just look at her. Face like a spatula you lick the cream from."

Once we were back on the boat, we pushed off. In a

voice full of liquid washing stones, I sang, gave the baby a rag soaked in fish oil to suck on.

I saw that she was irreplaceable, like a star that falls into darkness from all points of itself, and this: her held body into which there entered molecules of air, like grief.

Molecules and their jostling: her little life pulled back and waited while I told her about the damselfly, water skeet, mollusk, the caterpillar, the beetle, the spider, the ant, as well as the longing and the distance between meadows of night-blooming flowers and the impossible hope of the firefly, which was hers. Which was ours.

Whatever else can be said, me and Dirt Bag had a baby to take care of and this was everything.

Which is to say that I miss the mind I had when we lost her. Which is to say I knew her. Her smallness. Her corpse, simple as a grain of rice.

Like a short picaresque story that's suddenly over, I set the child-sized table of her grave, like a sheet cake—my breath, mouse-soft.

Alongside the mound, my pain struck me, like the spirals in a ham: iridescent, fatty—and Dirt Bag, he folded, somehow fitting himself inside the silence he pulled apart with his teeth.

In that moment, I packaged my body smaller and smaller while waiting, eager as a kitten, to corkscrew into death.

As me and Dirt Bag walked away, passing from the woods where each leaf was a perforated heart above which the sky darkly shook, a horsetail flicking off blood flies— that infant, intimate as injury, howled inside us.

I was still a child, leaving behind an even littler child.

That I loved her, like a mass of stars winking out, this glistened and glowed like the weapons in heaven.

Me and Dirt Bag, we felt we had no choice but to leave her where we had found her and because death is how we know our kind—I died, but only on the surface, feeling the many things I had not yet seen.

As we walked away, the moon leaked yellow light onto the water. This, as we emptied a bottle of red wine down our throats, knowing we needed one another like a bough being sawed in half.

While every yellow spread, like a clink of ice, impelling us further, beyond the long dark bodies of the conifers—where everything wavered like a question or a headstone, we became the meat of nothing.

Back on the boat, I got drunk, punched the walls. When they were gob-smacked with giddy, delirious cracks, cracks that snapped, my father's belt, I passed out, mistook the toilet for my mother's legs.

Come morning, I was topside with the sky above me, pressed like the pleats of an accordion.

Dirt Bag must have carried me there. He sat beside me, fed me slices of an orange, as though each were a portable shrine.

I didn't say anything. What was there to say? That my body expressed the thingness of a thing? A thing called girl? With hands like concrete balloons?

My hands, these bled. Dirt Bag, he just held me, purpling like a radish, you know, the red one with the bright white in the middle once you cut it all up.

"I'm dying, I'm dead," I moaned, "just like that itty, bitty baby."

This while we listened for the sound of that baby sucking the milk we didn't have and the sound of my breath, a wound that fed itself closed.

And because there wasn't even a drop of milk on that rag, not one drop, only the faint odor of spume, me and Dirt Bag tried to feed her the rat we caught. It was skinnier than the thinnest grief and slick as a pacifier.

"No teeth yet," I said as I chewed up meat stale as a brain, then passed it into the baby's mouth. And her voice, this was louder than thunder as she screamed, the meat spewing like blear.

"Christ," cried Dirt Bag as he grabbed her from me. He cuffed her ankles, hung her upside down—his arm, a croquet mallet, thwacked her back.

She coughed. The sound of it, child's play. Her bald head a squeaky toy as her face went blank as the underside of the river.

Like a hammock, I tugged on her arms, Dirt Bag her feet—no, not like a hammock, but a Chinese finger pull. Around us, the air snapped, like chewing gum. Or sockets, popping.

A swing, then. Had my mother ever held my right hand, my father the left? Had they ever swung me between them, a pendulum?

How the baby slipped from our hands, I'll never know, but the sound of her body, a loaf of bread but stale. A crackling like plastic, then nothing.

Me and Dirt Bag, after we buried that baby, we walked for miles, holding our suffering deeply and courteously, as if holding a package for somebody who would never come back.

While we walked, we were scoured by cold air, the

sheen of waves, the lengthy light, like nice, fine milk, the best of all milk, the milk we didn't have for the baby—the universe, this was cast in consequences.

When we got back to the boat, we picked stones up and hurled them. The shattering glass, prickly as a hand grenade, thrilled us.

Like a room with an open window, we were haunted and when the boat sank, we knew paradise had no winter like this.

A winter where the baby slept the sleep of the dreamless mind, so far from us, she no longer resembled anyone, like the motes that rose in the light and rested, which made each year harder to live within, each year harder to live without.

After the bear and the baby and stoning the boat, me and Dirt Bag wandered into a town that looked like sickness.

It was hailing. We were holding tin pots above our heads—life and death, by then, were the same.

"I don't care about my gloves," I said, as I tossed them into gutters that glittered, like particles of space shuttles, or a shattered moon.

"We will be richer than anyone in heaven," I said, after stealing from the Poor Boxes in churches. I was counting change under a tree whose fizzled leaves clanged like spoons.

Our shopping cart, the one we also stole, squeaked down the cobblestone streets. Saw-toothed lightning slashed the sky.

While a hawk floated down, a frayed paper crane, snagging its claws on electrical wire, we listened for the heartbreak in the heart of things.

We crumbled the dollars we stole from the Poor Boxes into our pockets. Beneath the cathedrals were underground trains, and we rode every one of them to its end, eating stale crusts of bread.

Each station was a burned-out lantern, and I couldn't help but wonder if I'd ever go home, where the television blinked and snowed, where my brothers and sister sat, watching black and white pictures flash.

This while my mother came into my room reeking of gin. I waited for her blows as she barked, "You're really worthless, aren't you?"

Coffin-legged, she staggered over to my bed. A photograph of a ghost, Mom stood there. She sucked her breath in. It was elastic, snapping.

"Don't get me wrong," she said, "I want to wake you."

She raised her arms. Skin sagged off them. Her blows wore shark skin, were follicle and meat and terror.

Heavy as wet cement, Mother climbed on top of me, lay down, passed out. The gravity of her breath pulled the sky from me like steam from an arch.

Underneath her, I was hard and quiet, a floorboard from a tree long gone, a floorboard sanded down, shellacked, hammered in a scrubbed, painfully immaculate house no one lives in anymore, a house where the vacuum scattered dust like sniper rifle fittings.

Who was she? Never enough time to know, but when Marie used the ping pong paddle to beat our dolls before hosting her one and only Barbie BBQ, I began to comprehend.

She dressed all our Barbies in their traveling clothes, put foreign words in their frugal mouths, then rounded them up.

"Make a wish," she said, as she put one doll's leg in my hand while she held the other. A surgeon of time, she gave a yank. Thighs split open from Viking hips. Flecks of skin cracked like gluten. I heard a bright wailing.

Marie took a knife. Used it. Split Barbie's face open. The noise echoed. A tiny hammer in the metal brain.

The grill, it was smoking when Marie lay the dolls on the blackened grate. Hotdog Barbies. They look suspended, like heroines, each one a blond stillness.

The flames foliaged, especially their chests, which were riddled with holes while their ash-riddled limbs tingled.

"How would you like yours done?" Marie asked.

I didn't answer. How far, I wondered, is instinct from such a thing? I grabbed one barbecued Barbie off the heat-crippled grill, her arms raised in a strike-or-embrace position.

I looked through what was left of the skull, saw how her face equaled mine, then looked through again until looking meant looking back, back through the skull into the self I always was.

That this, my holding a baby bottle to my doll, was the most exquisite instance of my childhood never changes. The slight buckling of her burnt face made her demure as a doe as she dissolved, an egg in acid.

When I tell this to Dirt Bag, my voice, a purple softness, it's what I cannot say that matters—how my mother was a shard inside my skull where the monsters of my childhood appeared like saints with erased mouths.

Also what I cannot say—how Marie, years later, leapt onto my mother's back, a bear cub, how she throttled my mother's head, like a drum, pounding, screeching, hyena-bright.

High-as-a kite she was, and her whine put a dark crease in me. Her freckles menaced, like ticks intent on blood and so, I pounced on top of her.

Behind us, the fire danced, like a painting looked into from more ways than one. Oh, how that fire danced, the flames long as grace, given to some, but not us.

Lowly, wretched, my work was to pull my sister off of my mother, she who was yanking her hair out in batches, then stuffing it down her throat.

My mother choked, bucked, but couldn't scream. I screamed for her. My scream was a whip, snake-lean and just as mean.

The tiny crucifixes of my nails, these I dragged down my sister's back. I gored her and in goring became unconquerable.

Wrung and wrung, we were ghostly, the three of us, our cruelty, God-given and so pure, it was nearly miraculous.

All along, my father, his eyes ripe as swords, watched. In doing so, he had been made happy, even whole.

While watching, his shadow staked us, his three little women, to the disastrous blue shag carpeting where we burned, were leaf litter in darkness the four winds scattered, *scattered*.

IV.

After the baby's death, all I wanted was to bring her back, but—like sewing patches of sunlight onto the water, it couldn't be done.

Instead, I remembered how her right leg had swung, a manic pendulum, skinny-looking but strong.

Like junk in the bottom of the junk drawer, me and Dirt Bag were off, knowing we couldn't stay wherever we were, nor could we be other than scrum and scrub.

Even when the winds started, there was only me and Dirt Bag, so much longing, always circling death. And birth? This was the blackest ice and, some say, irretrievable.

It was so delicate—stars quiet as parrots, the great darkness, the great darkness—at night, we sat by the fire's light like a flower that opened, closed—it didn't burn red, it burned white like snow and voices, words in a magic order.

It was so delicate—hope beyond belief, hierarchies of dream—as long as time went on.

Delicate, so delicate the light and there was so little of it—and the darkness so huge—the night sky, vast and wide, trees like stubble, and Dirt Bag's voice lifting, high and clear as a flock of blackbirds, "What the hell do we do next?"

"Keep moving," I said. My eyes were bright and toxic, my brain a ring.

"Alrighty," said Dirt Bag in a voice like burnt flan as he took a big swig, then passed the bottle to me.

My eyes, these crawled out of my head. Was this heaven?

Nothing around for miles, but the mountains bleak with the cold and a world that didn't ache, like I did, to be anything other than it was.

We boiled water in a kettle in the woods where I could hear the train grow louder, but also I couldn't. Then Dirt

Bag was shaving in front of a mirror while I, like a nurse, watched him.

I went to the river where a boulder dug into my shoulders. I released every muscle against it, gave it all my warmth. The long body of the river was still, but I listened like a sleeping child, to see which one of us would wake.

Neither of us did. Not me nor the child I was, but I can say I've come this far in order to speak. I've come to ask some speechless thing, but what?

Maybe I've come to ask forgiveness, it's hard to tell. Forgiveness because that baby is somehow still inside me, a manhole.

Snow shook onto my chest, quick as table salt. The branches above me were full of pine needles: when the river, lit with secrets, was done with me, I would belong to the evergreens.

Despite the funeral in everything, me and Dirt Bag, we stayed together. Much trouble was at hand, still we bided our time—by now we were used to the hell in our bodies.

Yet, when we went to hop another train, there was the wreck, which we found with its terrible engines, spilled freight, unbelievable mess.

The mystery. This is what stunned us. The silence of it. In the middle of nowhere. No ambulances, no nothing.

Along the tracks, ice in escutcheons. And beyond, the snowy fields and stone silos and the fugitive cows known for escaping their borders—the fences a mess of Hs.

From a distance, the fields looked blue or white, and in the air, birds of every ilk, and beyond them, like a long-lost love, the train wreck, which felt strange, a green pit, hollow, just like me, or my family, or Dirt Bag and the baby.

The bodies. Stranded, like a bunch of sad clowns, or jokes. Bad ones.

Each like the edge of a paragraph, or buoyant if bloody milk. We touched them, pillaged them, each a magnificent still life, a long, awful, silent scream.

We tore along as we pocketed watches, compasses. We took things and saw ourselves as smaller, stranger while waiting for a slow suffocation, which did not come.

Hollowed out, Dirt Bag held my chapped hand. Did stutter. Did slur. Did shush my open mouth. Rich with failure, terror and dither, he pulled me away.

When we went back, as if to check on the dead, like babies in an orphanage, the bodies were gone. Had a clean up crew come? Had they shoveled the bodies into a ditch?

But their vanishing. This spooked me and Dirt Bag. Like jellyfish clear as plastic bags they vanished, or worm prints in snow. And in their absence, not even phosphorescence, not even a glow.

Just the cold. Which we drank. After which my life fell like tears from windowsill of a drowned house.

The blue dress. Unlike the bodies, it was left behind. It was silk, was the river, water seeping into my sleep, winter stars stitched into brocade.

The dress, a cloud at my feet. There in the flooded field where the water dripped from the mouth of the river, its bleak, bruised hallway.

I put it on while me and Dirt Bag harvested icicles. Each was an ecstatic grammar, a cylindric column, inflating and deflating.

We made sculptures. The color of resin, vellum, wax—they were translucent, skin-like. In the sunlight, they glowed, took on the look of light penetrating the thinner parts of the ears or hands.

This felt formal. Me and Dirt Bag tied the icicles together with rope. A rigid umbilical cord of ice surrounded each one, as if composed of malleable metal.

The train wreck. This made us want to know what went wrong. In the cellular, microscopic parts, in the lipids and tissue. But the body is what it is: a combination of organs, bones, and tubes, resisting all sense.

A memorial, the sculptures resembled dried intestines pulled through a wall. Like the catgut used to string instruments, we hoped they would last.

It was very moving, visceral of course, but restrained. While the ice insisted that there was time to consider shape, the shape itself decayed, deteriorated.

Our creations couldn't be handled, let alone installed. Like the people in the train wreck, they were no longer their original selves.

Each sculpture, when first made, was softly draped, understated, organic, erotic, like the meninges, the protective tissue just under the skull. All too soon, each became a rigid tawny heap.

Maybe what we really wanted was to cut out a sizable cube of brain, to see what patterns developed, but the icicles didn't last. Each pliant, fragile, and resistant shell melted.

Still, the work had momentum, even if it was tenuous. And I didn't mind that. There was tension even as the sculptures flexed, moved, and poured themselves back into water.

The sculptures held life, but of the most bizarre kind. Did they cry? Grieve? Did they sin? Lie?

Me and Dirt Bag, we placed our hands upon the icy

flesh. Each crenelated texture stained our fingers a pensive, murky color, the color the hours take on—like pews bowing beneath their weight.

Our sculptures were grotesques, had a demonic aura. And when I strangled them one by one, wasn't it because dying requires practice?

As my hands tightened, each one became a slipknot of water, an arrangement of chainmail, a little whitely at the knuckles.

Each blank, lightless pupil, flush as a thumbtack, held the universe in place and fed upon our faces until we became the door that leads in and in, but never out.

While a kind of forever died inside our bodies, the purest emotions invaded us like sharks.

It was February. The month of blind, bald leaves under drifts of snow, bitchy as quicksand, of pink snails shut in dark waters, of gales that roiled like sick poodles.

Everything felt gluey, parasitic. Around me and Dirt Bag, drops of rain disappeared into an underground garden so sinister, the clay-infected snow sucked in our loose, vicious sculptures.

They disappeared, like small monoliths, into a heavy-as-honey grayness. Sky-like. Unfinished. About-to.

After that, we only traveled at night. One of my hands always went into one of Dirt Bag's. Silent and exhausted, unwashed for days, I asked myself, had the people in the train wreck ever existed? Had my family?

Night slid the moon behind me, pulled in the home I'd made from hollow innards, this I wanted still a moan out of, as I dreamt about my father emerging, like an alligator, from the room's shadows in darkness that always obeyed.

V.

After the bodies disappeared, time had a voice like a wood-shed full of dead mice or my sister's nail polish, which put me back in my bedroom, where the dark I shuttered in was the hole my father winked me into.

The angle of everything had shifted. There was no sun and there I was, starched, appalled. The something I had become was truly unbecoming.

For hours I thought: I want to take a bath.

Instead, I did nothing but talk. "Dirt Bag," I said, "did you know that the eye chews the apple, then sends the brain an image of un-apple. Which is similar to the way I throw my voice like a Frisbee, or salt over a shoulder, as a kind of party trick."

All this while Dirt Bag, who smelled like rusted oysters, or a dead cow's eye, rocked back and forth on his heels.

We left the train wreck behind us. We had to. Like a dirty story, it made us full of fuss and buzzkill. All those boxcars on the hill.

The world rolled oceans between us like a bitter gate—and wrought from us a kind of grace, a kinder rot until we became just what we were: a miracle without solace, heaving a burden of light, or death.

Like the debris we had sprung from, we bore what we could, moved on, but when we saw a massive body in the river, floating, as though it were a punched lung, we stood at the railing on the old bridge and stared.

Sky clear as water in a bedside glass. The last fat stars. Downriver. Still dark.

We could tell it was a woman because her hair was un-braided, frayed back toward one hundred streams and springs, toward the horrors of origin.

This is how it was. She had legs like Christmas-hams, breasts like piped icing, like tectonic catastrophes.

I was terrified. What if she took my hand and said, "I'm going to show you everything, even the two worlds." What if she was my mother?

We ran. The night was long and the wind—like friction, like the train when it derailed, was howling.

Only she could have done it. Her eyes like plastic spot-lights. Energy in the atmosphere, the sea vaporizing. Birds cawing and falling around us.

I held onto Dirt Bag, his pant leg like a flag in the wind signaling, *I surrender.*

"Me too," I said, "me too."

After that, we lived like a shroud—pitiful, wretched as the pigeon that, shivering in manic flashes, had spun its head off atop the bridge, close to where that body floated, like an infinite set of dreams.

In the still of the night, not a nightbird calling, not a fine light flickering, no crickets, no crickets singing, no far, far away train whistles calling, not a rustle, not a shimmer, the way a petal falls on its own away from all the others with no one watching, that's how what's human leaves us. Like that pigeon's head. Quiet as error.

Quiet as me and Dirt Bag as we stole away.

When we got hungry, we stole. Among the shopping carts, I fortressed. Among the plastic bags I affirmed: "Everyone crawls before flight."

Dirt Bag agreed while his hand plucked a bag of rice like a woman's head off the shelf.

When we stepped out of the A&P, a Ferris wheel rolled over the highway. It sounded like a gutted tambourine.

But the memories, these amputated us like the gunshot that killed the bear.

When it popped, we followed that slab of sound until we stumbled into the clearing where the bear was splayed, an inflatable raft.

Without thinking, I put my hand in the deep red envelope of its flesh. Saying goodbye is like this. You put your hand in and then you take it back out.

I wanted to suck the wound's stretch mark. Instead I ran off like a delicate dictator, shoes spattered by the night-wet grass.

Dirt Bag, he called after me. "Pit," he yelled, "don't you dare go running off on me, you hear?"

Of course I ran right back to him where I clung to him, as I once did my mother's skirt.

When he pulled out a flask, I grabbed it, took a big swig.

Soon I was so drunk all I could see was the sea monster of my vomit, luminous in the toilet bowl. It was nearly erotic.

Dirt Bag, he held me, cocooned around the toilet. He rearranged me into no more hurting, no more skin-sunk fear. No more deaths.

While the sickness crawled around my brain, I thought of my father, who like me, was unstable as a chandelier hung by its teeth. I remembered how he drove us one dawn down a twisting road to a bomb's test site.

While Marie kicked my shins, Dad yelled, "Stop it, stop it right now," and so we did as we watched a plaque of heat, a roar like a diesel blasting, heatwaves ricocheting

ELIZABETH KIRSCHNER

off gray mist, melting backward, shockwaves rippling to grip the car, shaking us like flames dimly seen inside the brain.

Confused by a father who was visibly elated to see the blast shoot up arabesques of mud and grit from the snow-fringed hole, we were delirious.

As the flames mottled into black slag, they got mixed up with blueberry pancakes and strawberry syrup or waffles, corrugated like the earth, or stacked like half-dollars, drenched and sticky.

My father—gone for years, and still I see him climbing the concrete steps out of the bomb shelter, his chilly body feeling sunlight on backs of his hands, the brightness making his eyes blink.

How to weigh this against char and flare, against the blast melting into whatever it was, then not—the air sucked out in a vacuum of fire calibrated in a brain like my father's?

I once showed him da Vinci's drawing of mortar, which we admired for its precision, shot raining down over the fortress walls—softly pattering, hailing down shrapnel, lulling to the ear and eye until it took shape in the unforgiving three dimensional, as when the fragile, antagonized, antagonistic human face begins to slacken unto death.

That picture—in it, my father's face smoothed into slate, like drenched paper.

"Life," he said, "is an exercise in preparing to die."

I believed him. Wasn't my skin the color of wood lice, their sordid meats and bloody organs arranged like a bouquet of crushed roses, paling, exhausted?

In rain that dangled. While the door to elsewhere

opened us, a cut.

VI.

Me and Dirt Bag didn't talk about the train wreck nor the bear and especially not the baby whom we had left unnamed because this made us hysterical like the birds that jammed the trees, in cold little knots.

As we went on in sun the color of tuna, Dirt Bag dwindled. Even so, he managed to construct a language all his own like a system of silkworms—everywhere, utter, sheer, lifting stranger and more urgent words to the same sentence, *we shouldn't have.*

Like a game of Hangman, I filled in the blanks. Shouldn't have burned the bear, left the baby, been born, had a secret handshake.

Shouldn't have tried to rob the liquor store with me twirling my pig tails, saying, "Stick 'em up. Pretty please."

Because I was splitting into smaller versions of myself, I believed we wouldn't get caught.

Just then, my nose began to bleed. Feeling punched, I decided that being a robber wasn't all it was cracked up to be.

When the police arrived, I was hauled out of the liquor store, pinned against a wall. While my blood aproned the officer's chest, my name got lost in his cigarette smoke.

The blood in my mouth, this tasted like a dimmer switch. While Dirt Bag was shoved into the cop car and driven away, my screams cracked, a hammered lollipop.

Arms flailing like the fleshy swords, I yelled, "Go, you go, don't you go, don't go, don't go now, don't!"

The sting of sharp dew settled into the corners of my eyes, as I stood all alone on the street, which was a temporary tomb.

Dirt Bag was thrown into jail. Not long after, I crawled among rats thin as whips, yelled up to his cell window where he had written, FOR SALE, in backward letters. Pursing my lips, I cried, "Oh, oh, I'm alive!"

And when he didn't answer, I remembered: language is a form of crying. Like his voice or the sculptures with their buttery waste.

As I walked away, trees lay down, throbbed. And the ground drank me in, a tall drink of water going down easy.

It swallowed me faster and faster. But I didn't worry. Eventually, we all wake up as forest, moss thick.

Under a scrap of sky foreign as a foreign country, or the self one seeks, I fingered a postcard filched from the corner store, its crenellated deeps, outmoded as paraffin.

Why it smelled like summer or sand I couldn't say, but on it, I wrote to Dirt Bag. My words were smudged like the bruises under my fingernails. "Here," I wrote, "still here."

The stamp, this held the earthy feint of sage and after I dropped the postcard in the mailbox, I found a wishbone in the dirt, delicate as a forceps.

Of course, I made a wish. After all, I was still a child.

I wished for Dirt Bag, the baby, and my family, but my wish was a lungful of air blowing out the candles caged in my chest, one for each of the days Dirt Bag had to spend, like the lone wisp of a life, in a cell tight as killer heels.

My family, weren't their bodies handcuffed to their own ghosts or the shadows in the hospital room where I was sloughed from my mother like a desiccated grape?

And after that, the shadow of my father's kiss on

mornings when he woke feeling like a tooth in the devil's mouth, mornings after he'd strolled through me, like a park he has known since he was old enough to forget the difference between praying and thinking about praying.

VII.

Needing to get Dirt Bag out of jail, I started to scheme. Because I still believed in what we'd begun together and because I wanted him back, badly, I had to plot, to plan. To get into the prison. Visit him. And so, I did.

As I walked up to the jail, sweat glued my blouse to my back. Before me, the fence, topped by a high tech crown of thorns, glistened in light hard as a switchblade.

The building itself was made of brick, like the house in the story of the three little pigs, the one the wolf couldn't blow down.

The heat bore down and the sun, it just hung there in what felt like a self-destructive sky.

I entered the prison through glass doors, sat down, waited.

After twenty minutes or so, a guard came down, led me and the other visitors through a metal detector, the kind one finds in an airport. We could not fly away.

Led down a hallway bland as the unborn, pictures of the guards were hung on the walls. These men, whose faces had jawlines set to throw epithets like darts, they were the keepers of the only friend I had in the whole wide world.

Into the visiting room we went. It looked like a sparse café. Small tables surrounded by chairs hard as cadavers.

No red-and-white checked tablecloths, no silverware, no napkins.

Who would serve us? The guards who stood in the corners like coroners?

Dirt Bag leapt up to greet me, to welcome me into his small, circumscribed world. His arms sobbed around me. No, they hula-hooped my waist. His smile looked like a snail had crossed it.

"Pit," he said, "you look just like store-bought cake. One that needs a whole bunch of candles."

We found a table near the door which lead outside. A block of genie-like light was painted on the floor.

"Tell me," Dirt Bag began, "what the hell happened to us?"

"Nothing, I swear it. Pinky swear, but maybe it's like this dream where my heart is a salted pretzel, which is better than the one where my body is a looted ship, which isn't a dream at all."

Dirt Bag, he laughed like something we buried long before we had words for the reek of it, something we no longer knew how to explain, like the baby.

"Well," I asked, "what's prison like?"

"Piss on the floors so gilded I mistake it for a trinket, or your locket," he replied as he removed the necklace and put it over my head, a lei.

"Listen," I said, "I'm not going to let you rot in here. No, I want your blood to rollercoaster down your veins again and for you to become the splendor your momma loved, if only for a little minute."

All around us, locked up words grew boundless. Voices floated, like runaways. Eardrums trembled, were drones tracking targets.

I hit the wall of vending machines because inmates weren't allowed to approach them. Like a gambler in a casino, I produced quarters fished out of the public fountain.

The candy the machines released was an indescribable treat. Snicker bars, Charlestown Chews, Butterfingers. While talking, I downed one soda after another.

"What do you think, are our bodies more like paper or scissors, or a long knock on a slab of wood that hasn't decided yet whether it wants to be a wall or a door?"

Dirt Bag, he just hung his head, which was long as a horse's. His hand reached over as if to wipe the flesh from my skull, a blind spot.

I swatted it, prattled, "Do you remember the hotel we went to that one time where I was happy as bubble-wrap while jumping up and down on the bed, eating ice like Crackerjacks?"

"I hoped I'd wake up finding a little square of chocolate on my pillow, or even a hand towel forced into the shape of a swan."

"Mostly I was hoping you'd take shorter cigarette breaks, in order to help me forget the sound a body makes when being struck."

Dirt Bag's hand, familiar and terrifying as the family name, when it reached for mine, it was lighter than frost or ashes. "Knock, knock," he said.

"Who's there?" I asked.

"Robin."

"Robin who?"

"Robin the piggy bank."

I sighed. I was afraid that Dirt Bag would be locked up for the rest of his life.

Did the presences of the harsh men around him haunt

him like a braid of dying onions? Were their hands like fugitives, or were they broken promises, still as the bottom of a pool?

Or were their hands, like ours, those of the burglar's slick with moonlight, hands smelling like lemons or whiskey as they reached for a gun or a knife?

"I'll come out dead or alive," Dirt Bag said, "if I come out at all." I sighed again. For once, he was telling the truth.

Dirt Bag's face turned into a gray-green landscape, a place where song could travel without remorse, as he added, "When I get out."

To which, I added, "When I get you out."

All too soon, it was time to say goodbye. Grief diffused the saturated room. I stood on tiptoe for a hug, which was warm and inviting. In it, I wanted to linger.

Suddenly, the line-up began. The inmates stood, shoulder-to-shoulder, in a derelict splendor, as though before their executioners. We visitors bowed our heads, wept.

Slowly, we wandered down the hallway. Door after door locked behind us, a thunderbolt—no Greek gods frescoed the walls, no Matisses, no Mozart climaxed in our ears, only the walk away.

As we went through the glass doors, I kept turning my head to look back at Dirt Bag, who stood stock still in his tan regulation uniform. His eyes opened and shut like lenses.

Going back down the hallway, I entered empty space and a world without gravity. As I stepped outside, I was stunned by sunlight that glared like five layers of spite.

In the prison yard, I kissed my locket for luck, remembering how the baby's leg had swung, a pendulum.

Kneeling in the dirt, I drew an escape route, like a treasure map, on a scrap of paper, put it in a baggy with a stone inside it, and tossed it at Dirt Bag's window like a misfit key.

Impossible to know—just as the glass shattered in kaleidoscopic shambles, Dirt Bag was putting a rope around his neck, his head hard as an armadillo's.

Because the hurt body needs to hurt the hurt, he kicked the chair out from under him and swung.

VIII.

After his death, I went back to where the train went missing, to where God invented everything out of nothing, until nothingness shines through—this was where we had tried to become different humans, where we left ourselves among the statues we carved like depressed guests.

They had bookended our life with the twin ghosts of hollowness and want, which put me in a void sharp as a paper cut, and in me, in spite of it all, was my own species of insanity, familiar as the family name.

Among the things me and Dirt Bag carved, not a single effigy captured the operatic rising and sinking of the bodies, their mythic images shrinking, pulling in on themselves like wintering frogs.

Because violence is necessary, even expedient, all I wanted was a corner to hole up in and so, I found an old barn.

Up in a hayloft full of must, I carved Dirt Bag's initials

into an orange—all was lost, was devastation.

Still, the peel and pith of the orange held its essence in its skin. Peel and pith, its bitterness too.

I struck a match to it, felt along its ragged side. In the beauty of that flame, I saw how we don't really get any older—we just fold down into ourselves.

Clutching that orange like an astral world with mirrors on its skin, a world that came half-furnished and half dead, I remembered the last time I stood in my mother's kitchen.

Water dripped from the ticking faucet like the bloody juice from a turkey baster.

Old kernel of a voice, she kept saying, "It's no use."

The sadness on her face, this was a canvas bag. It was no good to try to console her. She couldn't be consoled. It was too costly.

"You look so pretty in that blue dress," she said, while sucking on the spongy stuff inside a thick, yellow bone.

"What does one do," she continued, "after the meat is gone?"

When I didn't answer, she threw the bone at me.

While it boomeranged toward me, I ran out the door, went down to the river's strip of blue ice where I knew spring would turn my footprints to water, water fragrant as star anise.

I imagined shrimp, like coins from another realm, how they would froth—rice-paper shells bandaged around a bit of milky gray whiskers.

Small vehicles of life, they moved from one end of the river to another, their legs the oars of many men.

For them, spring was a continent of water. It was all

they needed to survive. There was nothing else. No apparent food for them to feed on, as if they sprouted from the rock itself—a deep pact between stone and water.

I wondered what it looked like to them whenever I dropped my net. A fibrous constellation pulled out of the sky, descending, penetrating the defenseless water with ease, carrying them towards the edge of the unknown.

The constant pressure of water—suddenly gone: a strange lightness, unbearable.

Were they aware of the body and the not-body? The mind and not-mind? In air as blind as they had ever been.

Fresh out of the water, their shells bloomed like rust under oil.

 But that night in the barn. I took a big swig from Dirt Bag's old flask.

The liquor went down into my liver like a dirty pet. It then hit my spleen, and also my stomach like Brueghel's monkey on a chain.

My heart, this felt hacked out with an ax: to live beyond the brain, like a country scissored from the map: *this was it.*

Dirt Bag, he used to tell me, "Pit, you need to think big, real big, like Saturn or something."

Even if I had been warned about what men like Dirt Bag could do because of what he had done in Nam: bayoneted women in their full-moon bellies, forced fathers to fuck their daughters, and afterwards taken photographs—little trophies to remember the war by, what of it?

Dark-skinned and dark-eyed, with long, straight hair like the fibers of falling stars, he had assured me, they're not like us, not like us at all.

Meaning, think of the angels, then their opposite.

Meaning, think of all the things we ache to hide flung open, soft, too soft, like a newborn barely formed.

After Dirt Bag's death, all my selves spread out like a deck of cards.

My whole body became warm and sticky like a child's car seat.

In my mind, I was back home. I knelt beneath the pine tree, lowered my head, and placed my hands in front of me like two plates, together but lightly, so they wouldn't break, just like this.

With my hands barely touching, I stared at the laundry on the line and felt skinned.

But I stayed there, smelled the pine, my face a breeze made of wood and metal.

I looked up into the stiff green needles of the pine tree and it seemed like my father was looking down on me the way fathers do, but the limbs moved like my mother's, and suddenly I wasn't alone.

There were boys. One of them held my arms while another held my legs while another pulled down my pants while another grabbed a branch, waved it in front of my face, yelling, "We're gonna stick it in you."

Years later, when the electrodes were strapped like quarters to either side of my temples—the world lit up, all the grayness was wiped away, and for a few minutes, I saw everything.

Those boys, their stick, the bomb Dad took us to go see, shooting up into the air, skylines blossoming and wilting, the baby, the bear, the whole cycle running over and over.

Fifteen seconds. There were thousands of aggregate voices joined in cacophony, but I heard every one and their harmonies and their contradictions and their swarm.

I saw Mom, blanched and narrow, in the old brown chair, her eyes gone milky. Dad, like a waxwork, surrounded by unfamiliar children, who stared at his face, which looked like the palest of spiders.

I saw radium and radon gas, embryos made in Petri dishes and frozen in place, the tiny eggs like planets, and I saw huge planets in orbit around a dying star, around thousands of stars careening into themselves.

Soldiers slamming rifle butts into skulls, soft as ostrich eggs, Dirt Bag among them.

There were whole worlds spun together by wire that transected the globe, like synapses, like my synapses, aglow, throbbing.

Ten seconds. While pain wrung me, I watched as my atoms were split, over and over, their whispered lament sung like the song of a whale hunting for a long-beached mate.

I counted the extinctions as solitary birds, like savage fighters, rolled their way into death. And it was all death, floating like carnations in milk.

Death and erasure; the train with its ghostly remains and our statues; melting, then later, by a resurgent wood, a deer and wild turkeys picking bugs from the field where there had just been bodies.

Every tree grew like lightning, died like fire blown off a match

Five seconds. My left hand shaking—four seconds—and dust, men with globes for heads, insects dripping in muck—lights on the river, flickering.

Three—my hands in my sister's thick ruff, which smelled like Juicy Fruit—two—and I saw my mother, whose overly dark eyeliner tapered into a punchline or a study of a thousand or more hurts—one—and no one met me on the other end to pick up my hand and hold it.

With the eye of the universe cupped between the hemispheres of my brain, the lightning jumped, coin to coin across the gap, and like a whip I lost it all, even the sound of my name.

Like the song of the siren that hauled Dirt Bag away, his hands cuffed as if in infinity rings, the sound caressed me, then cut me into parts.

After he hung himself, flakes of coldness bit and shivered and screamed and blended. Just like me.

Even in the asylum, or especially, I felt Dirt Bag's breath like snowflakes piled in my pocket.

Coupled by the cold the windows blocked out, the frosty windowpane became a cloud of amnesia behind which there was the skull-numbing pressure of nothingness.

In the day room, I pretended that a good book could solve it all, like a proper smile. Madness, I thought, wears the bloom out of silence.

Which was full of dunes and hell-colored waves. In the asylum by the sea. Where winter passed, white as boiled bone, a monstrous ravishing.

And the light was a vinegar-colored halo that, like hope, came and went, yellow as the poof of hair on the other women in the ward.

The nurses, they told us to stay away from the windows, but still I raised the pane and slipped a sparrow, black and shivering, into my mouth. I kept it there, wetting its wings on my tongue, letting it peck at the vault in my throat.

It tasted like lava, contagious and bitter. An hour when

the light went and the room grew walls.

That sparrow wept in the middle of my mouth. It sharpened my breath into little teeth. It was loveless. And I told no one. Especially not when I swallowed it whole.

On the table, the napkin holder was shaped like a garden gate. The other patients chewed graham crackers into the shape of guns, then set them down on dishes shiny as toys.

These were my paper-eating days. The wads tasted like the napkin I folded into a pillow for my doll's head, the one my mother decapitated after the Barbie barbecue.

Stationed at the window, the room flushed, red shadows licked the walls like a briar or a rose on a spit.

With my mouth half open, I stared into the cool glass and was back home at the front window which, like the pupil of an eye, was armless, legless, unable to move. Yet, all around me the walls flickered and the night, it was a lung.

No one in the day room saw the bear come from behind me, quiet like smoke, to swipe at my flesh. His breath on my neck and I knew the bite would follow.

Sharp as the knife they must have used to cut Dirt Bag down. The sound of his body hitting the floor, this is what I'm trying to say but can't.

And so, I ate paper. Like eyeballs, soft and chewy, I swallowed it whole. Gummy as a scream. The baby's. Her ears, with their bloodshot dust, ticking, like the minute hand of my father's watch.

I had clutched her, a hot water bottle—her lips, an isolated flower, its buds twisted into something like rolling papers the color of entrails.

What could we do but carry her over sludgy leaves into

a meadow that parted like a comb through hair across rodent tracks laid down under purple-tongued trees.

Onto the boat, which smelled like a mortuary, where I sang to her. Having beheld her eyes. Dull roadside pennies, dull overused thimbles.

Having beheld her skin, gray as the pattern on the gravel-laced riverbank. Having beheld her forehead like the dome of a mausoleum, knees naked as onion bulbs, I was besotted, harrowed, done.

Of course, we had no choice but to bury her as soon as she died.

Like a wolf at a live heart, the sun broke down. As the baby went into the ground, clouds big as an abscess, dipped and thundered and vanished, like rose leaves in closed jars.

In the asylum, where my body had little consequence, I collected eyelashes on paper.

This was my occupation—me trimming a curtain of lashes, then folding them into paper, which I stitched shut with red thread as if to immure them into a stray year.

When I swallowed the needle, the origami of my brain opened, like a weird geography that placed me alongside my parents, who I wanted to strike like chips of flint.

The house was burning. And their tongues were bloated, distended. Moments before, my father had pressed his cigarette butt into my arm. After he tossed it, my bedroom caught fire. Orange flames floated up like feathers, or exotic, hypnotic messages.

When flames ran toward my hair, I tried to grab the cat, but she wouldn't come out from behind the mirror, which was pinwheel thin.

In the flashing darkness, I saw her smoky silhouette,

which resembled a seahorse's, or that little baby's, as I backed out the door.

Outside, the air was smoke and when I looked back at the window of the room I just fled, each pane was filled with sparks, each spark bright as a plaque.

I wanted to run back inside but couldn't—my feet sunk like garbage into the mud while the trees reflected the house and their leaves, illuminated from below, were the palms of gospel singers.

And when I finally went back in, a skeleton, delicate as a sea urchin, or a Christmas ornament, but peanut-brittle crispy. A Greek perfection.

It was the dirt from the cat's grave that went into my locket. As did the dirt from that itty, bitty baby's grave. All around the mound, brown beetles crawled about and red flowers bent their heads in awful sorrow.

This was a dark time, a season of metal and tears, like a song with a lost room inside it, or the silence inside a syringe.

But that night. The fire, it clicked like shells, like an oven baking.

Still, when my father pressed the mole on my shoulder like an eject button, I let loose a cry, one that smelled like a headache. Ashes, these floated down, were the slightest scars.

VIII.

To get through the days, I often moaned. Like a deer, or the bear. I often sighed. The nurses said, "stop that." Another sigh. "Another stop that."

Moaning elicited laughter, sighing was upsetting. Perhaps each sigh was drawn into existence to pull in, pull under, who knows what; I could no more control these sighs than that which brought them about.

The sigh was the pathway to breath; it allowed breathing. No one fabricates that. I sat down, I sighed. I stood up, I sighed. The sighing was a worried exhale.

Even though remembering wasn't allowed, my memory went back, all the way back to the catfish heads strung on the clothesline.

Whoever skinned them had done so perfectly: each was a glistening ampersand of grief, a loose string of *es*, three repeated vowels pinned up to complicate the flesh and my obsession with it.

In the breeze's twisting of each wan, whiskered head: the obscene wind chimes. And the calm after it? Scale-glint, sonic nothing. Like them, my skin was wrinkled, greening the sky's bluer potion.

I wondered: did the soul do anything just before death—I mean, if it had wandered from where it first started: then, wouldn't it want to return to its source finally, the way seawater does?

Which I did. Return. To the house I grew up in. To the wind-cut snow, the ice honeyed in the branches.

After the lock-up. Where I went from oblivion to oblivion like that infant whose thin soul was bound and determined to fly back into the hands of nothingness.

Which wasn't terrible. To want that. The nothingness, vague as a shrug.

The day we inmates climbed the hill to breathe the sharp air through putrid lungs, I was the one who wandered off to find the baby's plot like an unstamped envelope.

When I found a steaming breast inside a footprint in the snow, I slipped it into my glove, held it close, a darling.

That night, I suckled it. Still warm, I draped it over my heart—then slept on my right side with the lavender breast tucked between my legs.

While my eyes fluttered shut, I dreamt of when my body was smooth as a crab, my fingers tip-toe soft. My hair, a shining crown—until the many little dyings.

By morning, the breast was shriveled up. Gone cold. A blue fish with one stone eye.

Still, I held it, like a window pulled shut and didn't I feel like I was being swallowed by a glass of ice water, then asked to live inside its imperious solitude?

When my bright pink pants disintegrated, bright pink with tiger stripes, the holes were old hungers, yawning griefs, and I couldn't have it. But I had to.

The pink so domestic, girl-canopy pink, or a vaginal whorl, and how to explain that when the pants acted napalmed and became flesh-eating, I shed them, twisted them into a ladder, then shimmied down into the muck and ran.

Under a nauseous sky, the algae of it effervescing, I fractured like a bridge or a bone, and this is what released me.

Of course, I didn't look back. The asylum, hard as a drill bit, and the world, suddenly a vast museum; no, I didn't look back, but ran.

In the old blue dress, I found my way back home. But there was nothing there.

Only the house, which like a grin and tilt skeleton, sank

as though it were the smallest calamity to do so. Of course, the trees remained, spectral and uncertain, a few doll dishes beneath them like flying saucers.

"Hello," I called out, "anybody home?"

Only the breeze, which smelled of cake mix, answered. Or was it the spirea, which reeked of sperm and Pinesol? The poppies swathed in testicular fur?

I went inside. The kitchen floor was split, an overripe banana, and glass was scattered everywhere like fistfuls of Jacks. There were pyramids of cans, hard as rolling pins, which smelled like zoos. And in the midst of it, a filthy mattress, an unlucky tarot card.

On the stairs, I stepped over dead birds, black and shiny as my Mom's good gloves. When I saw my room, dark as an anus, I went in. What had happened to my family? In the dimness, the sounds I made were foreign, my home not my own.

I sat on my bed, which felt like it was turning, a cake on a musical plate, then remembered how Dirt Bag told me that the corpses in Nam smelled like chocolate; and that once, when he yanked on an arm, it came loose, tugged free from its body like the limb of a lesser squid.

This I carried out to the garden where I started to dig a hole—soon, I unearthed crochet-hook snails, knowing that the greatest fables are about us, how we're varying shades of small—like when my father drowned the kittens, which I found floating down river, the mother's milk still warm in their dime-bag stomachs, the blood in them blood in a canteen.

I dragged them to the shore, put them in a hole while the future throttled towards me—and it was loud, reckless.

That summer, I walked out past the field, into the forest, toward the cleft in the hill, on the darker side of the river. Our entire house could have fit into this gap, this hole no one could explain, the one the kittens went into like paws.

Sitting on the edge, swinging my feet, I leaned back and fell, wrist-deep, into the body of a deer. Just a fawn, really, with no eyes. Her mouth was open, her tongue black, swollen, vibrating with flies.

I did not do this. But my appalled and appalling hand was inside her. Like the sword in Christ's side.

Only the rustling of darkness over the trees brought me to my feet. Never looking back, I left her there, surrounded by a mole's monastic corridors.

Back in the garden, I remembered that fawn, the kittens small as a jeweler's loupe and the fact that there's nothing more orphan than the heart with its reptilian insomnia, nameless drive, dim mission, bulging catalytic beat.

Above me, the night sky wheeled, as if thrown from a bowler's hand. Orion. Ursa Minor. I couldn't constellate desire, but I could name the wind, wind tethered to the earth like flame.

Beargrass. Monk's Hood Lichen. Methuselah's Beard. Old Man on the Mountain.

Taking my bearings from a belt of pulsing stars—Polaris, Dog's Tail—I thought of blood but did not bleed, as separate from myself as from anything.

The gap between then and now seemed a moment smaller. Hadn't I sat with myself, stood by myself, taken every step myself had taken?

I was no closer. I knew nothing more. But I was almost

used to it now, like two strangers in a waiting room or a woman in a garden.

Where once the tiger lilies, their tongues those of thirsty dogs, where once the pollen star-charted the rusty clitorises of the peonies, my sister tied me to the bed, forced me to eat orange slices, which I believed were goldfish.

"Do you know who's going to kill you? I'm going to kill you!"

Our limbs sounded like sand poured out of a Venus comb, our brains tidal pools.

When my eyelids closed like golden moons, tiger moons, zebra moons, my face felt wrapped tighter than anyone's else's.

My sister's unblinking eyes hovered from left to right, in the room where I imagined children nibbling the orange crusts she force-fed me.

Their faces like waxed paper, their bodies caked with the scales of dying birds, these remained locked inside what Dirt Bag would have named them: *spokes, spools, dying suns.*

This as he drank from his flask, as though it were half-filled with music. This as his voice, an oily gun, lifted me out of a repulsive sorrow like a strange resurrection.

The garden, it reminded me of a piano without keys, the one I used to play for my mother, in the afternoons, in the rusting light the parakeet preened its beak on.

My mother's hair smelled of oven cleaner as she ordered me to play. My notes, one by one, goldened her, made the room so red it felt like sleeping inside a heart, or maybe what she wanted was to sleep inside my heart but she couldn't, not with her body silent as molasses, nor would I let her.

And so I went out into the garden where my veins sang of chains, my mouth, lopsided as a fainting chaise, the one my mother slept on like an alibi for the brutally alive.

How could I not hope for someone to carry me across the threshold of my life? Wasn't that someone Dirt Bag, who was now the dust of a trillion distant, distant happenings which spilled into this bone-quiet garden: how could I stand being here, propped like a rifle?

Suddenly the valley was disaster, every chasm consuming. Because I could not recover a peace to rest in, I went down into my father's bomb shelter like a snake in subterfuge.

It had a trapdoor. Walls of canned goods. Here it was easy to see how madness can afflict anyone, even the dead.

Making noises which sounded violent, even suspect— all the things I ached for were flung open, soft, too soft, like skin flakes in moonlight.

In the bomb shelter, I feasted upon memory, pale as sand ground into glass and even my mother, who was nothing now, smelled like the inside of a suitcase.

Still she had put everything in the jars which glinted all around me, like tiny green cadavers: the slurry of the heart, its edgeless kind of soft, the grafted grin, vinegary light—one held a mortuary of rose petals, another teabags filled with dried wasps.

Blue as an embalming table, the bomb shelter was about the size of the boxcars me and Dirt Bag rode like morning sickness and the walls, weren't they a canvas of starlings the color of crocuses?

I was never coming back and now that I had, my mind was a brood of mannequins, a thing neutered with grief—

just like my family's shadows which I hung, a candelabra with no heads, on trees smelling like fat.

While I looped razor wire around their necks, their eyes told me, *from blood you come to blood you go.*

The flame I lit, this traveled like the one that set the house on fire, an indifferent lighthouse.

I watched it all but took in so little. My eyes were open, and I acted like someone looking into a box of catastrophes, saying as I once did to Dirt Bag, "Look at these. Which one would you like?"

The fire whirred, glimmering like fish that looked like blimps and fish-like blimps.

I wasn't a child for long and after I wasn't, I was something else. I was this. And that.

Like these burning effigies, all objects can be beautiful, yet when the rain came down, suffocating what was left of the fire, the ashes molted into damp, peeling wallpaper.

Which I stuffed into the mattress I had dragged into the bomb shelter. Here where the walls were as cold as unbroken bones, or eyeholes as they caved into the earth, I heard my father licking me, like someone he never loved. In moonlight white as a sturgeon.

By the next day, what was left of the ashes smelled like birthday cake and when I plucked a tiny spine out from among the daffodils, like popcorn needled with thread, I heard my father's camera shutter open and close like a tiny guillotine—*clicking.*

In the picture, my sister's holding my doll's head like an acorn without its cap and I'm screaming. After that, I spent my childhood inside myself, like a Byzantine painting, the questions old as light.

When I wanted to leave, it didn't hurt—I listened to the

flames in Dirt Bag's burn barrel the way an owl listens to air currents.

Since everything's a kind of violence—this was how we lived, the light cracking like scotch tape, or a grave full of fire which we believed gave us the power to crush or fray every living thing fiber by fiber.

And if my sister turned her head toward me, and said, "you," her eyes pepper-swollen, limbs thick with sinking—and if we float—*and we do!*—and I say, *here we are at the end of the earth!*—and if the sky immolates—magenta rimming the day as it dies—if it looks hopeless—and it is hopeless, then and only then is it perfect.

IX.

Fetal as seaweed, I howled. Somewhere in the empty house, I howled. Of this much I'm certain.

A shriek like gulls the color of glaciers, or a knotted, but erect hallucination.

The house itself seemed struck by its own animal dumbness—it panicked, sank, then took a deeper bite from its own foundation, reeking of earth and silt and bones.

Screaming, I watched the evening freight train as it pulled away in almost perfect silence, gliding at a low, inexorable speed.

It was tempting, if not yet compulsory, to think of this as history, a word I supposed was exiled.

The yard was locked down in fog. But what did I know? Only that the train rolled into the tunnel, after which no further reference was made.

There was a pause. Then the shrieking. There in the

attic, the cellar. Sealed between the walls, it had fur, or
was a fist in a glass jaw.

But the landscape like a verse in the psalter had weight
and ardor and eternity.

When I stopped screaming, I looked at the lilac—the
blossoms smelled like my siblings, or the back of the infant
Dirt Bag and I tried to care for, like someone I'd kill for.

Before she was born I wouldn't kill anyone. But now I
would. Now that she's dead. And think nothing of it.

When I was a little girl, I used lay in bed listening to
the river inside, also to the river outside—river of sun and
branch shadow, muskrat and mallard, heron, and the rattled cry of the kingfisher.

And the tree whose roots had been washed so often—
it stretched beyond itself, leaning out over the water
where what couldn't be said stirred beneath leaves, thick
as a medieval altarpiece, until there rushed a net of light
so loosely woven, I could almost hear it weave in and out.

Which made it all one—seamless as a lily about to open
from here into everywhere or the heron with its Corin-
thian neck flying over shallows whose bottomless surface
seeped, bloomed and retracted, in a flow that upheld the
bridge and the gate, the cormorants and the dragonflies,
which had no finish, no fragile end.

Unlike me and Dirt Bag, death invited us in many
times like the hidden salt in waves, its invisible flavors,
which tasted like collapsing shipwrecks and summits or
vast structures made by wind and snowdrifts.

Even our bodies hurt. Sometimes. So much. Like a
room of broken mirrors. Or owls. Or an amputated bell.

Yet when my family renounced me, or I them, and
their doors and paths were closed, such that my hands

could no longer touch their wounded existence, nor theirs mine, I went street by street and river by river, city by city and bed by bed, only to return without light, fire, bread, stone, or silence to burn the baby's blanket.

Which I put into the burn barrel until the sparks, like a spiral staircase, fanned into the tail of a strange bird, the one trapped in the story of its own ashes.

With these ashes, I washed myself. It was like washing the face of a dirty child—this, while my mind was swooped down upon by a larger, meaner, murkier story, one which, like a granite pestle, crushed my once soft, winsome self into something akin to caulk.

Holed up in the bomb shelter, I waited for something larger to pour over me like bruised ice.

I slept alone, curved inward like an almond, my shoulders lush as romantics. In my blue dress, which I wore like a soft fringe of hair.

While the rain came down like a vinyl-sided epiphany, my cheek was pressed against a pillow. My dreams, these I cursed, my voice shrieking.

I got up, inhaled: crisp vetiver, grapefruit and orange so pungent I was thrust back to another place, where I learned about the bitter oxymoron in the fruit Dirt Bag fed me piece by piece; from the cart humped on a concrete island, the left-behind grapefruit, a lost green sun.

When we first met, I stared at him like someone who didn't care how many times she got beat before pooling into the lower curve of the D like tea in a spoon. No sugar but still a revolting sweetness.

Back in the bomb shelter, I remembered what my father had said, "Only the dead suffer butter," in tones thin as shoestrings—tangled, hopelessly frayed, worn for the last time.

Meaning, *my beautiful family,* which like a whole flock of dark birds steered to avoid him, like a chewed gash, while singing a clear line of elegy, each note a dark pearl.

When he passed away, no one told me, but how could they? Hadn't I vanished like smoke from the underworld?

By the burn barrel, I imagined Dirt Bag telling me about what he built in his mother's basement—each mannequin's face, bloated with story.

"We are this now," he said, "inside the terror." The indifference of nature added to its weight.

How could I have known that I would drag the bones of everything into the bomb shelter—how each one housed a kind of brokenness. The ribcage a songbird loosed in snow. A skull which smelled like nutmeg.

It all became myth—hours where I waited, curled up around the bones, like quilled paper, storm clouds hardening over the stippled fields. The bones, these suffered.

And my body, it guttered in my mouth like the husks of dried crickets, their backs shattered violins. At some point the empty room became me.

This emptiness yoked me to a black hunger, one I shared with the raven. Which circled like a skate on a groove of air, the fur at the neck ruffed up.

The raven swooped down, poked its beak into the muff of a rabbit not yet dead, it pecked and pecked, until one red spot welled up.

A thin steam came from the rabbit, like a blown out wick. The snow sparkling. And the raven cocked its black eye, dipped its beak in the red pool it had made—ink for elegy.

The bones, these I collected. Even the rabbit's. With

them, I tried to build a bone chapel, a rookery made out of metacarpals and metatarsals, a memento I could pray to and confess and baptize.

Huts of bone. Like piled up combs, which smelled like tea gone cold and weighed less than a vein pumped full, or my soul, which had a trillion brittle wings and a billion black deaths.

While I tried to link the bones together like one word to another, as if struggling to turn a bunch of reclusive birds into a flock, I listened to their incessant clicking and chattering like many sets of tiny, wind-up teeth.

This sound carried, like salt singing its perfect punctuation. *We bones*, they said, as if they were sentient beings or the greeters at the Walmart. *We bones that here are, for yours await.*

I wasn't sure if they were my family or effigies or sculptures, but I knew I needed them like an improved corpse.

Dirt Bag was the cow's skull, bright as graph paper. I gave him hooves for feet, legs wrapped in pelts. His face was made from feathers, soft as a flurry of moths.

While building him, I thought about the bodies in the train wreck, how we had covered them with snow like sweets in a piñata.

One operatic head floated as if decapitation had made it a better singer. Each body held us without mercy.

Our eyes swelled and so did theirs, growing very tall and very soft. We abandoned all our plans, recited the creed of forgiveness, then drank whiskey to cleanse the wounds of the world: the sin of guilt, the sin of monstrosity.

We repented the weakness of our constitutions run

amuck.

But here in my own backyard, where the landscape smelled like vinegar, I saw nothing as it was; since my body was temporary, I imposed it anywhere it fit, like a throbbing under the gums.

"The shoeing of your mouth," Dad said. My cries, these had a blue interior and snapped like a bonfire stoked with dry rot.

They were a pitcher of ink that never spilled until it did, until it scrawled itself across the fields and up into the trees where it became the thread of black water in which death spawned.

On nights when I woke as the cry left me, it was my sister's hand that clamped my mouth shut, smelling of pennies and rain.

After which I went out into a field of weeds sharper than razors where I lay down among the palest flowers, the ones that smelled like meat—these made my body a small cave or a sick whale or maybe, just maybe, just like my mother's. Brutally alive. And without alibi.

Like my sculptures. As I built them, I began to see things in parts, segments, a pen drawn against the skin to show where to cut. And the owls, urging me all winter to *Go, go* while throwing my mother's bones behind me.

Under stars like empty silverware drawers, I tied their straw-thin wrists with baling wire—they looked like a mobile of warblers, their throats torn out.

The way they dreamed, the way I swelled like a cedar plank when the clouds opened their canning jars of smoke as I pressed my tongue to the wet ropy veins in each neck, their faces the color of spit.

With a few slits and a hard yank, I dressed them with

pelts that smelled like a snake in a woodshed.

These pelts, like some long paragraph about the dark, asked permission of nothing—here was something that would finally outlast me. Or would it?

If my mind was nothing more than a colorless thread of grief, then these naked, degraded marionettes in burlap hoods, which I strung up, lips blue as windchill, eyes fat as an Adam's apple; no, their eyes were halved hailstones, their skin the color of basement embers.

"Save us," they seemed to say, "Save us from death by water, from death by fire. Save us from being alive."

Which I would not do. My nails glowed as I dug into bones like sheet glass, which doubted all things visible. And invisible.

Because suffering does not destroy the possibility of suffering and living does not do away with death, the shells I pasted to the cracks in each bone hid an infinitesimal music, which marched towards a future where the light would scatter from the lowliest of places like coarse brown make up.

Yet, as I sat on the rubbish pile singing about the marriage of plastic and fire, a song which I believed would bring the dead up to the surface like a landscape for the unplanned, I understood.

Just like that. Suffering did not, does not destroy the possibility of suffering and everything will, once again, keep repeating until infinity. As it should.

And these figures, which I had sown into seal skin and crowned with bone, their eyes like nipples with splinters in them, these were what I had composed out of the tideline's litter—my hand dipping like a smile in the water to bring up a length of rope, plastic bottles, a lone shoe's laceless eyes bright among gobs of kelp and sea-worn bits, the shards of crab and mussel shells.

Each went into a string bag as I made my way through the thin, gray fade of evening.

Standing back, I memorized my sculptures, which gave me another chance to make the story I was given into a maze, a museum, a gallery of bones.

This was when I stepped into the girl I was—a pile of hand-shoveled remains, a body with its limbs crossed out.

Every story I've ever wanted to tell begins and ends with the blood and us longing for each other. My family, where had they gone? Were they reaching up and out of my throat in order to escape drowning inside me?

Last night, I dreamt I was running under a bone-white sky. I was wearing my blue dress. I was as human as could be. Which was unendurable.

I awoke in my father's bomb shelter. Because debris is part of every story: small tessera, nutshells, bones, milkweed pods; all were underfoot, as was a mouse's tail, with its small, terrible muscle and memory, which fed me until it didn't.

And in my mind, my thoughts ground their way into each and every bone, like bees on the edge of a blackhole or a fork in the throat, which is how this story goes.

My sculptures. Weren't they the briefest elegy on the tip of a match? The smallest of which was built from the bones my mother grew inside her, the colors like little gods on fire—hurtling in and out of each other's terrified skies.

Just like Dirt Bag, who used to make chess pieces out of stale bread. Those pieces constituted my rookery of bones, a lacework of bones whose lunar strength, brutal pull, was what my shadow invented every time the light failed to pass through me.

Because the whole world moved without me, I remembered how my fingerprints had stained the baby's coffin, and her face, which wanted nothing, this was swollen like the flicker of an eyelid.

The baby. The smallest sculpture. With my mother's bones in it. Her body a box, filled with a precious entanglement of kelp—and her head, which fit perfectly in the palm that might crush it.

Weren't mites living in the oniony layer that mummified her? Wasn't she the other me who was entirely free of pain like the idea of a rainbow inside a dying one?

Which is why, when in the ward, I sat at a table working the puzzle that was my head until it was swallowed by another head, which may or may not have been mine. Because the ultimate monster is the self, this brain told me that pain was a place where fire vanished like metaphors: moist, warm, soft.

The drugs they gave me had an underwater pallor, were a door locked in a dream. They made my head throb until it barked like a dog in an egg.

Docile, dully transfixed, I imagined shoving my family one by one off of a cliff like monsters stuffed with hammers. Or feathers. Or both.

I knew little of the world past the asylum, but the wind, this made the room whine, here where I thought I could stop time by taking apart a clock. Minute hand. Hour hand.

Nothing can keep. Nothing is kept. Only kept track of. I felt the passing seconds accumulate like dead calves in a thunderstorm.

I couldn't face it: the world moving on as if nothing had happened. The drugs, these kept thought after thought roiling like wind across water—coercing shape into shapelessness.

How could I go on when I'd been completely taken apart? Dismantled and made useless. Case. Wheel. Hands. Dial. Face.

When injuries began showing up on my statues—ruts the size of bullets, one arm broken at the elbow, another without a hand—the holes glinting like the slaughtered eyes of fireflies: I understood that pain is beautiful only because it can be transferred from one body onto another.

Knocked down they were. On the beaten hides, skin like a needle slipped into an orchid's throat. This was when I knew I'd be undone like that baby whose breath collected in the tiniest droplets on my neck.

Yes, I drank in her scalp's smell like the blue egg I found bulging in the grass, the one I pierced as if I could feed her its frothy soup.

The river, this smelled like the nail evening hangs on and her grave, which was a suitcase of rocks, was where the moths hatched from her chest like bits of glass from a harpsichord.

Surrounded by thorn bushes, oak, pine, warblers, crows, ants, and worms, I had this notion that if I lived long enough, there would be three or four stories in my life.

The story of a journey or a transformation. The story of love, which meant the loss of love. And the story of spiritual illumination, which for many is the moment of death, the story itself untellable, its beginning and middle and end collapsing into a brain broken past the point of suture until the damage and the beauty is passed on, a gene.

I realized that the shard, not the whole comprised a

life, the image, not the narrative and that one can be stacked inside the other like the after-hours in a library.

In my shrine of bones, a skull had been ripped off. I stitched it back on, as though it were a plot for the burying of corpses.

In darkness that never hurt, I layered gooey, amniotic plaster in joints strict as insects.

Singing to the baby, I told her to bring me her pain like fine rugs, silk sashes, or gold still hot in the body.

While singing, I gnawed on her sculpture as crazily as flowers eat meat. Its candied whispers. Translucent heart. Spine the color of peacock feathers.

Her hair, this smelled of sharpened pencils or a photograph, quiet as the echoes of a room without furniture or a corridor leading from the outside in.

Her cerebellum—I rested my length in its green shadow, there along the stone wall where I uttered a prayer with God washed out of it. It sounded like bones being broken.

What were we? A footnote in the order of its disappearance? An object rough as an emery board or little fish green as muscat grapes?

Or were we a precise light, like fender chrome, or the crystal ground down for frost—a formless moil, spread onto cold red leaves and successive clouds, each one edge-lit, its heart incinerate among the brittle sepals, rough as houndstooth.

This light made us if not the field, then maybe this: a green hour I can't stop. Or a green vein in my throat, green wing in my mouth, green thorn in my eye. I wanted that baby like a river goes, bending. Green moving green, moving.

I wanted her memory to be as permanent as paralysis, to live in this field as grass does, remembered with every passing year. Each and every passing year.

How nearly dead we were, but softer and more dangerous than an uncooked egg. How nearly perfect, like an ivory hairpin or a loose tooth. Unpleasantly the color of bones.

The sculptures, these linked us, a musical scale that sounded like shells wrapped in paper or a knife in a melon, the one that struck a note so plush—it came from the bells, or the graves, growing in the damp air like tears or rain.

Filled with the sound of death, which is silence, death arrived like a needle looking for thread as if to stitch a fungus back onto a tree. Florid, fluted, flowery, that fungus was a flounce on a girl's dress—or a ruffled fan, intricately ribboned like a secret.

At the outermost edge, a scallop of ivory, then a tweedy russet, then mouse gray, a crescent of celadon, an arc of copper, then butter because only the dead suffer butter, then celadon again, again copper and on into the center, striped thinner and thinner into the green moss-furry heart.

How could this be? Even in death, the baby and I grew, made more of ourselves with dozens and dozens of tiny starts under stars creaking like tulips—wasn't the air cool and wet and almost unbearably sweet?

I understood very little, but it seemed to me that we were the color of damp violets, of violets at home in the earth and because the face of death is green and the look death gave us was green, I gazed into the black flower of her animal eyes while the name she never had hurtled through me like honeyed rum. After which the stars collapsed.

By the river where me and Dirt Bag both found and lost her, I was and will be all-that-is absence, a blue light like one thimbleful of wet gold poured into another.

Because she smelled like an invalid, I drank from the water jetting her pale collarbones before I pulled her under four times, as though she and not the world was the cause of all my suffering.

When I brought her up, the chuff of her head was whiskered like my dead mother's belly and empty as a collection plate.

In that moment, I almost believed that me and Dirt Bag had been liberated from our horrible selves and had returned once again to the world's tumult and chaos where we could go quietly, like a little ending or a flame.

And yet, I felt caught, wanting to let go, to run, to be called back to wherever the dead suffer butter, to where I had been sprung like a room passing into a cloud. But did I feel pity? And for whom?

The eight-year-old I was once? The one stubby as a shoot?

And if I beat my mother between the mirror and the tie rack with the tips of her festive shoes, what of it?

The clouds of dust that mushroomed over her head while she ducked, these were beautiful the way family was supposed to be.

Both of us were in our nightgowns. While slapping her face the way I flipped through channels, I stared at her face.

When my father walked through the doorway, he said, *Brilliant*, his voice a symphony as white as a thief's hand.

On his shirt, lipstick smiled at me with the warmth of urine. It was as if somebody had thrown slices of skinned grapefruit at him.

Every time I hit her, he hit me back. The rhythm of it: a ball dribbling down a basketball court or a cache of weapons.

Look, I yelled, *look at what you've bred.*

Because he came at me, I can say that his gray breath tasted like gunpowder and yet he smiled—*finally!*—he could not stop smiling, his voice the singing in a cage of dead doves.

In a rookery of sea chill. In congeries of snow: and then, and only then, was I in clementine, like an infinity of ashes: a gasp of emeralds.

NOTES

"In Thy Kingdom Cut" contains references to Lucie Brock-Broido.

In "Because It's Nothing to Know One Moment Alive," the reference to a "fifty-year sting" is to Stanley Kunitz.

In the ending of "In a Scene Forever Dead," "like harnessed scorpions" is from Michael Simms.

"The Tenants of the Little Box" borrows from Vasko Popa's Little Box poems. "The elephantine shadow of my tears" is from Lorca.

Toward the end of "It's a Brief Death, A Brief Death," in the scene with the boy, some of the language is borrowed from Henri Cole.

The ending of "An Ode to Not" echoes Adam Zagajewski.

In "Only the Dead Suffer Butter," "You will not be spared, nor will what you love be spared" is from Louise Gluck.

"Lullaby with Exit Sign" is from Hardara Bar-Nadav.

"Like monsters stuffed with hammers. Or feathers. Or both" is a reference from a novel by Sebastian Barry.

Re: the baby's death and many of the references to the color green echo Neruda.

"An infinity of ashes: gasp of emeralds" is a variation on a line by Brenda Hillman.

ACKNOWLEDGMENTS

The following stories have been previously published:

"Mirror, Mirror" (under "Bright as Guilt"), *Vox Populi*, 1/1/19

"Jones Beach," *Vox Populi*, 8/4/19

"Dr. Flesh," *Verity La*, 9/27/19

"What It Is Like to Live," *Raw Art Review*, 11/17/19

"The Shipwrecked World," *The Red Wheelbarrow*, 4/15/20

"Cry the Dying Violet Hour," *Paragon Press,* 4/26/20

"In a Forest of Filleted Bones," *Finding The Birds*, 4/28/20

"Because the Sky is a Thousand Soft Hurts," *Vox Populi*, 4/29/20

"The Heft of Mercy", *Arlijo*, 4/30/20

"A Thousand Ways to Dissemble," *Gone Lawn*, 5/17/20

"Everyone Needs a Place," *Oyster River*, 5/24/20

"Murky as the Eye of God," *34th Parallel*, 5/28/20

"And the Rest is a Rose," *Southeast Fiction*, 6/5/20

"A Sorry of Scheme of Things," *Flying South*, 6/27/20

"The End Which Enveloped the End, A Bramble, A Rose," *Digging Through the Fat*, 7/9/20

"A Lullaby with an Exit Sign," *Storm Cellar*, 7/10/20

"A Siege of Herons," *Main Street Rag*, 8/10/20

"Tenants of the Little Box," *Ailment*, 9/10/20

"A Tornado's Soliloquy," *Toho Journal*, 11/20/20

"The Genius of Flowers," *Punt Volat*, 11/29/20
"Make Lasting Friends," *South Carolina Review*,
   forthcoming

ABOUT ATMOSPHERE PRESS

Atmosphere Press is an independent, full-service publisher for excellent books in all genres and for all audiences. Learn more about what we do at atmospherepress.com.

We encourage you to check out some of Atmosphere's latest releases, which are available at Amazon.com and via order from your local bookstore:

The Tattered Black Book, a novel by Lexy Duck
The Red Castle, a novel by Noah Verhoeff
American Genes, a novel by Kirby Nielsen
Newer Testaments, a novel by Philip Brunetti
All Things in Time, a novel by Sue Buyer
Hobson's Mischief, a novel by Caitlin Decatur
The Black-Marketer's Daughter, a novel by Suman Mallick
The Farthing Quest, a novel by Casey Bruce
This Side of Babylon, a novel by James Stoia
Within the Gray, a novel by Jenna Ashlyn
For a Better Life, a novel by Julia Reid Galosy
Where No Man Pursueth, a novel by Micheal E. Jimerson
Here's Waldo, a novel by Nick Olson
Tales of Little Egypt, a historical novel by James Gilbert
The Hidden Life, a novel by Robert Castle
Big Beasts, a novel by Patrick Scott
Alvarado, a novel by John W. Horton III
Nothing to Get Nostalgic About, a novel by Eddie Brophy
GROW: A Jack and Lake Creek Book, a novel by Chris S McGee
Whose Mary Kate, a novel by Jane Leclere Doyle

ABOUT THE AUTHOR

John Hauschildt / RumDoodle.com

Elizabeth Kirschner is a writer and Master Gardener. She's published six collections of poetry, most notably *My Life as a Doll*, and an award-winning memoir, *Waking the Bones. Because the Sky is a Thousand Soft Hurts* is her debut collection of short stories. She lives in Maine.

CPSIA information can be obtained
at www.ICGtesting.com
Printed in the USA
BVHW071414130821
613575BV00001B/6

9 781637 529324